The Gender Experiment
By L.J. Sellers

For Lynn,

JJ Sellers

The Gender Experiment

Novels by L.J. Sellers

Detective Jackson Mysteries
The Sex Club
Secrets to Die For
Thrilled to Death
Passions of the Dead
Dying for Justice
Liars, Cheaters & Thieves
Rulcs of Crime
Crimes of Memory
Deadly Bonds
Wrongful Death
Death Deserved

Agent Dallas Thrillers
The Trigger
The Target
The Trap

Standalone Thrillers
The Gender Experiment
Point of Control
The Baby Thief
The Gauntlet Assassin
The Lethal Effect

THE GENDER EXPERIMENT

Cover art by Gwen Thomsen Rhoads

ISBN: 978-0-9840086-3-6
Published in the USA by Spellbinder Press

Chapter 1

Monday, Oct. 10, 10:45 a.m., Denver, Colorado
The body was young and undamaged, except for the water-logged skin.

"Peaceful journey," Taylor Lopez whispered, pulling the white plastic sheet over him. She'd taken a quick peek to make sure the corpse matched the name and age on the paperwork: *Adrian Warsaw, age 21.*

"Can I go now?" The transport driver shivered in the cold autumn air. The blue sky and bright sun mocked the dark nature of their behind-the-morgue exchange.

"Do you know what happened?" Taylor asked. As a medical-legal-death intern, or MLDI, it was her job to help investigate the cause of death for the corpses her supervisor was assigned.

"He drowned in the pool at his apartment complex, probably early this morning." The driver's tone was impatient.

The dead man had probably been up late, drinking. So sad. Why did so many of her peers act so recklessly? He'd also died alone, poor man. One of her deepest fears.

The driver cleared his throat. Taylor didn't know what else to ask, so she said, "We're good." The man hurried back to his van.

She rolled the gurney into the lift shaft, pressed the button, and jogged upstairs to meet the corpse on the main floor of the Denver Medical Examiner's Office. In the wide hall, she pushed the gurney onto the floor scale and logged the dead man's weight, then rolled him into the x-ray room. Nothing unusual displayed, except a healed fracture in his right arm.

Preliminaries completed, Taylor took a seat at the shared computer desk and began the log-in process. After she keyed in his name, the digital form asked her to choose a gender by checking one of two boxes: male and female. The choice annoyed her every time. Only once had she encountered a form—from Microsoft—that gave a third option of *not specified*. The transport driver had said 'he,' so she clicked that box and moved through the rest of the brief form. More detail would be added to his file as they investigated his death.

Taylor stood and pushed the gurney farther down the hall, nodding at another intern who walked by. All six interns were female college students, but she was the youngest. Taylor had breezed through high school and started early at the University of Colorado with the help of a Pell Grant. When a girl in her advanced biology class had mentioned interning at the morgue, Taylor had been intrigued enough to apply. What better way to begin a career as a forensic investigator? The job was creepy at times and fascinating at others, but dealing with dead people was easier than interacting with the living.

Before moving the corpse into the cooler to wait his turn

for autopsy, Taylor stared at the young man's face. Lean, with sharp bones and symmetrical features. Almost androgynous. Much like her own profile, except he was pale and blond compared to her dark hair and toffee-colored skin. A burning curiosity consumed her. She pushed him into an empty autopsy room, grabbed scissors from a stainless steel drawer, and cut both sides of the spandex swimsuit he still wore. When her skin made contact with his flesh, she flinched. *Damn.* She'd forgotten to put on latex gloves. Taylor rushed over to the counter and pulled a pair from one of the six large boxes. They went through gloves like they were paper towels.

Taylor bagged the swimsuit in a plastic container, then turned back to Adrian's body. His genitalia caught her attention. He had a tiny, two-inch penis. A tingle ran up her spine. *Another one?* Cutting quickly, she removed the still-damp tank top clinging to his chest. Small breasts, like those of a thirteen-year-old girl. Sucking in a worried breath, Taylor pushed his legs apart. Was that a vaginal opening?

The discovery was disturbing. Not the mixed genitalia—that was familiar—but the fact that he was dead. This was the second intersex person to come into the morgue recently. Taylor tried to do the math. One in fifteen hundred people were born that way, and Denver had a population of 650,000. What were the odds? She shook her head. It didn't matter. Two dead dual-gender people in the same city within three weeks didn't seem like a coincidence—especially since they were about the same age. It was even strange that she'd seen both dead bodies. As an investigative intern, she didn't participate in the autopsies like the pathology interns did. Her job was to do everything else necessary to determine the cause of death. That usually meant asking the people who knew the deceased a lot of questions.

She couldn't get the first intersex corpse out of her mind. Maybe he was still in the cooler. Some bodies were never claimed. Other times, the family took weeks to arrange for burial services. Taylor covered Adrian and rolled him down the hall. The thick cooler door required a hefty tug, then she pushed the gurney into the walk-in. The 45-degree air penetrated her long-sleeved sweater, but she was used to it by now. She parked the gurney next to another one—which also held a body in a metal tray—and glanced around. Metal racks against the walls held a dozen white body bags. She didn't want to stay in the chilled room long enough to look at every tag, so she started with the first corpse that looked about the right size. The third ID she checked was Logan Hurtz. She'd never forget his name. His was the first body she'd ever seen that was like hers.

Logan had fallen from a balcony. Even bruised and broken, the genital confusion had been obvious to her. She remembered that he didn't really have breasts and that his gender on the check-in sheet had been listed as male. Shivering, she changed her mind about looking at him again. Now that she knew he was still in the morgue, she felt more confident about reporting her concerns to her supervisor.

She turned back to Adrian. Had he presented himself to the world as male? She would never know what he'd felt in his heart. Sometimes a person's private parts didn't match up with their self-identity. Her own body was much like theirs, but her mother had raised her as a girl simply because she'd wanted a daughter. Taylor had never related to other females, but she didn't feel like a guy either. She belonged to both worlds. Catching frogs and getting dirty had been natural to her as a child, but she hated team sports and wasn't competitive at all. Dresses and makeup seemed superfluous, but she loved to read, and her tastes ranged from historical mysteries to sci-fi. The past and the future, male and female, shy but aggressive about important things. Her life was a cluster of contradictions. So were her sex organs. Taylor touched herself, her own small penis tucked into soft cotton briefs. She'd been attracted to both men and women but had never acted on her impulses. Except that one time with a prostitute, who'd been amused by her body, but accommodating anyway.

Footsteps outside the cooler made her jerk her hand away. She hurried to the door and exited into the hall. The head of the investigative unit had passed by and was walking toward his office. Should she talk to him about this? He'd hired her, and she both liked and trusted him. But what exactly were her concerns?

That these deaths weren't accidents? If not, that implied someone was targeting and killing young intersex people. But why? It seemed a little crazy. These could be well-disguised hate crimes. Transgender people had the highest murder—and suicide—rates in the country. But hate crimes were usually passionate, and the violence inflicted on the victims was obvious—with bullet holes or ugly bruises. If these two young people had been murdered, the killer had been careful. So it didn't really make sense. *Just let it go.*

She couldn't. The similar age of the corpses bothered her too. Counting herself, what were the odds of three intersex people all about the same age living in Denver? A statistical anomaly. A scary thought slammed into her gut. Was she next?

Dr. Houton, the lead pathologist, came out of the shared office across the hall. "Hey, Taylor. Who did we get this morning?" Tall, with a long neck and tiny face, Houton looked like an ostrich.

"Adrian Warsaw, age twenty, drowned in a swimming pool."

"That's a shame." The pathologist walked toward the cooler, shaking her head.

Taylor followed her inside.

Dr. Houton headed for the first gurney, a corpse that had come in the night before.

Taylor worked up her nerve. "Would you look at this new one?"

Houton turned in the dimly lit room. "Sure. Why?"

"He's an intersex person, like the young man a few weeks ago."

The doctor scowled as she walked over. "Are you sure? That seems odd." The pathologist peered over her glasses at the waterlogged flesh on the white sheet. With gloved hands, she probed his genital area. "An opening, but no cervix. Still, he does seem to be mixed gender. I'll know more when I open him up." Houton stepped back. "I only processed one similar body the whole time I worked in Los Angeles. And now, we have two here in Denver in a few weeks. That is peculiar." She locked eyes with Taylor. "Who was the investigator on the first one?"

"Briggs and I handled that case too." The details came back to Taylor. "Logan Hurtz had been raised in foster care, and his foster mother refused to claim the body, calling him an abomination."

"It'll be interesting to see if you find any similarities between the cases. Keep me posted." Dr. Houton grabbed the other gurney. "Get the door please."

Taylor pulled the latch and stepped back to let the pathologist pass through, then followed her out. She headed upstairs to her workspace, a cubicle in a crowded office partitioned by cabinets. Only one investigator was at his desk. Taylor glanced at the time on her monitor: 12:40. Everyone was probably at lunch. *Good.* She could make some calls without being distracted. The first thing she wanted to determine was their birth dates and locations. A quick review of Logan Hurtz's file revealed that he'd been born July 5, 1996 and had worked in a Walmart warehouse. He'd also been a volunteer firefighter. They hadn't located his biological parents, and his neighbors and co-workers had referred to him as a loner.

She called the Denver Police Department. "This is Taylor Lopez from the Medical Examiner's office. We have a drowning victim from early this morning, Adrian Warsaw. I would like whatever information you have." The calls got a little easier every time. Her first day on the job, she'd stammered through them, blushing and sweating.

"Give me a minute." The department's clerk put her on hold for awhile, then cut back in. "I'll send you the report, but I can tell you that he's twenty and lived in unit five at the Meadow View Apartments where he drowned. No foul play is suspected."

"What's his birthday?"

"June 17, 1996."

The same year as Logan Hurtz. Her own birthday was four months before, February 13. They had all been born within seven months of each other. All in Denver? She had to know. "What's his birth city?"

"It's not in the report." A little exasperation in the desk officer's tone. "I'm emailing it now." The line went silent.

Icy fingers of fear wrapped around Taylor's heart. Something bad was coming, she could feel it. She jumped up from her desk, headed downstairs, and grabbed a mop from the supply closet. Dread gripped her torso, and her back muscles cramped as she furiously scrubbed the stained cement floor in the autopsy room. The exercise didn't help. She stopped and closed her eyes. Forcing herself to breathe deeply, she fought the familiar panic. *Everything is fine. Stay positive. Everything is fine.* Sometimes it took twenty minutes to calm herself. Other times, she reached for the anti-anxiety medicine she'd been prescribed at fifteen to combat the episodes. PTSD was the official label. But she'd never experienced any traumatic episodes—other than her mother's suicide—and the anxiety had started long before that. She'd endured some bullying, like most kids, but nothing that justified the panic attacks. Her mother, a veteran medic from the first Gulf War, had suffered from bouts of PTSD, and Taylor had started to believe she had inherited the condition.

Don't think about her! Not now. Taylor went back to her desk, put in earbuds, and cranked up her favorite song. This was her first anxiety episode at work, and she wasn't prepared for it. The music failed to soothe her. The deaths of the two young dual-gender people troubled her. Something wasn't right. As much as it terrified her, she had to find out if they were connected. But how? Whatever was going on may have started twenty years ago, and she wasn't a real investigator yet, just an intern with an interest in forensics. She would start by finding out where the two dead people had been born.

A wild thought hit her. What if there were more intersex kids from that time frame? Had their mothers all been exposed to something toxic? No one knew what caused babies to be born with mixed genitalia. But now that transgendered people were becoming accepted, Taylor hoped gender-fluid people would be eventually as well. For now, she couldn't imagine showing her naked body to anyone. Yet she thought about sex all the time. Her hyper-sexuality seemed like a cruel joke—like being jacked up for a party she wasn't invited to.

"Taylor!" Her supervisor was shouting her name, and he wasn't smiling.

She fumbled to shut off her music, face flushed with heat as she looked up. "Sorry. What can I do?"

"I need you to enter lab results." Ron Briggs, the MLDI she was assigned to, stepped toward her.

Taylor turned away. He had the worst breath! But he was usually pretty nice, for an older guy.

He shoved a stack of files at her. "I have to attend a death scene, and I'm behind on paperwork."

"I've got this." It was her job to do whatever was needed to assist the investigator she was paired with. Ron walked away, and Taylor logged into the main database to enter the case number for the lab results.

While the file loaded, she checked her email and found a message from the police department. The brief note said the report for Adrian Warsaw's death was attached. Taylor downloaded the report and printed it, feeling a little guilty about putting her own stuff ahead of the lab results she was supposed to process. But she was eager to find out what she could about Adrian.

She skimmed the pages, struggling with the police jargon, and learned little. Except that the cops had found Adrian's parents names in his phone. Burt and Ellen Warsaw, both with Denver area codes. *Good news.* The drowned man had probably been born right here. Now that she had his parents'

ID, she could probably find his birth records. But what about Logan, the guy who'd fallen off a balcony? Without knowing his biological mother, she might never find out where he was born. But he'd lived in Denver since he entered foster care as a kid, so she would just assume, for now, that he'd been born here as well. Her own entry into the world had started at Fort Carson Community Hospital on the military base an hour south, but she'd been a breach baby, and they'd rushed her mother to St. Paul's in Denver.

Taylor pushed the troubling thoughts out of her mind and tried to focus on the data entry. She'd had nothing but good performance reviews so far, and she intended to keep it that way. If she wanted a career as a forensic investigator, she needed a good reference from her internship. Yet sometimes she worried she wouldn't even make it through college, let alone find a good job. Interviews terrified her. She was sure the only reason she'd landed this position was because Briggs had been a military investigator at Fort Carson and had felt a kinship with Taylor when he learned her mother had been stationed there.

As soon as she finished entering the data, her brain spun back to the dead men. She had to figure this out. But how could she investigate something that might have happened two decades ago, if she was afraid of talking to people? And afraid of getting hurt? She would have to find the courage somewhere.

Chapter 2

After work, Taylor entered her apartment and headed straight for the fish. The coffin-sized glass tank occupied the space where a dining table should have been, but she didn't mind. "Hey, kids, I'm home." The silliness of her daily greeting made her smile. She tapped food flakes into the water and watched the little beauties gulp them down. The clownfish were her favorites—she related to their shyness—but the Mandarin was the most stunning, with its wavy turquoise and orange patterns. As she watched them swim around, the tension of her long workday melted off. The long shifts three days a week left her free to take classes on Tuesdays and Thursdays, but they wiped her out.

Hungry, she put a bag of popcorn in the microwave—a dinner she could eat in front of her laptop—then checked her messages. An email from her dentist, reminding her of an appointment, and two texts from a classmate who wanted her notes from a microbiology class. How pathetic was her social life? Her best friend had dropped out of college to take care of her sick mother, so Taylor didn't hear from her much anymore. She texted Jonie just to let her know she was thinking about her, then set her phone aside. She had an Instagram account, but didn't use it unless she took a picture of something really interesting. But pictures of dead people didn't go over that well with her few followers.

Eager to discover everything she could about the accident victims, Taylor opened Facebook in two tabs and keyed each of their names into a search field. Adrian Warsaw's profile came up quickly with no other exact name matches, but Logan Hurtz didn't have a page, at least not under his real name. Adrian's profile listed his birthplace as Colorado Springs, the town sixty miles south of Denver near Fort Carson, where she'd lived as a child. Adrian had attended community college in Aurora, then lived in Denver.

His collection of photos stood out, and fire was a dominant theme. Campfires, candle flames, even a few images of forests burning, but few pictures with people. A loner pyromaniac? Had he ever started a fire? Taylor opened the Denver newspaper website and keyed Adrian's name into the search field. He'd been a *person of interest* in connection with a fire at an abandoned factory. Was that why someone might want him dead?

What about Logan Hurtz? The police report had listed him as a volunteer firefighter. It seemed weird that he and Adrian had a common interest that was potentially dangerous. Taylor keyed Logan's name into Google, then plowed through several pages of sites that linked to an older businessman with the same name who'd started a windmill company. About to give up, she spotted a headline at the bottom of the page: *Obstetrics Clinic Hosts 20-year Reunion*. She clicked through to the website and found a year-old story by the Colorado Springs newspaper. The clinic, an off-base extension of the Fort Carson Community Hospital, had thrown a party for people who'd been brought into the world by staff doctors in the past twenty years. Logan Hurtz had attended and been singled out for being the oldest of the birth babies.

Taylor glanced at the time: 4:45 p.m. The facility might still be open. She keyed in the number but didn't press the dial icon. What would she say? Voice trembling, she practiced her introduction a few times. The questions would be the hardest. She wrote out several in longhand, then practiced asking them. Finally, she popped in her earpiece and made the call.

A tired-sounding woman answered on the fifth ring. "Carson Obstetrics Clinic."

"Hello. This is Taylor Lopez from the Denver Medical Examiner's Office." She had that part down pat. The woman was silent, so Taylor blurted out her opening line. "Logan Hurtz, one of your birth babies, died in an accident a few weeks ago."

A long pause. "I'm sorry to hear that." The voice sounded weak and soft, like an older woman.

"Adrian Warsaw drowned in a pool early this morning. I think he might have been a clinic baby too."

A strange sound escaped the receptionist's throat. "Why are you calling here?" She sounded distressed.

Taylor gulped in air. *Just say it.* "Both men had genital abnormalities. Do you know anything about it? Or who I should talk to?"

A longer hesitation this time. "That information is confidential, and I'm not at liberty to discuss patients."

"Can you tell me if Adrian Warsaw was one of the clinic doctor's deliveries?"

"Technically no, I can't."

That meant he probably was, and the receptionist wanted her to know.

"How long have you worked at the clinic?" The question

popped out of Taylor's mouth, surprising her.

"Twenty-three years. But you should forget what you think you know about Logan and Adrian." The woman ended the call.

Taylor's pulse quickened. Was that a warning? The receptionist had been at the clinic the year Adrian and Logan were born, and she knew something about their condition. Feeling shaky, Taylor paced in front of the fish tank, thinking everything through. Logan and Adrian's mothers had both been patients at Carson Obstetrics, where they'd received prenatal care around the same time. Then they'd both given birth to intersex babies. Taylor's mother had been stationed at Fort Carson during her pregnancy, and she'd started labor in the military hospital. She had probably been a patient at Carson Obstetrics that year too.

A startling thought hit her brain. *How many more were there?* Taylor knew she was one of them—whatever they were. Two clinic babies from 1996 were dead. A chill ran up her spine. Was she in danger?

She ran to the end of the hall. On the closet floor sat a white plastic tub that contained everything she had left of her mother. Taylor pulled it out and dug straight to the bottom for the bundle of paper, trying to ignore the soft fabric of her mother's favorite scarf and the scent of vanilla wafting from her jewelry box. *Please let there be something!* A receipt, a note, or maybe the doctor's name was on her birth certificate. She would check that next.

Taylor scanned the military papers first, but nothing medical surfaced. Her mother's high school track-and-field awards made Taylor smile, but she pushed them aside. A few handwritten letters from her father were also in here somewhere. He'd sent them when her mother had been overseas during the Gulf War. Or so she'd been told. Her dad had disappeared when she was four, and her mother had never talked about him. She'd never used the word *died*, so Taylor sensed he was still out there somewhere. Some day, she would take the time to find him, if only to ask him why he'd abandoned her. Right now, it didn't matter.

She found the stash of letters inside a folder, remembering that she'd tucked them there for safekeeping. The first one was brief, written on lined paper, like she'd used in grade school before they got laptops in the classroom. *I love you...I miss you...I'm keeping the bed warm.* Taylor's cheeks flushed, and she flipped to the next letter. They'd all been written before she was born. *No help.* That was her mother's expression, and she'd subconsciously started using it soon after her death. Along with a few other choice phrases. It was a way of keeping her close.

Pushing to her feet, Taylor reached for the small metal safe on the top shelf. The code, made up of her favorite numbers, three and seven, was similar to her password for everything she did online. Keep it simple was her motto. Inside the safe was her birth certificate, high school diploma, social security card, pearl earrings that had belonged to her mother, and a hundred dollars she kept for emergencies.

Taylor scanned the birth certificate, not finding the doctor's name. She looked again more slowly. There it was, near the bottom, in the middle box. But what the heck did it say? The first two letters of the first name were CH, and the rest was a squiggle. Charles? Chuck? There weren't many options. The last name started with an M, then the signature shot out in a dramatic line. No help at all. *Damn.*

Maybe she would skip her morning classes and drive down to Fort Carson tomorrow and talk to the receptionist in person. Show the woman the birth certificate and see if she recognized the obstetrician's name—then find the doctor and talk to him. What if he was retired now? That would make it more challenging, but she'd try anyway. She also needed to track down Logan and Adrian's birth certificates. But how? From their parents?

The thought made her cringe. This was really out of her comfort zone. But talking to grieving people would be a big part of her internship, so she had to get used to it. She closed the safe, keeping the birth certificate in hand, and pushed the plastic tub back into the closet. "Later, Mom," she whispered, closing the door. Respect for the dead was a military motto, and she'd learned it young. Now that she worked with corpses all day, it was ingrained. Or maybe her acceptance of death had compelled her into the morgue as an intern. *Whatever.* She had to start a load of laundry, eat some protein, and write a paper for her sociology class.

By ten o'clock, her eyes hurt and she was exhausted. Taylor grabbed her laptop and phone from beside her on the couch and heard the familiar ping of a text. Probably Justin again. He usually texted late, after he'd had a beer or two. He'd been bugging her to hang out with him, but she only liked him as a friend. If her body were normal, she would have hooked up with him just for the experience, but she was a freak and didn't plan to get naked with anyone she would ever see again. At least not yet.

She tapped the message icon, not recognizing the number of the text, but the sender was obvious: *Your call stirred up a lot of old memories. I looked back through the files and found a list. Give me your email address and I'll send it to you.*

A list! Taylor sucked in her breath. That meant there

were more dual-gender babies born through the clinic. She quickly texted: *Thnx! Taylor73@gmail.com*

After a short wait, she checked her email, but a new message hadn't come yet. She texted the receptionist again: *Why so many intersex babies? What happened at the clinic?*

Her phone stayed silent. Taylor walked over to the fish tank, knowing it would help her keep calm. The biggest clown fish swam by, and she watched it dart through the rocks. The old woman's contact had surprised her. Taylor certainly hadn't expected to get a text from her. She didn't seem the type. Where had the receptionist gotten her number? From her earlier incoming call?

A beep in her hand made Taylor jump. She looked at the phone. An email this time. No message, just an attachment. Taylor left the file unopened and hurried to her laptop on the couch. She wanted to open the list on the big screen where she could scroll, save, and print it.

The email was from an anonymous Hotmail account. The receptionist was being careful to mask her identity. Or was the woman trying to hide the communication from someone else? Fingers trembling, Taylor opened the attachment, a plain-text file with a long list of names and birth dates. A fast count tallied thirty-three. Four had checkmarks by their names. Her chest tightened. Logan Hurtz and Adrian Warsaw were both marked. So were two others: Zion Tumara and Seth Wozac. Were they also dead? Or targeted for death?

After a second run through, she found her own name. No check next to it, but a little asterisk instead. What did that mean? A thorough scrutiny revealed that hers was the only name highlighted that way. She hoped the receptionist had just noted it for her convenience, but Taylor didn't believe it.

Someone was coming for her too.

Chapter 3

Tuesday, Oct. 11, 6:05 a.m.

Running hard, breathing heavy, her heart gripped with fear. Past the burnt-out rubble that used to be buildings. The road beneath her bare feet turned to dirt, and the wreckage gave way to open fields. Were those dead bodies? Out of nowhere, the earth in front of her exploded. For a moment, she flew through the air, then landed in a heap on the cold, hard ground. The silent aftermath hurt her ears. Was she dead?

A piercing scream cut through the quiet. But it wasn't human. Taylor opened her eyes. The dreaded alarm drilled into her still sleepy brain. She reached out and slammed it off, heart pounding. That damn dream again. Whatever it was about. She'd never been in a war or seen an explosion, so it didn't make sense. She hated the alarm almost as much as the dream, but at least its intrusion was short. When would she become a morning person? It was supposed to be easier now that she was twenty.

Taylor took a long shower to wake herself up and finally made up her mind about what she should do. She wasn't scheduled at the ME's office, and she only had three classes. Skipping them to drive to Colorado Springs and talk to the receptionist face-to-face seemed essential. She had to find out why her name had been noted and why the others had been checked—and possibly murdered.

She pulled on yoga pants to be comfortable during the drive and topped them with a pale-blue, button-up shirt to look sort of dressy. Plus ankle boots of course. They made her feel taller and more confident. She ate a banana and washed it down with instant coffee. Not her fave, but it was all she could afford and make time for. She grabbed her canvas shoulder bag, locked her small apartment, and headed down to her beat-up Jetta. Someday, she hoped to own a Prius or maybe a hybrid like a Trax. After getting gas, her first stop would be on campus to turn in her homework, then head south on the highway.

She'd finished writing her deviant-behavior paper for sociology class late the night before, then had stayed up searching online for some of the names on the clinic list. The task had been challenging, and she'd only found three before she was too exhausted to continue. Two were still in Colorado, and one had moved to L.A. The first two names she'd googled were Seth Wozac and Zion Tumara. Seth hadn't turned up at all, but she'd found Zion on Instagram. His photos also included a lot of fire scenes, which had startled her. It was as if the marked men shared some DNA. Zion, who lived in Denver, was an artist and liked outer space too, posting pictures of comets and supernovas—explosions in the cosmos.

Tempting as it was to track down Zion right away, Taylor thought it would be best to get more information. Her mother's voice in her head kept nagging her to contact the police, but she wasn't ready. The thought made her queasy. What could she tell them? That two young men had died in accidents? It happened all the time. Their connection to the same obstetrics clinic was also common. The people of Colorado loved their state and tended to stick around.

The list—and vague warning—from the clinic receptionist was the only inexplicable part of her story, and it sounded a little crazy. Taylor suspected the receptionist would deny everything if detectives questioned her. Otherwise, why hadn't the clinic worker contacted the police herself? Taylor decided that when she was ready to take her concerns to the authorities, she would contact the female police detective who'd attended Adrian's autopsy. At least the detective had seen one of the bodies and would understand what Taylor meant by intersex. Talking to a woman would be easier than being questioned by a man with a badge and gun.

But she wouldn't call the detective yet. Taylor wasn't even sure she should contact Zion. He might think she was a paranoid type who stirred up drama just to feel alive. Yet, not warning him seemed wrong. Logan and Adrian had died seventeen days apart. If Zion or Seth came into the morgue next week, she would freak the hell out. And if she hadn't tried to contact them, the guilt would be unbearable.

The closest parking spot was six blocks from the sociology building, so her errand at the college took longer than she'd planned. But she managed to slip the essay under her professor's door without encountering the woman and only had to stop and chat with one person, a graduate teaching fellow who always bugged her about her internship.

"Who'd you cut open this week?" he asked with a smirk.

She didn't do the autopsies, but she was tired of explaining that to him. "A young person who drowned."

"Bet he was drunk."

She'd also assumed so at first too. "We don't know yet. The toxicology report takes weeks." Taylor had been surprised to learn that. TV made death investigations seem so fast and high-tech. She'd learned otherwise, but it hadn't disappointed her. "Sorry, but I have to go. I'm late." Taylor gave the guy a half smile and hurried away. She didn't want to encourage him, in case he was actually flirting with her in his own peculiar way.

Once she was on the highway, she set her music to shuffle through her favorite songs and punched the address of the clinic into her GPS app. The big Colorado sky was blue and clear the way she liked it, and the mountains were topped with a light frosting of snow for the first time in months. The changing season and its new challenges suddenly made her anxious. Structure and predictability were her friends, but they never stuck around long enough.

Carson Obstetrics was just off Nevada Avenue on the south end of Colorado Springs, not far from Fort Carson. The original red-brick building had been added onto with a two-story structure of glass and mauve concrete. Taylor sat in her car, working up the nerve to go in. She had two strategies mapped out and rehearsed, but her legs shook just thinking about the potential conflict.

What's the worst that could happen? Her mother's voice echoed in her head.

They could call security and have her thrown out.

Then what?

Get in the car and drive away.

See? You'll survive.

Taylor smiled sheepishly and climbed out. She remembered the first time her mother had talked her through a fearful situation. A big black dog had lived in the middle of their block, and she'd been afraid to walk past that house to her school around the corner. Her mother had sat her down and asked, "What are you afraid of?"

"It might bite me!"

"And if the dog bites you, what happens then?"

"It'll hurt and I'll bleed," she'd responded, even more worried.

"Then what?"

"I don't know. I might need stitches."

"Then what?"

Taylor had shrugged, not wanting to admit the next part.

Her mother had supplied it. "We'll put on a bandage, and you'll go back out and play."

Taylor had reluctantly walked to school after that, and the dog hadn't left its porch. The lesson had stayed with her.

Now she walked into the clinic, trying to look confident.

A pretty young receptionist sat behind a long, curved counter. "May I help you?"

Taylor had expected the older woman, so the script in her head was suddenly worthless. *Oh no.* She'd have to wing it. "I want to see the older woman who answered my call yesterday afternoon."

"Bonnie? She didn't come to work today." The girl reached up and adjusted her tight blonde bun. "I think I heard someone say she retired."

Since yesterday? "Do you have Bonnie's contact information? I really need to talk to her." Taylor had the printed list of names in her pocket, but the thought of showing it to anyone else in the building worried her. They might see her as a threat.

"I'll see what I can find out." The receptionist turned

away and made a phone call.

The door opened behind her, and Taylor turned to see a pregnant woman walk in and plop down in a waiting chair. Taylor hoped the baby inside her was okay. On the surface, the place seemed comforting, with thick carpet and soft chairs in pale-blue and peach colors. But knowing what she did, she wouldn't come here for prenatal care.

After a hushed conversation, the young receptionist turned to Taylor. "Bonnie did retire and she won't be back."

Had the older woman known she was leaving the clinic when she sent Taylor the information? Or had someone discovered the leaked document and forced her out? An icy knot of fear formed in Taylor's stomach. She started to say something, got tongue-tied, and stopped. Then tried again. "What I'm trying to determine is whether Bonnie's retirement was planned. Did she know that yesterday was her last day?"

The receptionist shrugged. "Why do you care?"

Time for her second strategy. "Is there anyone else on staff who worked here twenty years ago?"

The tight-bun girl laughed. "I have no idea. I'm a temp who only fills in sometimes, but I'll see if the director will talk to you."

"Thanks."

A moment later. "Karen Thayer is busy, but she said you could email her if you have questions." Tight Bun handed her a business card with little pink and blue bows around the border. "This is the director's contact info. Now excuse me." The receptionist waved at the pregnant lady and called her to the counter.

Taylor pocketed the card and stepped back. She needed to speak with the retired woman. "What's Bonnie's last name?"

Tight Bun gave her a look. "Yost."

Taylor hurried out, disappointed. So far, she'd been a crappy investigator. But she had learned her contact's name. That was something. Could she find her? Colorado Springs wasn't that big.

In her car, she googled *Bonnie Yost Colorado Springs*. A crude approach, but it made sense to start with the easiest and most obvious things. That's what her mentor at the ME's office always said. The search phrase came up twice, once in an old news article about library volunteers and repeatedly in a story about condominium owners fighting a rezoning ordinance to stop the development of high-rise apartments near the adjacent golf course. Dated two months earlier, the article indicated Bonnie still lived in the Fairfield Greens Complex. Taylor keyed the neighborhood name into her GPS and set off, following the directions.

After a minute, she realized she knew where she was going. She'd lived in Colorado Springs as a child and remembered passing the golf course every time she and her mother went clothes shopping. Finding the right condo would still be a challenge. Yet, she had to try. Bonnie's abrupt retirement seemed suspicious enough to check out. Or maybe the receptionist had known it was her final day, and that's why she'd sent the list of names, believing it was her last chance to access the data and share the secret—whatever it was.

A waist-high rock wall surrounded Fairfield Greens, but the gate stood open after another car pulled in, so Taylor drove through. The homes were clustered in groups of three or four, and each condo had two levels and one shared wall—somewhere between an apartment and a house. Dozens of sandstone-colored units spread out in a meandering maze, dotted with small pine trees and rock paths. She didn't spot any mailboxes with names, only shared mail stations with numbers.

Taylor parked in front of the first condo cluster and shut off her car. This would be impossible. If only they still made phonebooks. Taylor laughed at herself, pulled out her phone, and brought up the white pages for Colorado Springs. Bonnie Yost was listed, but her condo number was not.

Footsteps made her look up. The man who'd pulled in ahead of her had parked and was walking back. An older guy with a permanent golfer's tan. He probably wanted to know why she'd snuck in behind him and what she was doing. Taylor scrambled for something plausible to say and rolled down her window. "I'm looking for Bonnie Yost. She knew my mother when she was pregnant. Now that my mother's gone, I'm trying to figure out some things." True, but Taylor had a flash of guilt for using the dead-mother card.

The man hesitated for a full five seconds. Finally, he pointed at the third cluster of condos on the left. "On the end, farthest from the gate. That's her Volkswagen in the driveway."

"Thank you."

Taylor rolled up the window, waited for him to get into his car, and drove toward Bonnie's home.

Loud knocking didn't bring anyone to the door. Taylor called out Bonnie's name and waited. Maybe she was out for a walk or playing golf. The mint-colored VW bug in the driveway suggested she was home though. Taylor hurried around the side of the condo and peered over the short white fence. Bonnie wasn't in her small backyard either.

Taylor decided to get something to eat, then try again.

Back in her car, she took a few deep breaths and called Zion. Warning him that he could be in danger suddenly seemed more urgent. His phone rang six times and went to voicemail. *Please let him be okay.* Taylor introduced herself, then left a message, stammering her way through an explanation and trying not to sound paranoid: "I need to talk to you about your birth, and it's best if we meet in person. This is a little complicated . . ." She trailed off, then plunged in again. "I'm worried because you're one of the marked names, and I think you'll be targeted. I'm sorry to sound dramatic, but I think your life could be in danger. Please call me."

Relieved that she'd finally done the right thing, she drove to a KFC she'd spotted earlier. Taylor took her time and ate a chicken breast and coleslaw, one of her only fast food weaknesses, then headed back to the Greens. After twenty minutes of waiting, another car came through and opened the security gate. Taylor followed it in and drove straight to Bonnie's place, as if she belonged.

While she walked to the door, she pulled off her sweater and tied it around her waist. The day was warming up. Bonnie didn't respond to her knock. On impulse, Taylor stepped off the porch and peeked through the window, in case Bonnie was napping on the couch or had headphones on.

Oh god. The old woman was sprawled on the floor looking lifeless, and a lot of blood had spilled from her head into the pale carpet. Heart pounding, Taylor ran to her car, climbed in, and locked the doors. *Damn!* This was bad. What now? Her chest hurt, and she couldn't get enough oxygen into her body. *Just get away!* It was all she could think. She backed out of the driveway and turned toward the entrance. *Be calm. Don't speed. Don't draw attention.* Hands slick with sweat, she gripped the wheel and drove through the gate after it opened automatically.

Someone had killed Bonnie to keep her from talking. Someone who might kill Taylor too. She knew she should call the police, but the idea terrified her. The cops might think she murdered the receptionist, because they always suspected the person who found the body. They would take her into a little room for intense questioning. She couldn't handle that. If she told the truth and mentioned the list, they might send her to a psych ward. Her mother had been institutionalized against her will for a few months and had come home a different person. She'd killed herself a year later.

Taylor wasn't taking that kind of chance. She would stop and make an anonymous 911 call in case Bonnie was still alive, then find another way to figure this out.

Chapter 4

Wednesday, Oct. 12, 8:15 p.m., Denver

Jake Wilson stumbled down the dark alley, choking on the stink of garbage. How much farther was the park? As he passed another dumpster, his foot caught on something and he tripped. Smashing down on one knee, he cursed in pain. Then he cursed the growing despair in his heart. When the throbbing subsided, he turned to see what he'd fallen over. Big, yet pliable. What was it? He crawled forward, curious and a little stoned. *Oh shit.* A human body. A homeless drunk who'd passed out?

No. A young person in nice clothes. With bullet holes in the chest and pelvis. Jake could smell the blood and piss and other disgusting things that still seeped from her body. His stomach heaved, and he fought the urge to vomit. He'd never seen a dead person before, even though he'd covered the crime beat as a reporter for six months. Before they'd fired him and he lost everything.

He moved closer and stared at the pale face illuminated only by a half moon. Not a woman after all. A young man with a narrow, sculpted profile. A rent boy? Maybe killed by an angry client or a gay-hating bigot? Was the guy really dead? Jake felt his neck for a pulse and didn't feel one. He glanced around, suddenly fearful. What the hell was he doing here? What had happened to his life? If he didn't get it together soon, he could end up just like this poor guy. Tears welled in his eyes. Grief for the dead young man, and for himself and what had become of his promising life.

Jake shook off the dark thoughts and pulled himself into a squat, ready to stand and move on. He had to find a place to sleep soon and something to cover up with. His jacket alone wouldn't be warm enough tonight.

The shrill sound of a cell phone cut into the dark silence, startling him. The dead man's pocket chirped, his ringtone set to an unsettling electronic beat. A creepy feeling ran up Jake's backbone. Whoever was calling didn't know the guy was dead. But the phone tempted him. This dude no longer needed it. Jake slipped his hand into the nylon jacket pocket and pulled out the cell. A phone would be useful for his job search and for calling about rooms to rent. He'd pawned his phone to a friend for cash—to hold until he could buy it back. But it wouldn't be any time soon. For a long moment, he hesitated. His life would be so much easier with a phone . . . even for a few days. When the ringing finally went silent, he slipped the cell into his own pocket. Jake glanced around. Was anyone watching him? He shook it off. Probably just a little pot paranoia.

Maybe the dead man had a little cash too.

Guilt twisted his gut and made his stomach heave again. Disgusted with himself, Jake promised to make up for this bullshit by doing volunteer work later, when he got it together. With shaky hands, he searched the body's pockets and found a set of keys, followed by a wallet with a driver's license showing through a clear-plastic sleeve. Zion Tumara, age twenty. The guy looked younger, with a smooth face and a skinny body. Who had shot him and why? Jake's natural quest to find answers—buried recently by his overriding struggle just to survive—surfaced in his pot-spacy brain. The need to know had driven him through journalism school and into an investigative reporter position at the Denver Post. He'd loved every moment of his job there.

But he'd failed a random drug test and been fired—even though pot was legal in Colorado! Soon after, his car had broken down and he'd been evicted. His father, who hated the pot smoking, refused to help him, except for keeping him on his phone service. New in Denver, Jake only had one good friend, but the guy lived with roommates who hadn't been willing to let Jake crash with them. He slept in his car for a while, then sold it when he needed cash and ended up on the streets. Somewhere in his brain, he knew the weed was a problem and that he had to quit, but he hadn't been able to yet. At the end of a miserable day of being homeless and stressed, smoking a joint was all he had to look forward to.

Jake flipped open the man's wallet and checked the cash compartment. It was too dark to know for sure, but the wad of twenties probably added up to three hundred dollars or more. He started to pull out the cash, then changed his mind and shoved the whole wallet into his pocket. If he could find the address, he might be able to sleep there tonight, then rent a cheap room tomorrow with the cash. All he needed was a place to shower and sleep until he could find a job and jumpstart his life again. Right now, he had to get out of this alley before someone saw him with the body—and before the police came to investigate.

He glanced at the dead man again and impulsively reached out to touch his head, a gesture of compassion and apology. Jake's fingers came away sticky with blood, and he noticed a gaping wound in his temple. Had he fallen against the dumpster when he was shot?

Jake pushed to his feet and looked around for something to wipe his hands on. A candy bar wrapper near the brick wall cleaned up most of it. He would rinse off the rest at the earliest opportunity. After another backward glance, Jake jogged down the alley. He'd been heading to Cheyenne Park to maybe sleep on the bench near the bathrooms, but now he would hop on a bus and cross town to find Zion's home. If the dead man had a roommate, Jake would be out of luck.

The address turned out to be a small complex near an art school, an older neighborhood with a mix of apartments and retail. The lights were out in the upstairs window in unit three. A good sign. Feeling less high now, Jake moved quietly up the steps and let himself into the apartment. Afraid to show his face before he knew what he would encounter, he used the light on the cell phone to look around. Leather furniture, potted cactuses, and bizarre paintings. Was Zion the artist?

Jake heard a soft thump in another room and held his breath, not moving. If a roommate came out and turned on the lights, what would he say? *Oops?* Maybe this had been a stupid idea. It might be better to just use the cash and find a cheap motel along the highway. For a long moment, he waited, listening for footsteps or voices and expecting a light to come on. Something brushed against his leg and he jumped. The cat let out a meow at the same time, and Jake laughed. Not exactly a roommate.

Still, he had to check the apartment to be sure. He hurried into the hallway where two of the three doors were closed. The open entry led into a bedroom. A nightlight in a wall outlet shimmered with a purple glow, illuminating a large empty bed with a dark purple comforter. Jake stepped back and tried the other doors. A bathroom and a messy art studio. Zion had created the bizarre paintings, and he appeared to live alone. Except for the cat, which was following Jake around.

His stomach growled, and he headed for the kitchen. He hadn't eaten since his free breakfast at the Food Bank that morning. The day had been devoted to job searching at the employment office and renewing his food stamps, then he'd smoked a joint with a street friend and started looking for a place to crash. The Mission filled up early so no point in going there. He hated the shelter anyway. The preaching was hard to take, and the smell of that many homeless people in one place was overwhelming. He'd only spent one night there, and it had been enough.

In Zion's refrigerator, he found half a leftover pizza—the first normal thing in the apartment—and shoved it in the microwave. While he waited for it to heat up, the phone in his pocket rang. *Shit.* Getting calls for the dead man was too creepy. Jake pulled out the cell and silenced it. The caller information caught his attention. Whoever it was had called twice already. This was the third time. A family member trying to reach Zion? Jake had a pang of guilt for not reporting the death. He would do that soon. For now, he put the phone on the table, retrieved the warm pizza, and sat down to eat. No newspaper or magazines to peruse. A vase with fake purple flowers instead.

Out of curiosity and boredom, he accessed Zion's voicemail and played the newest message: "This is Taylor Lopez again. I need to talk to you about your birth, and it's best if we meet in person. I'm very worried about you. Your life could be in danger. Please call me."

Jake's pulse raced, and he put down his slice of pizza. Who the hell was Taylor Lopez? The voice had a pleasant tone that wasn't distinctly male or female, and the name could go either way too. More important, how had Taylor known Zion was in trouble and would be murdered? Jake itched to grab the phone and call back. This was a news story and he wanted to know! But he had to think everything through and not get himself into trouble. He could call Taylor and pretend to be Zion, then figure out what to tell her before they met. Or maybe he should just be honest and tell Taylor about Zion's death over the phone. If Taylor knew where Zion lived, he or she might eventually show up. The police would too.

Another wave of guilt rolled through Jake's gut. The cops wouldn't be able to identify the body and inform Zion's family. What the hell had he done? Jake put his head on the table. He would leave the apartment first thing in the morning and make an anonymous phone call to the police department. Then he would sign up at one of those day labor places and work whatever crappy jobs they offered. He would quit smoking pot too. He needed a clear head.

The phone seemed to exert a magnetic pull, and Jake reached for it. He hit the callback button, and scrambled to think of a plausible connection between him and Zion—and a reason why he was in the dead man's home. Taylor's smooth voice answered right away. "Zion. Thank you for returning my call. I'd like to meet as soon as possible. Are you available now?"

Jake's curiosity overpowered his sense of decency. "What's this about?"

"I'll explain when I see you. Where do you want to meet?

I'll come to you."

Had Taylor ever seen the dead man before? Or know what Zion looked like? If not, Jake could pretend to be Zion just long enough to hear her story. Then he would tell her the truth. Jake remembered passing a coffee shop two blocks away and gave her the name and location. "I can be there in a few minutes."

"Give me fifteen." A pause. "What are you wearing?"

Jake glanced down at his stained hoodie, embarrassed by his appearance, but relieved that Taylor had never met Zion. "A blue Broncos sweatshirt and jeans. What about you?"

"Red sweater, black pants. See you soon." The call went dead.

Taylor was a woman, Jake decided. Men didn't wear red unless it was a football jersey. His own dirty sweatshirt bothered him even more now. How could he make a good impression? He had more clothes in a small storage locker downtown, but they were all just as crappy. Reflexively, his hand went to his chin. He could shave. That would help.

In the bathroom, he searched for a razor and finally found a small, unopened package of disposables. Zion didn't keep any shaving gear on the countertop, so bar soap would have to suffice. The leisurely shave in the bright lights of a clean private bathroom was the best grooming experience he'd had since he'd lost his apartment. For months, he'd been using the Catholic Community Center, a crowded space he couldn't get out of fast enough. Did he have enough time to shower? No. He would do that when he got back. Jake grabbed his backpack and headed out. He felt upbeat for the first time in ages. Taylor and her mysterious circumstances might be just what he needed to pull himself out of this slump. He was so ready for a comeback.

Chapter 5

Taylor stood outside the coffee shop, zipping and unzipping her sweater, having second thoughts about going in. Warning Zion that he could be in danger was the right thing to do, but he would probably think she was a nutty drama queen. Now that she was out of high school, she wasn't bullied or humiliated anymore, but if he mocked her, she didn't know how she would handle it. Everything she'd learned about Zion from social media indicated he was a troubled, but decent, human being. *Just do it and move on!* She could always walk away if things got uncomfortable.

Taylor reached for the door and stepped in. At nine on a Friday night, the coffee house was nearly empty, and she spotted the man in the blue Broncos sweatshirt immediately. Something wasn't right. He was too big, too masculine. Only the side of his face was visible, but he wasn't Zion. She froze, and a bolt of fear shot through her. He could be the hit man. Maybe he'd killed Zion, taken his phone, and listened to her message. She spun toward the door and bolted outside.

Why would an assassin meet her openly in a coffee shop? Wouldn't it be smarter to follow her and attack her somewhere private?

The door opened behind her, and a voice called out. "Taylor?" Low pitched, but kind and soothing.

Her mind screamed *Run!* But her body turned back. "Who are you?"

He blinked, started to speak, then stopped. After an uncomfortable pause, he said, "Jake Wilson. Please come in and sit down. We have a lot to talk about."

His voice was like a salve that penetrated her defenses.

He held open the door, and curiosity drove her through it. She eased over to the booth where he'd been sitting and slipped in.

Jake sat across from her.

"Where is Zion?"

His eyes pinched with distress. "There's no way to put this gently. He was shot."

No! "Is he dead?"

Jake nodded. "I'm sorry."

She was too late. *Why hadn't she called him earlier?* An ache settled into her heart. She hadn't known Zion, but she'd felt connected to him. They were both part of an accident or cruel experiment that she suspected was still going on. "How do you know Zion? And why didn't you tell me on the phone?"

"This is complicated." Jake leaned toward her and kept his amber eyes locked on hers. His face was pleasing, except his mouth was too big and he'd cut himself shaving. His dirty-blond hair was getting long enough to show a curl at the end.

Taylor was suddenly aware of his smell—sweaty clothes and unwashed hair. Was he on the run? "Tell me the truth. At this point, not much surprises me."

"I tripped over Zion's body in an alley." Jake touched her hand. "I'm sorry for your loss."

Reflexively, she pulled back. "You didn't know him? How did you get his phone? Why are you here?"

A darkness washed over Jake's face. "After I found the

body, I took the phone, looked up the address, and went to his house for a place to sleep tonight. I know—" He held up his hands. "I'm ashamed of all that. But I've had some tough breaks and just needed to feel human for a moment. Then you called, and your message was so urgent and intriguing, I had to meet you."

He was homeless? Yet Jake seemed articulate and clear-eyed. She wanted to walk away from this confusing stranger, but not yet. "I want Zion's phone." The assassin might have contacted his target to lure him out. Or Zion might be in touch with other people on the list. She desperately needed information. Someone had to stop the murders and find the military doctor who was responsible for all the intersex kids.

"What's your connection?" Jake reached in his pocket and handed her the cell. "And what made you think Zion was in danger?"

"Why should I tell you? You're just an opportunistic moocher." Another of her mother's expressions.

"Ouch!" He recoiled in hurt.

Was he mocking her?

For a long moment, they stared at each other in silence. Finally, he said, "Let me buy you a cup of coffee."

"Make it hot tea, please."

Taylor watched him walk to the counter, admiring his body. Long and lean but with a nice butt and strong thighs. She pictured him naked, those muscular legs wrapped around her. Then she imagined herself rubbing against his warm flesh. *Stop!* She made herself visualize skin lesions all over his body. A sure way to shut down her need. Hyper-sexuality had been a problem since she was thirteen, but she'd finally learned to control it. She'd always assumed it was related to her gender duality. But now she wondered if it was caused by whatever the military had given those pregnant women long ago. Probably some kind of pharmaceutical. But for what purpose, she had yet to figure out. Had they tested a drug they thought would produce better soldiers?

She made a note of Jake's name in her own phone, then perused Zion's call log. He had few contacts, and almost all of his calls had been to or from people he'd created contact files for. Only one call, three days earlier, had come from a number with no association. She searched for it on Chrome, but didn't get a direct result.

Jake came back with her tea and another charming smile. "The reason you should tell me what's going on," he said, sitting down, "is because I used to be a reporter. So I'm good at tracking things down and getting the whole story."

He looked too young to have been one for long. But still, a newspaper connection could come in handy. "Were you fired?"

"Sort of. I was lucky to get the job in the first place. My father told me not to major in journalism."

"So why did you?"

"I love writing. And as a kid, I loved every movie with a reporter as the hero who exposes the bad stuff going down." Jake shrugged. "I'm not giving up on my career, but right now I just need a job."

A romantic and an idealist—who smelled like old carpet in a rental trailer. But it would be nice to have someone to brainstorm with. She was still trying to figure out why they were only targeting certain people on the list. But the dead guys' love of fire could be a factor.

"Are you going to enlighten me?" Jake prodded.

She had to tell somebody. If Jake believed her, maybe the

police would too. She took a sip of tea and eased into the story. "I work in the morgue as a death investigative intern. I like figuring things out too." CSI had inspired her, but he didn't need to know that.

"That's unusual. But cool."

"In the last few weeks, two similar bodies have come in. Both young people who supposedly died from accidents."

"I'm intrigued." Jake leaned forward. "What about their bodies was similar? The way they died?"

"One fell off a balcony and one drowned, but they were the same age."

"Both male?"

"Yes. Sort of." Taylor squirmed in her seat. Could she tell him without admitting she was the same? Was that why she hadn't talked to the police yet? She'd spent a lifetime hiding the fact.

Jake scowled. "What do you mean by *sort of*?"

"They were," Taylor paused, "intersex. Living and presenting as males, but with some female genitalia."

She watched his face for signs of revulsion or judgment but saw only curiosity.

"Two intersex people the same age dying accidentally around the same time." He rubbed his chin. "I see why you think that's odd. I don't know how common the mutation is, but that must be a statistical anomaly."

She winced at the word *mutation*. "It's more common than you think. Gender is more of a continuum than a category, and intersex people aren't mutants." *Unless some military asshole had purposefully designed them that way.*

Jake grimaced. "Sorry, that was the wrong word. But I know there's more to this. Like Zion. How does he fit in?"

"I think he was targeted too." Taylor took a deep breath.

"I did a brief investigation of the dead guys and discovered they were both connected to an obstetrics clinic in Colorado Springs. So I called there and mentioned their names. The receptionist warned me to back off, then later that evening she emailed me a list of people. Four had checkmarks. Logan Hurtz and Adrian Warsaw are both currently in the morgue. And now Zion is dead too. I can't find the fourth person, Seth Wozac."

"Get out! Seriously?" Jake's eyes popped open and he sat up straighter. "You need to go to the police."

"I know." Taylor took another sip of tea and stared at the mug. She was ashamed of this next part.

Jake tapped her hand. "Why haven't you?"

"I was afraid they wouldn't believe me. So I went to see the receptionist. She's dead too."

"That's too bizarre." His voice tightened, but his eyes looked more excited than afraid. "How did she die?"

"I saw her on the floor through the window at her house, and it looked like she'd been hit on the head."

"You went to her house? When?" He looked both alarmed and impressed.

"Yesterday. The clinic said she'd retired, so I tracked her down."

"She was older? Maybe she fell."

Taylor didn't believe it. "Her retirement seemed very sudden. I think she decided to leave the clinic after she sent me the list. Or someone forced her out."

"What's her name? I want to find out what I can about her death." Jake reached in his backpack, then swore. "Can I have the phone back for a minute? I don't have mine with me."

Taylor pushed the cell across the table. "Bonnie Yost. I've been checking the news and nothing has been reported." She shifted in the booth seat, worried about how to say the next part. "One of her neighbors knows I was looking for her and that I went to her house. I'm afraid the police will want to question me."

"So? Tell them everything." Jake grinned. "We can still investigate, even if the cops take it seriously and look into the whole mess." He keyed something into the phone.

Her gut clenched, and she suddenly regretted the tea. "I can't handle an interrogation. I'm easily intimidated and could end up being one of those people who confesses to something they didn't do just to get them to leave me alone."

Jake started to laugh, then stopped. "You're serious."

"Yeah. I'm working on the issue, but look." She held out her hand. "I'm trembling just from visualizing myself in one of those little rooms with a mean cop."

Jake cocked his head and gave her a funny smile. "Yet you tracked down the receptionist and you came to warn Zion."

"Both were difficult for me, but what else could I do? I can't let them kill any more subjects."

"Subjects?" He stared at her, eyes narrowed. "What's your theory?"

"A medical experiment conducted twenty-one years ago. Probably by the military to test some pregnancy drug. The clinic is connected to the hospital at Fort Carson. Another reason I'm so worried about going to the authorities."

Jake nodded. "If the military is behind it, they're probably testing drugs they hope will produce superior soldiers."

The cafe door opened, and Taylor looked up, worried. An older lady entered, and she was too distracted by her cell phone to notice anyone. Taylor continued. "Somehow, a lot of the women had intersex babies, which is probably not what the researchers had in mind."

"Who knows? Maybe intersex people make better warriors."

She didn't feel like a warrior.

"Why kill those kids now?" Jake had started taking notes in a small paper tablet.

Did people still use those? "I don't know, but Logan, Adrian, and Zion all seemed a bit obsessed with fire. Logan was even arrested and questioned about an arson."

"Fascinating." Jake looked down at the phone again. "Still nothing about Bonnie Yost's death. Maybe she wasn't murdered." His shoulders slumped. "I need to get my phone back with all my contacts. A friend of mine has it." His face brightened. "But now I have the money to retrieve it."

Was he asking her for a ride? "What contacts?"

"With the Denver police and a woman in county records. I worked the crime beat for six months."

"I'll take you to get your phone if you can arrange a way for me to tell all this to the police without being arrested or stuck in an interrogation room."

"I appreciate the offer of a ride. I'll see what I can do." He shook his head. "But no guarantees. I haven't been at the paper for a few months, and the only person I know at the Colorado Springs Police Department isn't an officer."

"Can you, or the woman you know at county records, help me find Seth Wozac, the fourth guy? We need to warn him."

Jake snapped his fingers. "Maybe we should contact the FBI. If this is a military thing, the feds will have more clout to investigate. It's also better than involving two police departments."

Oh great. The FBI could make people they questioned disappear. "I don't know about that."

"Can I see the list? How many names?"

"Thirty-three." She had a printed copy in her pocket but wasn't ready to let him know her name was on it. Because then he would know she was intersex too.

"Just four were check-marked? All males?"

If she wanted his help, she had to be honest. Taylor unzipped a jacket pocket and handed him the list. "Yes, four with checks, but I don't know if Seth identifies as male or female." She couldn't hold back. "I look forward when we can stop using gender-specific pronouns and forcing people to label themselves. It's so unnecessary." She already used the term *they* as much as possible, and it had become acceptable in the papers she wrote for her university classes.

Jake eagerly scanned the names, then stopped and looked up. "You're on the list. And your name has an asterisk." He blinked and swallowed hard. "We have to find a place for you to hide."

Chapter 6

Through the glass storefront, Devin Blackburn watched the girl enter the coffee shop and sit down across from a young man. A boyfriend? The background search she'd done on Taylor Lopez indicated she was a busy college student with little social life. A loner. That hadn't surprised her. Most of the subjects were. But no, this guy wasn't a boyfriend. They weren't touching each other, and Taylor's expression was distrustful. Devin moved into a better position and snapped a photo of him, then stepped away from the window to run the facial recognition app. Jake Wilson, no military service, no criminal record. Last employer, the Denver Post. Current address unknown.

Shit! A journalist. The last thing the Peace Project needed was a reporter snooping around. At least he wasn't still with the newspaper. How had he gotten involved? Was Lopez telling him about the subjects that had come through the morgue? Maybe her visit to Carson Obstetrics too. If the clinic receptionist hadn't accessed the data and triggered a software alert, they might not have known about Lopez's inquiry.

In some ways, terminating Bonnie Yost had been harder than taking out the subjects. The old woman had reminded Devin of her grandmother, and she'd had a moment of doubt.

Yet Bonnie was old and had used up most of her life, so that eased Devin's guilt. She was still coming to terms with assassinating the fire-obsessed subjects who had the potential to cause trouble and draw scrutiny to the project. The three men had been so young. Devin pulled up her sleeve and glanced at the fresh tattoo she'd had inked last week. Another flame, like the first subject, to represent Adrian Warsaw's passion, and with his initials blended into the flickering light. It was the least she could do to honor the life she'd taken.

She would get one for Lopez and Wozac too after she terminated them. But they were all like her—a gender mess. Killing them was an act of kindness that would spare them a life of freakish loneliness. Or a long stretch in prison. Unlike the other subjects, Devin felt lucky to have a purpose. *The Greater Good.* It always took precedence over individual lives. That's what the military was all about. Sacrificing a few to save the many—and the innocents.

Devin stepped in front of the window to observe her targets. They seemed to be engaged in a lively conversation. She knew what her orders would be, but it was essential to update the major. She walked to the corner to get away from the entrance and called his private cell phone.

"What's the situation?" The major was direct, as always.

"Taylor Lopez is talking to an ex-journalist named Jake Wilson."

"Dammit all to hell! You were supposed to terminate her."

Devin had only received the assignment thirty-six hours earlier, and the clinic receptionist had been the priority. Followed by Tumara, who she'd been watching for a few days. But making excuses would only worsen the reprimand. "I'm sorry, sir. I was waiting for the right opportunity to make it look accidental."

An unexpected pause. "I've changed my mind. Bring Lopez in. New information leads me to believe she'd be a good candidate for operative training."

That surprised Devin, even though two other subjects had entered the program. "Yes, sir. What about Wilson?"

"He needs to be terminated. But get Lopez first, then wait a day or so and make Wilson look like an accident as well."

Faking accidents was more challenging than a bullet to the brain, but she would pull it off. Again.

"Better yet, make him disappear," the major added.

Damn. Disposing of bodies was a pain in the ass. "I believe Wilson might be homeless, sir. I can give him an overdose and leave him on a park bench. No one will even care."

"As long as he's never connected to the clinic."

"I'll handle it." She heard footsteps and glanced over at the front of the coffee shop. It was just an older woman entering.

"You'd better. I'm already concerned about the subjects' bodies. You must have left too much of them intact or Lopez wouldn't have been able to connect the deaths and start snooping around the clinic."

Devin had failed him and deserved the reprimand, but this time she had to explain. "The fall from the seventh floor should have damaged the first body more than it did. I left Warsaw intact because it needed to look natural, and he never left his apartment complex. But the third one, which I just completed, will not be identified as intersex. I put several bullets in his groin and chest."

The major grunted. "It's unfortunate that the morgue attendant is one of the subjects. It's in her file, but no one foresaw that it would be a problem."

He was letting her off the hook. A rare moment. She checked the coffee shop entrance again. Still quiet.

"Report to me when you bring Lopez into the complex."

"Yes, sir."

The major ended the call. Her father liked to keep their relationship formal. Most likely because he thought of her as male. She'd never tried to correct him since that one time when she was a kid. Her Army-short hair, workout buff muscles, and wide face helped her pass as male, and she was glad to be treated like a man. The major wouldn't have told her about the Project or let her into the program if he'd raised her as a daughter. Devin had known from the age of twelve that she'd been part of an important experiment that would help keep America safe. Her sniper training had started at fifteen, and she'd taken out her first target at eighteen. *For the Greater Good.* She'd played the motto over and over in her head to suppress the unexpected sense of loss and shame. She'd expected the assassinations to get easier, but she was relieved not to have to terminate Taylor Lopez. Why? Because Lopez identified as a female?

Devin stepped around to the front of the coffee shop. Lopez and Wilson weren't at their table. *Fuck!* Devin opened the door and scanned the cafe. They weren't at the counter either. Yet, they hadn't come out the front door. She would have seen them from her post on the corner. Had she missed them while focusing on the major's orders?

No, they'd snuck out a back door. She'd lost her targets. Devin sprinted down the side of the building. As soon as she had Lopez and Wilson in sight again, she would move quickly to silence them.

Chapter 7

A few minutes earlier

Jake grabbed Taylor's hands, and this time she didn't pull away. "We need to leave now," he urged. "And go out the back door, in case you were followed." An equal mix of fear and excitement pulsed in his heart. He hadn't felt this alive since he'd lost his job. Or maybe ever. This was big, a news story unlike anything he'd ever investigated. He pulled his backpack over his shoulder and stood. "I'm serious. Let's go."

Taylor's green eyes searched the small cafe, as she clutched her cup. She looked terrified, but he couldn't help that. Four people were already dead, and she could be next. For a second, her face caught his attention. Smooth skin, angular cheekbones, and hauntingly attractive. Yet not distinctly feminine or masculine. Was she intersex too? Like the others on the list? He would ask her eventually, but it didn't matter. He liked her already for her courage, even though she didn't know she was brave.

The door opened again, and they both spun toward it. Two teenage boys. Jake turned back to Taylor. She was already standing and pulling on her sweater.

"Is there a back door?" she asked.

"There has to be. I think fire codes call for it." Jake rushed toward a small alcove at the back of the cafe, finding a bathroom door on the exterior wall plus an unmarked door on the right. After glancing over his shoulder to make sure Taylor was behind him, he pushed open the unmarked door and entered a small kitchen. The middle-aged woman who'd served their drinks turned in surprise. Jake grinned and kept moving. He'd spotted a door with a push-bar handle tucked between two steel refrigerators. But the exit didn't lead outside. They found themselves in a dim hallway that connected to the business on the other side of the building.

"Oh no. Can we get out?" Taylor asked, keeping a half step behind him.

"I think so." If the business was still open to the public, and if its back door wasn't locked. *Shit.* Jake didn't know this area well. Denver was a big city, and he hadn't lived here long. He spotted an opening to the right and turned. Another door with a red Exit sign. He pushed through, and a cold blast of air chilled his face. The dark alley reminded him of finding Zion's body, and he repressed a shudder.

Grabbing Taylor's hand, he ran left, away from the coffee shop. If a hit man was waiting near the corner, watching the front door for Taylor to exit, the assassin might still be able to see them. Or at least see their movement. The low-wattage bulbs over the doors didn't offer much light.

Jake didn't look back until they'd reached the sidewalk at the end of the alley. He let go of Taylor's hand and asked. "Where is your car?"

"On the next block, not far from the coffee shop."

If the killer had followed Taylor, then he knew her car and might be watching it. "We'll circle the block and see if we spot anyone lurking."

"I can't abandon my car!" Taylor strode down the sidewalk, passing a closed storefront.

Jake hurried to catch up. "I know. We need it to drive to Colorado Springs."

Taylor glanced over at him. "We need a plan, and for the record, you're not in charge." Her voice was soft, but determined.

Jake laughed. "I know. I tend to be bossy. Especially if I'm worried."

"I think you might be overreacting. My name wasn't checked. It just had an asterisk, and maybe Bonnie did that, just as a note to herself."

Wishful thinking. "Maybe. But now that you're investigating, they'll want to shut you down."

Taylor didn't respond.

They reached the end of the block and stopped. Once they stepped past the edge of the building, they could be seen by someone in front of the cafe. *Just go for it.* Jake put his arm around Taylor. "Hug me back. We'll look like a couple with no worries."

Taylor reluctantly slid her arm around him, her body tense. She was so lean! No softness to her at all. After a lone car passed them, Jake pulled her in close and took off across the street. On the other side, he kept going. They would circle the block and come back on the next avenue. "Where exactly is your car?"

"Parallel to us one block over." Taylor pulled away. "It's not directly in front of the coffee shop. I think this will work." She made an odd sound in her throat. "If anyone is watching, I would expect them to go after Seth first."

"The fourth name?"

"Yeah. I couldn't find him."

"I may be able to help with that too." Cold air squeezed his chest, and Jake realized he hadn't zipped his jacket before they bolted. "We need to warn Seth even if we go to the FBI with all this." He didn't know what to call the collections of deaths, correlations, and list people. Evidence? Theory? Taylor had referred to the births as an experiment. "The feds may not take us seriously enough to act quickly. Seth could be living his last moments."

"Don't say that," Taylor snapped. "I feel bad enough that I didn't warn Zion in time."

Jake patted her arm as they hurried around the corner. "You tried, and you're still doing everything you can."

Two couples pushed past them on the sidewalk, talking in loud, drunk voices. Jake suddenly craved a tall mug of dark ale, with a joint chaser. But he had to keep his shit together. This could be the most important journalistic endeavor of his life. Getting it right and selling the story to a major newspaper or magazine could be the break he needed to make a career comeback.

"My car is just around this next corner." Taylor picked up her pace. "I'll unlock it as soon as I'm within range, and we'll run for it."

"What's the make?"

"A white Jetta, in the middle of the block." Taylor stepped around the building and pressed her key. They heard the beep and both charged forward. As he ran, Jake glanced to the end of the sidewalk but didn't see anyone lurking or watching them. He jumped in the passenger's side. He would rather be the driver, but it felt good just to be inside a vehicle for the first time in weeks.

Taylor started the car and eased onto the street. "Do you see anyone back there?" She glanced in the rearview mirror.

"No. I think we're good." Had he been too paranoid? Maybe Taylor wasn't in danger. A wave of doubt rolled over him. Was she making all this up? Some people were loony enough to fake their own kidnappings or other bizarre events. But he had found Zion's murdered body. How could she have known about Zion? Unless Taylor was the killer. Oh god. Was she a psychopath?

Taylor touched his arm, initiating contact for the first time. "Thanks for taking me seriously. It's nice not to be alone in this."

Jake buckled his seat belt and leaned back. He would investigate everything she'd told him, including her claim to work at the morgue, but his instinct was to believe her. "Let's go get my phone, then drive to Colorado Springs and find a cheap motel. We'll visit the clinic first thing in the morning. Only this time, I'll try to access a computer and see if I find relevant files."

Taylor gave him a look. "Do you have money for a motel?"

He had Zion's cash and bankcard. "Sort of. Do you have any resources?"

"Sort of."

"Once we contact the FBI, they might put you into protective custody."

"That sounds horrible." She shook her head and turned left at the intersection. "Another good reason to not contact authorities." Taylor glanced in her rearview mirror. "There's a car back there, but I can't tell if it's following us."

Jake looked over his shoulder. The headlights were a block and half behind them. "Probably not."

"Maybe after we warn Seth, I should just run," Taylor suggested. "I have an online friend in Oregon who would probably take me in for a while."

Jake felt a chill. If the military was behind the experiment and the killings, Taylor might not be safe anywhere. Now that he knew, he might not be either. "Let's see what we can find out, then we'll call the FBI. We can keep you in the background until you feel comfortable talking to them."

Taylor was quiet for a minute. "Perfect. Thank you."

He gave her directions to his friend's house, then texted him to make sure he was home. Ryan was happy to hear Jake could buy back his phone, and he couldn't wait to get it. Giving up his connection to the internet had been like losing an arm. The worst part of being homeless.

"Why does he have your phone?" Taylor asked.

"I needed some cash, and Ryan loaned it to me. But kept the phone as collateral."

"It must have been a lot of cash or he's not much of a friend."

Jake laughed. "A little of both. I haven't been in Denver very long."

"Where are you from?" Taylor pulled into the turning lane.

"Illinois. After college, I applied for jobs everywhere and got lucky in landing the Denver Post. What about you?"

"I grew up in Colorado Springs because my mother was stationed at Fort Carson. I'm currently enrolled in UC."

"Why the morgue?"

"I like forensics, and dead people are easier to be around than most living people." Taylor let out her first small laugh. "That makes me sound weird, and I am. You've probably guessed that I'm gender-fluid. So I've been a shy freak my whole life. College is easier than high school because gender issues are finally becoming more open."

"I hope this isn't inappropriate, but I'm curious. Are you attracted to men or women?"

"Both, but I keep to myself."

What a unique person. Taylor was quiet after that. They made a quick stop to get his phone, and Jake took a moment to make an anonymous call to the police about Zion. Then they got on the freeway and headed south. After a long silent stretch, Jake brought up the investigation, and they discussed it for while, then Taylor went quiet again.

An hour later, they exited on Nevada Avenue and soon pulled into the Rocky Ridge Motel, an old, flat-roofed building with only a few cars out front. "Carson Obstetrics is only five minutes away," Taylor said as she turned off the car.

Jake had been worried about how they would handle the sleeping situation, but he hadn't wanted to bring it up and spook her before they got here. "I think we should get one room and stay together for safety and economy." He met her eyes. "You can trust me."

"I know. You wouldn't be in my car otherwise." She opened her door. "We'll work out the sleeping arrangement."

Perfect. She wasn't going to be weird about crashing together. He climbed out too, and they walked toward the neon office sign at the end of the building. "I have some cash," he said, "but maybe we should save it." He didn't want to use Zion's card unless it was an emergency. The police might start watching the murdered man's bank for activity.

"I'll put it on my credit card, then we'll settle up." Taylor paused. "I mean when this is over and we part company."

Jake touched her arm. "I hope we'll stay friends."

"Sure. Why not?" She didn't look at him.

He liked her and hoped she would warm up. As an extrovert, he sometimes got frustrated with shy, quiet types, but he'd learned to be patient. Growing up, his mother had hardly talked to him, but he'd spent every weekend with his father, a talkative fun-loving extrovert, so his childhood had been unusual, but balanced. He and his dad weren't talking now, but Jake hoped that would change.

He stopped in front of the office door and blocked Taylor with his arm. "Wait. Let me check in on my own. It's better if the manager doesn't even see you."

"Good idea." She handed him her credit card and hurried away.

Chapter 8

Inside the car, Taylor shivered, more from fear than cold. She was going to die. She felt it in her bones. Her only hope was to get a fake ID, ditch her car, and buy a train ticket to somewhere far away. She desperately wanted to do just that, but she couldn't. She wasn't a soldier but she'd been raised by one. And soldiers didn't run. They didn't leave anyone behind either. All those intersex people who'd been conceived in the experiment felt like her siblings, her people. What if they were all murdered because she'd been too scared to fight for them? She couldn't live with herself if she were the only survivor. Even if most weren't targeted for death, they still deserved to know the circumstances of their birth and the reason for their sexual differences.

Taylor glanced back at the motel office and saw Jake come out. He was willing to risk himself for this investigation, and it wasn't even personal for him. She hadn't figured him out yet. He seemed to have integrity, and she instinctively trusted him. So how had he ended up homeless and desperate enough to take a dead man's wallet and phone? She watched Jake walk toward a room near the other end of the motel, so she grabbed her satchel and ran across the narrow parking lot. He had the door open by the time she reached it, and she darted inside. Jake bolted the chain lock behind them, and she felt a sense of relief. She was safe—for the moment.

Jake glanced around. "It's not bad."

They both laughed. The walls were stained with nicotine, the carpet smelled like a wet dog, and the orange-and-beige motif hurt her eyes. "We'll find another motel tomorrow. It will be good to keep on the move anyway."

"Speaking of which, we need to move your car. It's too obvious from the road."

Taylor handed him the key. As he walked out, she had a moment of dread. What if he stole her Jetta and took off? She shook her head and plopped on the bed. No, that didn't make sense. She pulled her laptop from her satchel and plugged her phone into it. The crappy motel probably didn't have Wi-Fi, but her cell might pick up a tower. She wanted to check her messages and search for more names on the list. Most of her classmates had switched to tablet computers, but she still loved her lightweight laptop. So much more functional.

An Instagram message from an acquaintance popped into her phone, asking why she'd missed classes, but Taylor didn't respond. She didn't like to lie, and the truth was too complex. She'd never been a big social media user. Her mother hadn't allowed much of it when she was young, and Taylor hadn't had enough friends in high school to make the effort worthwhile.

Her mind shifted to the sleeping arrangement. She couldn't make him sleep on the floor. Too rude and prude. But she couldn't risk Jake flopping around in his sleep and making contact with her body. The problem wasn't just her weird private parts, it was her hyper-sexuality. She didn't trust herself not to respond if he touched her, even accidentally. And she couldn't risk him being freaked out by her small penis.

Pillows and jackets. They would make a barrier in the middle.

Jake came back in. "Hey, mind if I turn up the heat?"

"Please do." She hadn't noticed how chilly the room was until he mentioned it.

Jake sat in the worn padded chair. "Let's figure out a game plan for tomorrow at the clinic. One of us needs to create a distraction while the other accesses a computer and downloads files. I'm pretty good with data, so I should probably be the one to take that risk."

"A distraction?" *Oh god.* That meant drawing attention to herself in a big, messy way. "I don't think I can do that."

Jake gave her a charming smile. "Sure you can. Just keep it simple. Put on a little show of not feeling well to get their attention, then fall on the floor."

Taylor cringed. She'd never participated in a school performance of any kind, and this was completely out of her comfort zone. "Maybe I should access the computer instead."

"Have you done any programming or coding?"

"No."

"Then you get to be the distraction."

"But I've been inside the clinic before. The receptionist might remember me and figure out that it's staged."

Jake stood and grabbed a small pillow. "You could pretend to be pregnant. Plus pull your hair back and wear some fake glasses."

It could work. Her hand shook as she reached for the pillow. What in the hell had she signed up for?

Chapter 9

Thursday, Oct. 13, 9:05 a.m., Washington DC

Andra Bailey walked into the monitoring room where five agents watched giant screens, scanning the world for trouble. The nearest one looked up at her.

"Anything happening in Colorado?" she asked. The recent cluster of mass shootings in her home state had triggered a need to watch it closely. She feared a militant group like the Bundys was primed to take over a federal building or seize state-owned lands. As a key member of the Critical Incident Unit, it was her job to be aware of these possibilities so the Federal Bureau of Investigation could get a jump on them—maybe quash them in advance.

"A missing teenager and a murdered old woman." The agent, a young man still in training, gave her a devilish grin. "Also, Owen Granger was arrested for assault with a deadly weapon."

Bailey smiled back, knowing it was expected. "That'll keep him out of circulation for a while." Granger was an anti-government zealot they'd been watching for years. She turned to leave, then changed her mind and spun back. "What do we know about the murdered old woman?" *What if she was connected to Granger and he was on a personal vendetta?*

"She worked for a medical clinic and was attacked in her home. Bludgeoned with something heavy."

Probably not related. "Give me her name."

"Bonnie Yost."

Why was that a familiar surname? Bailey nodded and walked to the door, then realized the nod wasn't enough. She turned back. "Thank you." Niceties weren't natural to her, and she had to constantly check her own behavior. She didn't care what the agent thought about her on a personal level, but she was next in line to head the CIU and would do whatever it took to land the position. Anything short of sabotaging the current leader. Bailey knew exactly how she could set up her boss to fail, but so far, she'd resisted the impulse. Most sociopaths wouldn't have that much restraint. She was lucky to be on the low end of the spectrum. She didn't take any pleasure in hurting people, she just didn't feel guilty if she did.

Bailey hurried through the maze of corridors to her office near the back of the building. At her desk, she ran the name Bonnie Yost through the database. There was the connection. Bonnie had been married to Roland Granger, Owen's older brother. Roland had died in prison, while serving a long sentence for illegal firearms possession and assaulting a federal officer. Now Owen had been arrested for aggravated assault and his sister-in-law had been murdered in the same time frame. Bailey needed more information, such as who the militiaman had attacked.

Two more searches revealed that Owen Granger had assaulted a man named Clay Richmond, who'd once been a member of the Freedom Guardians but had left the group after the incident that sent the older Granger to prison. Richmond had been hospitalized from the attack, and attempted murder charges were being considered against Granger. Why assault Richmond now? Bailey leaned back in her chair, working though the possibilities. It could just have been a drunken brawl. Or maybe Owen Granger blamed Richmond for his brother's imprisonment and death.

But why kill his brother's widow? Bailey loaded the Denver Post website and keyed in the dead woman's name. The news report was brief, and she learned only one new detail. Bonnie Yost had retired from the clinic where she'd worked the day before she was murdered. Probably a coincidence, but still odd. Bailey googled *Carson Obstetrics* and learned that it was an offshoot of Fort Carson Community Hospital. The army angle deepened her interest. Like the bureau and the CIA, the military was a keeper of secrets.

Other than their connection to Owen Granger, how were Bonnie Yost and Clay Richmond linked? Had they both testified against Roland Granger? If so, Owen might be carrying out his revenge.

Bailey tried to set the puzzle aside. She had other sites to monitor and should be looking for anti-government militants and young Islamists with bomb-making plans. But the Granger incidents nagged at her. She would do one more brief search before she dropped the idea that the two crimes were connected. Yost's death right after her retirement bothered Bailey the most. She keyed in the clinic's name and landed on a news article about the medical center hosting a twenty-year reunion, celebrating the babies that had been delivered by its doctors. Completely unrelated. She skimmed the article and came away with two names. Logan Hurtz, age twenty, had been mentioned as the oldest of the children in attendance, and Dr. David Novak was cited for the most deliveries. Bailey filed the information in her methodical brain, then went back to investigating the murder of the militiaman's sister-in-law.

She searched for a morgue in Colorado Springs and came up with the El Paso County Coroner's office. She made the call. "This is Agent Bailey with the FBI. I'd like to see the report on Bonnie Yost's death."

The woman started to speak, but Bailey cut in. "Yes, I'll give you my badge number, then you can send the report to me at the bureau." Bailey rattled off her ID and her long government email address.

"Can I ask what this is about?"

"I'm looking into a militant group. Please keep that to yourself." The information wasn't classified, but it made people more willing to help if they thought it was.

"We have our share in Colorado." The woman's voice was hushed. "What else do you need?"

"That's it for now, but I may call back." Bailey pressed off the call and realized she'd forgotten to say thanks. *Oh well.* The woman got paid to do her job. Next she called the Denver Medical Examiner. If Owen Granger, the militia extremist, was on a personal vendetta, he might have put other victims in the Denver hospital or morgue. She gave her name and badge number and asked for a list of all the dead bodies they'd processed in the last few weeks. The receptionist said she would compile the report and email it soon.

Bailey's private cell phone beeped. A text from Garrett: *Lunch today?*

Garrett was her twenty-five-year-old lover, which technically made her a Cougar. The thought always made her smile. At forty, she might be too young for the term, but maybe not. Most people didn't seem to notice the age difference because her attractive face and thick ginger-red hair made her look younger than her years. She texted back: *Poppy's at noon?*

He agreed to meet her, then signed off, saying he had to get to class. Garret, who'd lost a foot saving a child, was studying to become a physical therapist. She admired his commitment to a career helping others. She liked to think of her job that way too, but in reality, working at the bureau was self-serving. It challenged her intellectually, gave her an opportunity to seek and use power, and kept her from acting on some of her worst impulses. She'd been questioned by an FBI agent in college—about a boyfriend's fraud activity—and had coveted the agent's authority and investigative focus. A life-changing moment.

A ping let her know that the email from the Colorado Springs coroner had landed. Bailey opened it, then downloaded and read the autopsy report on Bonnie Yost. The woman had been struck on the head with a heavy instrument that left a crescent-moon shaped wound. Most likely the end of a flashlight. *Interesting.* Cops carried heavy flashlights. Further reading revealed that a matching flashlight had been found on the premise and belonged to the victim. No fingerprints or signs of trauma to the body and no mention of motive. Had Yost been robbed? That was critical information. If nothing had been taken from the victim's house, then her murder was probably personal. Bailey called the Colorado Springs Police Department and asked to speak to the detective handling Yost's death. The desk clerk gave her the name Brad Miller and patched her through. She got an answering machine, a male voice. She used a soft tone with a hint of distress to leave a message asking for a callback.

A few minutes later, an email from the Denver morgue

came through. Bailey opened the list of deceased names, each accompanied by a date and a cause of death. Heart attacks, stabbings, accidents in the home. One drowning and a fall from a balcony. *Logan Hurtz?* He'd been named in the article about Carson Obstetrics, where Bonnie Yost had worked. Two people associated with the military medical facility had died in the last three weeks. What if Hurtz had been pushed? Had he and the receptionist been silenced? But why?

Bailey's bloodhound neurons were firing at full capacity. Something was going on in Colorado, and the deaths were likely connected to an armed militant group. This was exactly her kind of investigation. Time to take it to her boss, then get on a plane for Denver.

Special Agent Lennard waved her in but continued her phone call. The woman was tall even sitting down and wore cropped platinum hair that should have worked against her but didn't.

The irritation in her supervisor's voice made Bailey consider waiting for a better time. But she wanted Lennard's job, so she decided to listen and file away what information she could. The conversation, obviously about money, heated up quickly. Agent Lennard fought to defend her decision to send a team to Florida to stake out a motel in Tampa where a Cuban drug runner was rumored to be keeping teenage girls for company. Bailey had not been involved, thank god, because it had been a waste of time. Her cases were usually more high profile. The drug trade was just not interesting.

Lennard finally ended the call. "Sorry. The director is on my case about wasting the team's resources."

The director was right. "The drug runner didn't meet our critical incident standards."

Her boss' mouth tightened. "What do you have for me?" Her tone was curt.

Oh hell. Bailey realized her mistake in blurting out the truth. Her filter hadn't caught it, but she couldn't apologize. "A few incidents in Colorado make me think a militant group might be quietly killing people. Owen Granger, specifically, as the key perpetrator."

"Granger isn't known for quiet tactics."

That was a key sticking point in her theory. She also suspected military involvement, but wouldn't bring that up yet. "I know, but this is worth looking into. Bonnie Yost, Granger's sister-in-law, was murdered the day before he was arrested for another assault and possibly attempted murder. In addition, a young man connected to the clinic where Yost worked died rather mysteriously a few weeks before." Now that she'd said them out loud, the connections seemed lame.

Her boss' blond eyebrows arched. "That's it? You're not going to Colorado on that intel. The director would fire me."

That would work out well for her. Bailey felt compelled to argue her points, but forced herself to hold back. She stood. "I'm still waiting for a return call from the Denver police. We'll see what else I can come up with. Thanks for your time." She hurried out before her boss gave her a different assignment. Bailey could afford to be choosy about what cases she took because the director loved her work. She'd tracked down a power-mad CEO who'd kidnapped scientists—and a North Korean cryptologist—in his quest to dominate the cell phone market. In doing so, she'd averted another crisis with the North Korean government, and that had moved her to the top of the director's list of rising stars. Yet Lennard was still her boss, and Bailey had to play every situation to her advantage. She should have tried to show empathy for Lennard, but that emotion wasn't real to her, and she'd never learned to fake it.

On her way out to meet Garrett for lunch, her phone rang with a Colorado area code. She turned back to her desk. "Agent Bailey."

"Detective Miller with the Colorado Springs Police Department returning your call. Why is the FBI interested in Bonnie Yost's murder?"

"She's the sister-in-law of Owen Granger, leader of the Freedom Guardians, an armed militant group that doesn't recognize the authority of the federal government."

A pause. "I hadn't learned that yet." The detective cleared his throat. "On the surface, the homicide looks like a burglary gone bad. But her car was in the driveway, so the perp had to know she was home."

"What was stolen?"

"Her cell phone was missing and there was no computer in the house, but we're still trying to interview people who knew her. She was mostly a loner."

The missing items could have been taken to make the homicide look like a robbery. "Have you run prints?"

"There were none on the murder weapon, and those we took from the house didn't match anyone in our database."

"Any witnesses or leads?"

"We have a suspect we're hoping to pick up soon."

"Who?"

"We don't know her name yet, but we're watching for her."

A woman? That surprised Bailey. "What's her connection to the case?"

"We don't know that either, but she was seen outside the victim's house at the time of the murder." A pause, as though he hesitated to give her too much information. "The suspect was seen at the clinic right before as well."

"What's the description?"

"Young, slender, maybe still a teenager. Straight dark hair and attractive."

A teenager? Odder still. "Will you update me if you find her?"

"Sure."

Bailey gave him her cell number but didn't expect to hear anything. She'd had to drag every nugget of intel out of him. After she clicked off the call, the young ages of the two accident victims in Denver came to mind. Particularly, Logan Hurtz, who was connected to the clinic. This was all related somehow, and she felt an urgent need to figure it out. But was it a federal matter that could justify the attention of the Critical Incident Unit? Her boss didn't think so. Yet.

Bailey called the Denver police again. Maybe they could tell her something about Hurtz's death that would connect him to Owen Granger, who was someone of interest to the CIU. The transfer took a few minutes, but she finally reached Detective Pat Delphy's phone and was asked to leave a message. The voice wasn't distinctively male or female and neither was the name. Bailey didn't particularly care, but it would be nice to know before they talked.

Her cell phone rang, and she looked at the ID. *Garrett!* She'd been on her way out to meet him for lunch and had gotten sidetracked. *Oh hell.* Garrett understood the nature of her job, but this kind of thing bothered him. He would also be upset to learn she might be leaving town again soon. The thought of his distress caused a tug on her heart. Not guilt. She never felt that. But some level of empathy. A new experience since she'd met him. He was the one person she'd ever really connected to—besides her father. Yet she didn't empathize with her father because he didn't feel much pain. Garrett was a kind soul who felt everything, and she loved him more than she expected to. Their deep connection was a first for her, but she knew their relationship probably wouldn't last. They never did. Men always wanted more from her than she could give.

Chapter 10

Bailey hurried into the restaurant, found Garrett near a window, and kissed him before she sat down. "I'm sorry. Thanks for waiting." Her boyfriend was the only person she apologized to and only when she was blatantly at fault.

"Something important came up?" The tension in his face was obvious, but he was still handsome with bright blue eyes, great cheekbones, and a strong chin.

Bailey nodded. "Several deaths in Colorado seem to be connected to an anti-government group, and I may have to fly out there soon."

His jaw tightened. "How long will you be gone?"

"I don't have any idea." She gave him a sly smile. "But you know how fast I work." Garrett was the son of a kidnapped scientist she'd located and rescued six months earlier. They'd fallen for each other during the investigation, and he'd moved to Washington DC to be with her.

"I knew your job was demanding, but I didn't realize you traveled this much."

His discontent had started. He would break off with her before the year was over. A sadness overcame her. Bailey would miss him, particularly the sex, but she wouldn't fight for the relationship. Her ego wouldn't allow it. "Don't be upset. I haven't left yet, and we should make the most of our time together." She picked up the menu. "Let's order."

While they waited for their food, she asked Garrett about his classes, and he seemed to relax as he updated her on his academic progress. Then he abruptly switched back to her impending travel. "Hey, you said 'Colorado.' That's where you grew up, right?"

"Yes, Denver. Why?"

"Isn't your dad in jail there? You should go see him."

The thought had briefly crossed her mind. "I won't have time, and it doesn't sound like fun." Her father was also a sociopath. He'd instilled a code of ethics in her from a young age but had less control than she did, at least for violent tendencies

Garrett shook his head. "Sometimes family isn't fun, but you make the effort anyway."

Bailey laughed. "Maybe you do. Not me."

The food came, and they ate in silence for a minute. Garrett put down his burger and stared at her. "Do you ever do anything that's just for someone else's benefit?" He blushed. "I mean other than within our relationship?"

Her sacrifices for him were minimal, but she appreciated his acknowledgement. She shrugged. "I give money to charity." It was the best she could do. She just didn't feel empathy, except for Garrett, and she couldn't make herself endure discomfort just to help someone else feel better. She had tried when an old friend from college had been sick with cancer, but witnessing the pain and deterioration had made her avoid contact. In the long run, the experience had taught Bailey to limit her friendships.

"I still think you should visit your father," Garrett pressured. "If I had the money, I'd fly home to see my mother every few months."

Bailey bit her tongue. He was such a momma's boy. But that was probably why he was attracted to her. She told him she'd think about visiting her dad just to get him to change the subject. They talked about rescheduling their plans for the weekend if she had to travel, then moved on to discuss an art show they'd seen together recently. When the server picked up their plates, Bailey asked for the check. "I have to get back to work."

"I think we should get couples' counseling," Garrett blurted out.

Oh hell. She'd been honest with him about her sociopathy, but she wouldn't discuss her nature with a counselor. Never again. Bailey patted his hand. "No. I'm not capable of change. You know that. You're either in or out."

She paid the bill, kissed him again, and walked away.

Chapter 11

Thursday, Oct. 13, 7:35 a.m., Colorado Springs

Taylor woke with her pulse pounding. A building had exploded in her dream this time. She'd known in her heart that it was full of people. Why was she dreaming about explosions every night? She sat up, confused by her surroundings. *Oh god.* The motel room. The plan to steal clinic files. The panic in her pulse spread to her stomach. What the hell was she doing? Taylor glanced over at the other half of the bed. Jake slept with his mouth open, but he didn't snore. The first time she'd woken up with someone in her bed. Her lack of panic surprised her. Jake was starting to feel like an old friend. Yet the new stubble on his chin made him look older, sexier.

She jumped up and hurried to the tiny bathroom. Maybe she could get out of this whole thing. Just grab her stuff and go. She didn't owe Jake anything. The names on the list played in her mind, especially Seth Wozac. What if he was killed because she was afraid to make a scene? Guilt pulled her back in. She could do this. What was the worst that could happen to her personally?

Arrested and dragged to jail in handcuffs.

Then what?

A few days in jail. What would they charge her with? Conspiracy to commit data theft? Was that even a real thing?

Taylor locked the bathroom door, showered, and pulled on yesterday's clothes. She wished they could have stopped by her apartment to pick up a few things and feed the fish, but she'd be all right. As a busy student—and compulsive worrier—she carried emergency supplies in her satchel, including some cash, a toothbrush, and a travel-sized tube of Crest. And in one of her pockets, she always carried a small, all-purpose, knife-like tool, a stocking stuffer from her mother when she was thirteen.

When Taylor came out of the bathroom, Jake was brewing coffee. He turned and smiled. "It's the cheap stuff, but at least it's caffeine. And it's fast."

"Thanks, but I'll grab a soda from the vending machine. I may be the only person in the world who doesn't like the taste of coffee."

"I'll try not to judge you for it." He reached for his paper cup, looking sleepy and disheveled but still cute. "I need a flash drive for downloading. Do you have one in your bag?"

"Of course. Do you have a comb?"

"I think so." He started to grab his backpack, then caught her meaning and laughed. "You meant for me. Don't worry, I'll get myself together before we head to the clinic. Coffee first."

He didn't have a beard, so she assumed he carried shaving stuff in his pack, among other things. She couldn't imagine what it would be like to be homeless and have to worry about where to brush her teeth twice a day. She wanted to ask him, but didn't know him well enough to get that personal. *They'd just slept in the same bed!* The thought made her smile.

"What? Is it my hair?"

"No. I'm just wondering what it's like to be homeless."

"In one word? Challenging. I hope you never find out." He gulped down the rest of his coffee. "The hardest part was selling my laptop and not being able to sit down and write whenever I wanted." He shook his head. "But I'm making a comeback." He squinted at her. "I'm worried about having enough time to access the files today. Are you game for breaking into the clinic now before it opens?"

Was he serious? "It's a medical facility, run by the military. I'm sure it has an alarm."

Jake laughed. "Right." He started brewing another cup of coffee. "Hand me the flash drive, then give me five minutes to get ready. I say we do this right after it opens at eight. The administrative staff probably doesn't arrive until nine."

Fewer employees was a good thing. "We'll park a few blocks away. If they call the police, we can run and meet at my car. That way, they won't get the description or license plate." She handed him the thumb drive.

"I like your thinking. Shows a criminal nature." He grinned and sauntered into the bathroom.

Thirty minutes later, they stood in front of the doors, with a soft morning sun struggling to illuminate the cold concrete building. Taylor fought the urge to shiver, keeping one hand under her fake belly bulge the way she'd seen pregnant women do. She caught her reflection in the glass and winced. Having children wasn't in her future. She had a uterus but no ovaries. Another reason she didn't feel like a real woman.

"Ready?" Jake sounded nervous for the first time.

"Not really." They had discussed at least five scenarios for how this might play out, but most of them ended with her leaving in a hurry. Jake was prepared to exit out the back or push through an alarm door if confronted. He'd pulled on a baseball cap to hide his face from security cameras, and she wore a scarf that covered her chin. Plus the cheap reader glasses they'd picked up at the pharmacy across the street.

"As the saying goes, just do it." Jake gave her a little push, and Taylor stumbled toward the door. His plan was to slide in, unobserved, once she had the receptionist's attention.

Inside, the heat helped her body relax. Only one patient waited in the wide, blue-and-gray themed lobby. The woman looked about six months pregnant, and a toddler slept in her lap. Taylor moved slowly to a seat on the other side, far from the door, and held her mouth in a grimace. The worry was real, but she wanted to convey pain too. The receptionist looked up. The same young woman with the tight bun. Not good. She spotted Taylor and scowled.

Oh no. Taylor's heart started to hammer. Had Tight Bun recognized her even with the glasses and scarf? Maybe the clerk was just annoyed that she hadn't come to the counter to check in. Taylor winced and leaned forward, hoping to keep the receptionist focused on her. She made small moaning noises and glanced sideways at the door. Jake was walking toward a drinking faucet near the front. Taylor sat up. Tight Bun rounded the front counter and came out into the lobby. Perfect. Tight Bun's back had been toward Jake when he crossed the carpeted room, and now Taylor couldn't see him at all. He was good at this.

She leaned over again, not wanting the receptionist to get a good look at her face, and let out a louder moan. *Oh god.* She couldn't believe she was doing this.

"Miss, do you have an appointment?"

Taylor ignored her and moaned louder.

"What's your name? I need to get you checked in so a doctor can see you." Annoyance overrode the receptionist's concern.

"I don't have an appointment." Taylor spoke slowly through her fake pain. "I think I'm in labor." She drew in a sharp breath and winced. Time to get on the floor. Taylor pushed up with one hand on the arm of the chair, the other gripping her padded belly. As soon as she was standing, she let herself collapse. Her knees hit first with a painful twinge, then she flopped over on her side. The scarf fell off the bottom of her face, but it didn't matter. The receptionist wasn't looking at her any more. Tight Bun had turned away and started yelling for assistance.

Chapter 12

Jake steered away from the exam rooms and hurried down a short, dead-end hall with three closed doors. In the lobby behind him, he heard the receptionist shout for help. A moment later, Taylor let out a sharp cry. The girl was giving it her all. *Sweet.* He'd half expected her to bail out. The door directly in front of him started to open. He grabbed the knob on his left and turned hard. Locked. *Damn.* A woman in a dark suit stepped out. With heels, she was taller than he was and either a rough thirty-five or a well-preserved fifty.

"My wife needs help," Jake said. "I think she's in labor." He reached for the woman's arm, expecting her to pull away.

She did, moving rapidly toward the lobby, her pumps clicking on the laminate floor. "Who's her doctor?"

"I can't remember." Jake lagged behind. "Give me a minute and I'll find his name." He pulled out his cell phone, as Taylor cried out in another room.

"Call for an ambulance," the director shouted over her shoulder. "We don't do deliveries here."

Jake waited for her to exit the end of the hall, then spun back and charged into her office. He had six to ten minutes at most. He closed the door and sat down in front of her computer, which she'd left on. After a few false starts, he found the shared server. He conducted a broad search, using the word *archive*, then tried again with the date *1995*, the year the drug had likely been administered. A list of files displayed on the monitor. *Yes!* The military had probably been the first major organization to create digital medical records. They likely still had paper copies too, but those could be in a storage unit on the base.

Jake pulled the flash drive from his jeans pocket and searched for an empty USB port. He found one on a hub behind the laptop. After inserting the drive, he scanned the file names. *Patients A-F, Patients G-M, Patients N-Z* were the top three listings. The intersex babies could be mixed in among all the other patients, and the files were huge. He didn't have time to download even one. He skimmed farther on the list and spotted two folders near the bottom of the monitor. An entry called *Gender Exp. Protocol,* followed by another file, *Subjects 1995/96.*

Score! An experiment, just as Taylor had guessed. He left-clicked on the file and chose the download option. A dialogue box opened and asked for his password. *Shit!* He clicked on the email app and typed *password* into the search bar. A message opened that contained a list of pass codes the director had sent herself, and the second one was labeled *work.* If he were a real criminal, he could have wiped out her bank account in the next few hours. But all he cared about was the medical experiment conducted at this clinic twenty-one years ago.

After he pasted the passcode into the security box, the files began to download. Jake glanced at the clock on the computer monitor, but the numbers meant nothing. He hadn't looked at the time before he started. How many minutes left? He listened for footsteps in the hall and bounced on his well-worn shoes.

Without warning, the door opened and someone said, "Karen." As the younger woman's mouth dropped open to process the scene, Jake gave her a charming smile. "I'm with IT. The hospital sent me over to correct a glitch in the data-sharing software." He nodded toward the front of the building. "Karen's dealing with an emergency out front. Someone's in labor."

"I heard." The woman turned toward the hall to listen.

Jake pulled out the flash drive and slipped it into a secret pocket inside his jeans. He'd bought the pants at the Goodwill, and they'd probably belonged to a druggie. Now he had to get out of the building and call Taylor when he was clear. Her ringing phone would signal her to shut down the show and get moving. "I think I fixed it. I'll test it from the other end." Jake moved toward the door.

The woman eyed him suspiciously. "I don't recognize you. Let me see your ID."

Jake kept smiling and walked into the hall. He patted his shirt pocket. "I think I left it in the car. But don't worry, I have it." He let out a stressed laugh. "I can't get back on base without it."

The emergency exit was around the corner and ten feet away. The front exit was more like fifty yards—and with a crowd watching. He strode toward the hallway intersection.

The woman followed him, talking excitedly. "I don't know how you got back here without your identification. Karen wouldn't allow that."

When he spotted the side exit, Jake bolted for it. "I parked out here," he called over his shoulder.

Behind him the woman yelled, "Security!"

Chapter 13

Two hours earlier

Devin pulled into the parking lot across from the obstetrics clinic. In the dark quiet of the early morning, she had her pick of spaces. Another hour of sleep—even in the crappy motel bed—would have been nice, but she couldn't lose her targets again. She'd watched Lopez's apartment for a while the night before, but she and Wilson hadn't shown up. Devin had driven south, guessing the pair would head for Colorado Springs and the obstetrics clinic in search of more information. She expected them to turn up sometime this morning. They would be in for a surprise.

For an hour, she sat, waited, and watched, as she had the night before in front of Lopez's apartment. Her training as a sniper had taught her to quiet her mind while remaining hyper alert. To get into that state, she tapped into her animal instinct, the part of the brain that didn't think or process but simply survived.

A car engine slowed, and she snapped to attention. A white sedan pulled into the clinic parking lot, and a tall blond woman climbed out. Devin glanced at the time on her phone. The director was early. The clinic wouldn't open for another hour. But Lopez and Wilson could be here already, sitting and waiting like she was. The challenge was the split mission: terminating Wilson and kidnapping the girl. She hoped to accomplish both in a single orchestrated move, but it might not be possible. Lopez had to be her priority.

Devin took inventory of the tool kit under the back seat. Chloroform, plastic handcuffs, duct tape, and rope. Yes, she was ready. But she couldn't conduct the grab here at the clinic. Too much risk of a witness, which meant it could make the news. Any media coverage that connected the subjects' deaths or disappearances could jeopardize the whole Peace Project, which was only weeks—or possibly days—away from its final phase. The second generation of subjects all seemed normal, with no deviant tendencies. The major and his research partner were confident the hormone-targeting drug was ready. They just needed a green light from the last operative to get into position.

A few minutes after eight, Devin spotted a young couple approaching the clinic on foot. They had come from the side, and the woman looked pregnant. Her dark hair was pulled back, and a scarf covered the bottom half of her face. The man wore a hooded sweatshirt and walked stiffly. A worried husband. They paused in front of the door and exchanged words. Why hesitate? Because they weren't patients! Wilson and Lopez had done well to disguise themselves, and the fake pregnancy was clever. But not clever enough.

What were they up to? Devin had expected a more direct approach. Their deviousness meant they might plan to steal files, probably from the year of the first experiment. Should she try to stop them? The pregnancy and birth records by themselves weren't incriminating, except for the anomaly of so many intersex babies born in the same geographic area at the same time. But that didn't prove anything.

In her head, the major's voice scoffed at her simplistic thinking. They couldn't afford to draw attention to the project, especially now that it was so close to fruition. The first seeds had been planted twenty-one years ago, and the operatives had been sent into the field a decade after. She admired her father's ability to think long-term and his patience in conducting a twenty-year mission. She was proud to be part of it. But her orders were to terminate and kidnap, and she couldn't do that inside the clinic. She would wait for the couple to exit and walk away. If they'd taken files, she would confiscate them when she completed her task.

She silently cursed the reporter. His interference had really mucked things up, and now she had to pull off a kidnapping. It would have been better to not let them access the data in the first place, but she couldn't stop them here without drawing attention to herself. To function successfully as the cleanup person, she had to keep a low profile. But she was good at that. After completing boot camp, she'd been assigned to her father's command and had lived in the shadows, keeping her face out of the public and out of the watchful eye of security cameras. For months, she'd trained in a secret research complex, an underground facility that few people knew about. She still had a sleeping unit there but preferred to live in her own apartment on the base. The major spent all his time inside the underground lab now, and she sometimes worried about his mental health. His recent decisions seemed almost reactionary.

She climbed from her vehicle, wanting to be ready for anything. Where was Lopez's car? She and Wilson had seemed to come out of nowhere, and it was troubling. Devin briefly considered creating a diversion, but anything big enough to get everyone out of the building would also bring the police. Her best choice was to wait, follow them to the car, then carry out the assault when the opportunity presented itself. As she visualized how that would play out, she reconsidered her plan. It might be better to find Lopez's car, break into it, and wait in the backseat. She could slit Wilson's throat without him ever sensing her presence, then chloroform the girl before she could scream. She would bind and muffle Taylor with duct tape, then retrieve her own vehicle to pick up the sedated target. How much time did she have to search for the Jetta? What if she didn't find the car and missed them when they exited the clinic?

From across the street, Devin scanned the parking lot but didn't see the white car. She pulled her hood over her head and hurried to the sidewalk. The brightness of the day made her feel exposed, so she put on dark glasses too. At a break in traffic, she jogged across the busy road, a main artery leading to Fort Carson. On the sidewalk in front of the clinic, Devin paused, trying to get inside the other girl's head. Where would she park? Someplace easy to get to but not out in the open. Lopez's caution had surprised her last night and now it troubled her again. Devin blamed the reporter and was still upset with herself for losing them.

After walking a few blocks in each direction from the clinic, she located the Jetta under a tree near a yoga studio on a side street. She strode toward it, moving rapidly without running, and pulled out the knife she carried. She would puncture one of the tires, just in case the pair got out of the clinic without her spotting them. Three women emerged from the studio and started across the small parking lot, cheerfully arguing about their instructor. They stopped next to the Jetta and continued their loud discussion.

Well, hell. Devin couldn't wait for them to move on. Her

targets could be leaving the clinic at that moment. If they continued their careful behavior, they might head away from the car or even abandon it. She spun around and jogged back to the main avenue, turning toward the clinic. The parking lot was still quiet, and she didn't spot anyone leaving. But a dark sedan was pulling in. Two men in business jackets. Police officers? Or FBI? *Damn it all to hell.*

No point in jumping to conclusions. She would watch and wait.

The sedan parked, and the men climbed out. One wore a navy-blue suit, and the other sported jeans with a gray tweed jacket. *Local detectives.* Were they investigating the receptionist's death? As the men walked toward the entrance, the glass door opened, and the female target came out, moving quickly. Devin was close enough to hear the man in the blue suit say, "Taylor Lopez? We need you to come with us."

Chapter 14

Police! Taylor's heart skipped a beat. Her gut screamed *Run!*, but instead she froze. What did they want? They weren't in uniform, and that made her even more nervous. "What's this about? Can't we talk right here?"

They stared at her belly.

She flushed with shame at the fake bump under her shirt. How would she explain it? Stick to the truth, without mentioning Jake. Why had she let him talk her into this?

"We have questions about the murder of Bonnie Yost." The younger man in jeans stepped close and grabbed her elbow. "I'm Detective Miller, and this is Detective Blunt with the Colorado Springs Police Department. You're coming with us."

To an interrogation room! Her heart raced, and she felt faint. "I never met Bonnie in person! She didn't come to the door when I went to her house." Taylor heard the panic in her voice and tried to calm herself.

"We'll talk when we get to the department." Detective Miller steered her into the parking lot.

Taylor's legs buckled, and she couldn't move.

"Cuff her," the older cop snapped. "The clinic reported a security issue, and I'm sure she's involved."

"Then we have to Mirandize her." The younger detective

had turned away from her, but Taylor still heard it.

"So do it."

Miller pulled her hands together and snapped cold steel around her wrists, while citing her rights to remain silent and obtain an attorney. Tears welled in her eyes, and Taylor fought back sobs. *No crying!*

The detective grabbed her elbow again and started walking. Taylor stumbled a few times before her weak legs started functioning. Suddenly, the wail of an alarm filled the air. They all turned to stare at the clinic. Nothing seemed wrong. No smoke or fire. No one running out the front door. Yet Taylor knew Jake had somehow set it off. She hoped he wasn't busted.

The detective put her in the back of a dark sedan and locked the doors. She was a prisoner! Her heart pounded so hard it ached. A full panic attack hit her, and she couldn't breathe. For a moment, she saw little stars around her forehead. Taylor lay sideways on the seat, closed her eyes, and took long slow breaths. She had to get calm before she passed out from hyperventilating.

Her phone beeped, indicating a text. It was probably Jake, and she hoped the cops hadn't heard it. *Please let him get away.* Worrying about Jake seemed to ease her panic. She took five more long breaths and talked herself through the situation. She hadn't done anything illegal. She would tell the truth, and this would turn out okay.

Or not. Hundreds of people were serving long prison sentences for crimes they hadn't committed. Most of them weren't young women though. Her light-brown skin might work against her, but her clean record should at least make them hesitate to charge her with murder. That's what this was about. Bonnie's death. Tight Bun must have recognized her and called the police. The cops might not even care about her little drama scene. But she would have to explain the fake belly. She could say she wanted to get more information from the clinic and thought they might open up more to a pregnant patient. She hadn't lied about her name, and it wasn't illegal to pretend to be pregnant. Was it?

Her mother's voice was suddenly in her head, soothing her and praising her for caring about the lives of strangers. But her mother was dead, and she had no one to call if things went badly.

The trip to the police department was a five-minute ride down the same main avenue. When she heard the car's lock release, some of the tension went out of her body. But the cuffs behind her back were still painful. Detective Miller opened the door and pulled her from the vehicle. As she awkwardly climbed out, the pillow fell out of her waistband and landed on the ground.

Detective Blunt picked it up. "What is this?"

Taylor's throat closed up.

The older man leaned in, a fierce expression on his face. "Answer me."

"I needed an excuse to go into the clinic. I wanted more information."

The younger detective pulled on her elbow. "Let's take this conversation inside.

They crossed a narrow parking lot and approached a three-story, red-brick building. The bright sun and big sky only made her feel small and hopeless in comparison. What if they didn't believe anything she said?

Inside the department, they led her to a small room with no windows. Her worst fear! Miller uncuffed her hands, then recuffed them in the front. She almost cried out with relief. After he searched her pockets, he took her cell phone pouch, the only thing she'd taken into the clinic. She knew her rights and forced herself to speak. "You're not legally allowed to search my phone."

"Don't worry. We'll get a warrant." Miller pointed to a wooden chair on one side of a metal table. "Sit down. We'll be back in a minute."

They were gone much longer. After a while, she stood and paced the room. What were they doing besides an illegal search of her phone? Breaking her down. That was probably the point. To make her so anxious she would tell them anything.

After what seemed like an hour, the two men came back. Detective Miller put a cup of water on the table in front of her. She noticed for the first time that he was handsome with a wide face and thick dark hair. His partner had sagging skin, a shaved head, and a mean expression. Blunt would probably play the bad cop. She would ignore him, as though he weren't important—a strategy that had gotten her through some tough times with one of her mother's boyfriends.

Detective Miller, seated across the table, told her the session was being recorded, then moved quickly to the real questions. "How do you know Bonnie Yost?"

"I don't." Taylor paused, hoping to steady her voice. "Except that she was a receptionist at Carson Obstetrics. I talked to her on the phone once."

"You were seen at her house around the time she was murdered. What were you doing there?" Miller kept his voice deadpan.

Should she tell them about the experiment? Would they think she was crazy? The list of subjects was in her satchel, which she'd left in the car. She would give the information to them slowly and test their reactions. "I wanted to ask her questions about my birth. My mother was a patient at the clinic in 1995."

"Why now? What prompted that?"

"I work in the Denver morgue. A guy my age came in a few days ago, and he had drowned." Taylor reached for the water with her cuffed hands and managed to take a sip. "The man was also a Carson clinic baby from the same year. It made me curious about my birth. My mother's dead, and she never talked about it."

Detective Miller blinked, jotted down a few notes, then asked, "Did Bonnie Yost refuse to give you information? Is that why you got angry and killed her?"

"That's absurd." Taylor shook her head, hoping to sound sincere. "I went to her house because she abruptly retired after I called the clinic. I thought maybe she'd been forced out, so I went there to follow up."

Miller scowled. "Why would a medical clinic force her to retire? Maybe you were the one who intimidated her." He leaned forward, his voice intense. "*You* were the last person to talk to her at the clinic. *You* were the last person to see her before she died. What were you *really* hounding her about?"

A flash of guilt. Had she harassed the old woman with her questions? *No.* The receptionist had sent her an email with a list of names. Bonnie had wanted to help her. Had the cops searched the old woman's computer? If so, why hadn't they asked about the list? "It wasn't like that." Taylor tried to explain. "I called and asked a few questions. Bonnie wasn't free to talk at the clinic, but she emailed me that same evening. She sent me a list of babies born that year to clinic patients."

Miller leaned back, perplexed. The other detective slapped his hand on the table. "Bullshit! Bonnie Yost didn't have a computer in her home, and I doubt she violated patient confidentiality just because you were curious about your birth. What the hell are you hiding?"

Taylor's lips trembled. "She emailed me. I have the message on my phone. I have the list in my car."

"Why did you want to know about the other kids born that year?" Detective Miller had softened his face and tone. "What's so special about them?"

This was the quicksand, and she had no choice but to step in. "I think they all share some abnormalities. There wasn't just one body that came into the morgue. A few weeks earlier, another young man with a similar body died in a fall from his balcony. He'd been born that same year to a clinic patient."

A long silence.

Blunt looked disgusted, and Miller looked skeptical. "What are you saying? You think those deaths weren't accidents?"

"It seemed too strange to be coincidence."

Blunt crossed his arms and shook his head. "This is a bullshit distraction. What's your connection to Bonnie Yost?"

"None. Other than she worked at the clinic and sent me the list of babies born in 1996."

Miller jumped back in. "Tell us what happened when you went to see Bonnie."

"Nothing! She didn't come to the door. I was worried about her, so I looked in the window and saw her on the floor with all the blood. I knew she was dead." This part was embarrassing, and Taylor felt her cheeks flush. "I panicked and drove back to Denver. But I did call 9-11 and report it."

"You never went inside?"

"No."

"Why were you worried?"

"Because Bonnie retired suddenly. Because two guys born that year were dead. Bonnie had tried to help me, and I thought maybe someone had silenced her too."

"Okay, that's enough." Detective Blunt stood. "We're not entertaining any conspiracy theory bullshit. When you're ready to tell the truth, we'll be back." He tapped his partner's arm. Miller hesitated, then got up, and they both walked out.

Oh god. They were going to leave her here in this windowless little hole, handcuffed and hungry for days. They would break her down. Taylor fought the tears, but they came anyway.

Chapter 15

The intensity of the security alarm unnerved him. So much louder than he'd braced for. Jake ran along the back of the building, hoping Taylor had made it out. He rounded the corner but didn't see her anywhere. Worried that the staff was looking for him—or even at him through the windows—he crossed the parking lot and took cover behind a minivan. He sent Taylor a quick text: *I'm out. Side parking lot.*

She didn't respond, so he called. No answer. Jake moved along behind the row of cars until he could see the front of the building. Two men walked with Taylor, who was handcuffed. She was being arrested! *Shit!* How had the police arrived so quickly?

If they hadn't already detained her, he would have tried to distract them and give her a chance to get away. But those weren't uniformed officers. They wore suits. Detectives didn't respond to trespassing or theft crimes. Her arrest had to be about the receptionist's death, and Taylor was probably terrified. He shouldn't have encouraged her to come back here.

His guilt was interrupted by the sight of someone in dark clothes barreling toward him from the back of the building. The man had a fierce expression and didn't look like a clinic staffer . . . or a cop. Was that a gun at his side?

Run!

Jake leapt over the low-growing hedge dividing the two properties and sprinted across the back lot of the carwash next door. A neighboring concrete building blocked his path, so he rounded the corner of the carwash to head for the street. A glance over his shoulder escalated his fear. The man was coming after him! He had to be the killer.

At the sidewalk, Jake turned away from the clinic and ran for his life. The guy wouldn't murder him in plain view of passing traffic, would he? Taylor's car was around here somewhere, but he didn't have a key. He either had to put distance between him and the hit man or find a great place to hide. Or both.

At the corner, he spotted a grocery store. Jake pumped his arms and sprinted as hard as he could for the automatic door. He had excelled at track in high school and prayed that he was faster than the man coming after him. An older couple coming out the entrance saw him barreling toward them and stepped aside. The woman cursed at him to "Slow the hell down!"

Inside the store, he ran through an empty checkout lane and bolted for the back. He considered hiding in their storage area, then spotted the stairs. Offices on a second floor loft overlooked the store. Jake climbed the wooden steps two at a time and ducked into an alcove at the top. From his position, he could see the man in black jogging down the same aisle he'd taken. Or was that a woman? The assassin's face was angular, but hairless, and the mouth was oddly feminine. The bulky black jacket hid the shape of the killer's body. It probably concealed the weapon he'd seen as well. No, not a woman. The killer moved like a man.

The assassin glanced up in his direction, and Jake's already overworked heart kicked up a notch. But the killer quickly looked back down and focused on the swinging rubber doors near the produce section.

Thank God.

"What are you doing?" A middle-aged woman stared at Jake from the landing at the top of the stairs.

"Uh." He scrambled to come up with something. "I have an interview, and I'm spending a moment preparing for it."

She blinked, her skepticism obvious.

Jake forced a smile. "Wish me luck. I really want to work here."

"You should have dressed better." She shook her head and moved down the catwalk.

Jake leaned over the railing for a better view and spotted the assassin pushing through the rubber doors into the back part of the store. Now what? Would the killer assume he'd left out the back? Then search for him behind the store? Or would he come back inside and head straight for the stairs? Jake felt trapped and regretted his decision to come up here.

He pounded down the steps and jogged to the opposite rear corner of the store where he could smell bread baking. He slid through an opening between the glass-front counter and a wall lined with wheeled trays. A heavy woman in a hairnet looked up from a table where she packaged cookies. He smiled and jogged past a row of industrial ovens toward a back exit. He felt the woman following him so he stepped outside, keeping flat against the building. He glanced to his right. *Shit!* The man in black was looking in dumpsters lined up against the back wall.

Jake hurried back into the bakery. He spotted a large recycling bin and climbed inside, sitting cross-legged on a pile of cardboard. The darkness, small space, and greasy smell creeped him out, but after some of the places he'd slept recently, it wasn't that bad. Being homeless had taught him to be grateful for every little thing. At the moment, he was just glad to be alive—and not in jail. He might still get arrested, depending on what Taylor told the police, but no one had seen him access the computer. They probably wouldn't find the flash drive and without it, could never prove data theft.

He wondered how long the killer would look for him around the store. Maybe the assassin had moved on to search the alley and businesses on the next block. Or he could be circling the building, just watching for Jake to exit. If the armed man was a trained military person, he might wait for him all day and shoot the minute he walked out. Jake decided to stay inside the bin until someone discovered him, then hide somewhere else in the store until dark. Or maybe he could figure out a way to sneak out of the store without being seen. Maybe attach himself to a large family and try to blend in. No, he was tall and obvious in his Broncos sweatshirt. He needed to hide inside something that was leaving the store.

Like a delivery truck. Those rigs usually backed right up to the giant overhead doors, then after unloading, they drove away. If he could sneak inside, he could get away. But then he would be inside a semi-trailer that might be traveling across the country. Not a bad idea, but cowardly. He couldn't leave Taylor. The bakery probably took deliveries too, and/or made deliveries to restaurants. He needed a local truck that would only travel around Colorado Springs.

Voices in the hall cut into his thoughts. He heard a woman say, "Only three stops today. The two Breakfast Pantries and the stale goods that go to the Mission."

A man responded, "Good. My back is killing me."

Footsteps moved away in two directions.

Perfect. Jake pushed up the metal lid over his head and peeked out the inch-wide opening. The hall was clear. He climbed out and glanced toward the kitchen. No man in black. He stepped out the exit door again, blinking in the bright sun. A blue box truck sat there, with the back roller-door open. The driver was inside the cargo area, dumping a tray of bread bags into a bin. Jake moved sideways against the building, hoping to get out of the driver's line of sight. He wished he had a cigarette to light, so he could pretend to be a store employee on a break. The driver clumped down the metal ramp, empty-handed, and walked back inside the store. Jake scooted up the ramp, glancing around for the killer.

Was that him by the dumpsters? His heart skipped a beat, even though the man in black wasn't looking at him.

Inside the truck, Jake rushed to the back and moved a load of boxes, then slipped behind them and sat down. Hopefully, the driver would be preoccupied with his back pain and not notice the change.

He didn't. The driver made two more trips into the truck to load bakery goods, then pushed the ramp back into its slot, and closed the overhead door.

An hour later, Jake scooted out when the driver took the old bread into the Mission. He stared at the familiar building and longed to go inside for a meal. But he would settle for the stale muffin in his pocket. Finding out what was happening with Taylor couldn't wait.

Chapter 16

Jake hurried back to the Rocky Ridge Motel, taking only side streets so he wouldn't be seen from Nevada Avenue. He didn't mind the walk, but his feet were cold from the holes in his shoes, and he wanted out of the killer's sight. The motel room might not turn out to be a safe haven, but right now it seemed like one.

He passed the manager's office and considered paying for another night but not yet. He had calls to make first, and it might be better to move to another motel. He put the card-key in the lock of room seven and hesitated. What if the killer was inside, waiting for him? He backtracked to the office. A different woman was on duty, older and reeking of cigarettes.

Jake nodded and gave his name. "Has anyone asked about me or my friend, Taylor Lopez?"

"No." She glared at him. "You can't have guests in the room." A glance at the clock. "And it's past checkout time."

"I know. I'm trying to decide if I want to stay another night. I'll get back to you in a bit." Jake scooted out of the office before she could respond. He glanced up and down the street, then turned his face back to the building and hurried into their room. He wished he knew what the assassin was driving. And it would be great to have access to Taylor's car. How would he retrieve it? The killer might be watching the vehicle now, assuming they would eventually come back to it. Abandoning the Jetta seemed crazy.

Inside the dark motel room, Jake finally felt his body start to unclench. He lay on the bed and listened to his heartbeat, grateful to be alive. He'd never come so close to death. Not even that time he'd nearly drowned trying to swim across Cedar Lake—while stoned, of course. He really wanted to smoke a joint right now but resisted.

When he felt calm enough to sound rational, Jake called his friend at the Colorado Springs PD. They'd met when they were both employees at the Denver paper. She'd left the Post to take a public relations job at the Springs police department for better benefits. They'd dated briefly, then decided they were better friends than lovers. But she moved soon after, and they'd lost contact. "Kari, it's Jake."

"Hey! It's good to hear from you." She lowered her voice mid-sentence, as if suddenly aware of her surroundings. "Is everything all right?"

"I'm struggling a little, but it's temporary. How are you?"

"Good." A pause. "I can't really talk right now. Can I call you after work?"

"Do you have a minute?" This wasn't a social call.

"Sure."

"I need a favor. I'm in Colorado Springs, and a friend was picked up this morning by detectives. I need to know what's happening with her."

"That doesn't sound good. What's her name?"

"Taylor Lopez."

"Do you know which detectives?"

"No, but one of them looked young. Dark hair and jeans with a tweed jacket."

"That's Brad Miller. Give me your number, and I'll see

what I can find out. But I'm not optimistic."

"Thanks." He ended the call.

Jake booted up Taylor's laptop and searched for inmate information at the local jail. Taylor's name didn't come up. At least she hadn't been booked into custody. A troubling thought hit him. If the assassin had seen Taylor being arrested, would he wait for her outside the police department? Maybe jail was the safest place for Taylor right now.

While Jake waited to hear back from Kari, he decided to search for Seth Wozac. He'd promised Taylor that he would, but he hadn't had time since they discussed it in the coffee shop. Jake checked Facebook and Instagram but struck out. He then tried Denver city records, in case Seth owned property or had been married in Denver. No luck there either. Seth could have moved away to attend college or taken a job in the oil fields. He could be anywhere. Or already dead.

Jake started to search El Paso county, which covered Colorado Springs, but his phone rang. *Kari.* "Hey, what's the situation?"

"Taylor is being questioned in the murder of Bonnie Yost," Kari whispered. "But they haven't charged her, except for criminal mischief. That's all I could find out."

"Will you call me when she's released?"

"If I can. I leave at five, but the detectives often work all night if they have a homicide and a viable suspect. Taylor could be released at anytime." Kari kept her voice quiet. "Or she could be booked into jail. I'll try to keep you posted."

"Thanks."

"Jake? Did she do it? Kill that old woman?"

"Get out! No." He wanted to tell Kari about the assassin, but it sounded lame without the whole back-story. "Taylor just wanted to find out more about her birth and maybe learn something about her father."

"Good to know. I'll call you later." Kari clicked off.

Jake paced the musty motel room. Was this his fault for pushing Taylor to go back to the clinic, or would the detectives have tracked her down anyway? It didn't matter. He had to help her. What Taylor really needed was a lawyer. Yet an attorney would want a retainer, probably several thousand, and they didn't have it.

Could he bluff his way into the police department, pretending to be her lawyer? He could pick up a suit at a second-hand store. Maybe even print a few fake business cards. Bad idea. Maybe he could find a lawyer who would take her case pro-bono. The criminal mischief charge was bullshit. The police might just question Taylor and let her go.

And the killer could be waiting—unless the man in black was still looking for him.

Jake had never felt so helpless. The least he could do was to track down Seth and warn him. It was the one thing he could accomplish while holed up in this motel room.

Jake plopped on the bed and grabbed the laptop. He would search every county in Colorado. If only he had access to national databases. He suddenly remembered the files from the clinic. He stood and pulled the thumb drive from the hidden interior pocket of his jeans. Running from the assassin and worrying about Taylor had preoccupied him so much, he'd briefly forgotten about the clinic data. With the drive inserted, he opened the white file icon on the laptop screen. Dozens of color-coded folders appeared, many labeled with yearly dates and a short group of seemingly random capital letters. The labels meant something though, and with enough data sifting, he would figure it out. The first thing he would look for was Seth's parents. They might still be in Colorado and know where to find him.

Loud knocking on the door startled him. The motel manager shouted, "Pay up or get out!"

Jake decided to pay for another day. If he moved to a new motel, it had to be late at night when he had a chance of escaping the assassin's watchful eye. Using Zion's cash, he opened the door a few inches and gave the manager the night's rate. "I'll get a receipt later."

The old woman eyed him suspiciously, trying to look past him into the room.

"Don't worry. It's all good." Jake closed the door and sat on the bed. His stomach cramped, and he realized he hadn't eaten hardly anything since he'd left Zion's home the night before. Guilt sent another stab of pain to his gut. When he could, he would locate Zion's family and pay them back.

For now, he had to eat. He ordered a sausage-and-mushroom pizza to be delivered and sat back down to open files. He couldn't stop thinking about Taylor. She must be hungry too. Maybe even handcuffed and thirsty. Would she confess to a murder she hadn't committed if they intimidated her enough? *Please no.* He didn't believe it. She was stronger than she thought. Her courage to pursue this investigation, knowing that two subjects had already been killed, spoke for itself.

He grabbed the laptop, leaned back against the wall, and opened a file dated 1995/96. Within it were hundreds of folders labeled with last names. To check what kind of data they contained, he clicked the top folder: Sandra Altman. Three documents displayed. The first was a medical history file with some personal data, the second contained birth records, and the third was her pregnancy record. A scan of the birth information revealed that the baby had been labeled *female*, with no notes indicating gender confusion or abnormality. Were these files even relevant? Maybe the test subject data had been destroyed or kept somewhere else. But the researchers had known not only where to find the three men who'd been killed, but they also knew the three subjects shared a love of fire. They were keeping track of the offspring.

Jake switched to Sandra Altman's pregnancy record and scanned through the data, looking for a prescription or injection and didn't see one. But he'd moved too quickly. He started at the top and perused it again, reading every word. Under a listing titled *Ges-Rx,* he finally found a short list of medications*: Prenatal vitamins, amoxicillin, ImmuNatal.* The vitamins and antibiotic seemed harmless enough, but what the heck was ImmuNatal? He googled it and came up with nothing. Was it the experimental medication that had created dozens of intersex children? It would be interesting to see if the mystery prescription showed up in other files.

But first he needed to check if Seth Wozac was listed. Jake scanned to the bottom of the folders and spotted an entry labeled *Julie Wozac, NPIN.* Did IN stand for ImmuNatal? Jake scrolled back to Altman's file, which also bore the label *NPIN.* Many others said *NPST,* and a few were marked *APST.* He would think about the coding later. Finding and warning Seth had to be a priority.

Julie Wozac had given birth to Seth Richard Wozac on March 15, 1996. The father was listed as Dale Wozac, and the baby's gender was male. Jake couldn't find notes indicating any gender confusion. Had the doctor ignored the obvious or suppressed it? Or was Taylor simply wrong? Or maybe most intersex babies used to be labeled with a single gender— because that's what society expected. Maybe they still were.

Or it might be the parents' choice now. He'd read that doctors often performed surgeries on newborns to force them into a single gender. Jake cringed and reached to protect himself. Was there a standard protocol in the medical field? He wanted to believe obstetricians and parents were more open-minded these days, but he'd never given the subject much thought. He would ask Taylor what she knew about it.

Out of curiosity, he looked up her mother's records: *Mariah Lopez, NPIN*. Baby Taylor was listed as female. He glanced at the Father box, which listed Miguel Lopez. Taylor hadn't mentioned him once. Jake kept scanning and discovered that Taylor's mother had taken ImmuNatal too. He checked to see if a doctor was listed. *Charles Metzler.*

Jake had occasionally spotted a second name, Dr. David Novak, but the Altman and Wozac files also listed Metzler as the obstetrician. Could he find him? Metzler might be pretty old by now. Plus, Seth still came first. Jake went back to the Wozac file, looking for an address.

A loud knock on the door made him jump. Jake looked around for a weapon or a place to hide. Someone called out, "Pizza delivery."

Relieved, he paid the driver and tipped him five bucks. Jake had waited tables in college and knew how important the extra cash was. Minimum wage didn't leave enough money to buy pizza after paying rent, utilities, and car insurance.

After scarfing down three pieces, he felt satiated enough to set it aside. He had to make this money last, and Taylor would be hungry if and when the police released her. Now he needed a little toke to compliment his meal and keep him from feeling cooped up. He still had half a joint in his backpack. Jake found his lighter in a jacket pocket and smoked it in two big lungfuls.

Ahh. Tension melted from his body and his thoughts mellowed. He reached for the laptop and opened the Wozac file. But the urgency had gone out of his task, and he had to reread information. After a few minutes, he put the data-intensive files aside. He tried searching for Seth's parents online and found Julie Wozac on LinkedIn. She ran her own consulting company and had multiple contact listings. Jake called the top phone number, then panicked about what to say. He couldn't tell her the truth; she'd think he was mentally ill. But he needed her son's information. With clinic files and Dr. Metzler on his mind, Jake opened with, "Mrs. Wozac? This is Dr. David Carson. I'm trying to reach Seth Wozac. Is he available?"

"Ahh, no. He hasn't lived with me in a few years." Sadness permeated her voice. "What is this about?"

"I'm sorry, but I can't violate patient confidentiality. Yet, it's important that I speak with him. Please tell me how I can reach Seth."

"Why don't you have his number?" A little concern now.

"This is the only contact information he supplied on his intake form. Some patients get the test but are afraid of the results, so they make it hard for us to contact them. But he needs to know."

A sharp intake of breath. "What's his diagnosis? Is he all right?"

"I really can't tell you, but I hope he will. Do you have his number?"

"Yes. Let me look in my phone for it. I hope I don't cut you off when I do." A moment later, she read the number to him, as though it were not one she was familiar with. "Please tell him to call me," the desperate mother pleaded. "I want to help."

"I will. Thank you." Jake got off the phone, heaved a sigh of relief, then processed a wave of guilt for making the poor woman worry. He rationalized it by reminding himself that he was trying to keep Seth alive. The next call would be even more difficult. He had no idea how Seth would react to the potential death threat, yet Jake had to warn him.

He called the number and rehearsed his speech while it rang. Seth didn't answer. Following Taylor's example, Jake left a brief message: "This is Jake Wilson, and I have information about your birth that you need to know. Your life could be in danger. Please call or text me so we can meet and talk about this."

He tried to read more of the medical files, but exhaustion from not sleeping much the night before overcame him and he lay down to rest his eyes. He wasn't just tired though; he was stoned. If he hadn't smoked, he might still be working this investigation.

Shit. Getting high had been a mistake. Again. He vowed it would be his last time.

Chapter 17

Friday, Oct. 14, 5:05 a.m.

The recurring strange dream disappeared the moment she opened her eyes. Taylor glanced around. The horrible gray room still held her captive. She sat up and leaned against the wall, her side aching from napping on the hard floor. At least she wasn't handcuffed anymore. But she was hungry, and her lips hurt from drying out. It had to be the middle of the night or early morning by now. How long would they hold her? She had to pee again. She fought the urge to cry. *Be strong. Get mad.* Her mother's coaching had gotten her through this so far. What she really needed was a lawyer. Did she know any?

The door burst open, and the older detective charged into the room. "Get up!"

His intensity drove her to her feet. The way he looked at her, as if she were some kind of lowlife. God, she hated him. Where was his partner? This was the first time Blunt had come in alone, and she didn't trust him.

"Sit in the chair. I want some goddamn answers." He slammed a fist into the table.

But he'd done that a few times already, so she didn't react. He was a bully, and she survived other bullies. But in this situation, she wasn't free to walk away.

"What were you doing in that clinic with a fake baby belly?"

"Looking for information."

"Who was with you?"

"No one." It wasn't exactly a lie. She and Jake had split up, and she'd been alone in the lobby. *Stop talking!* That's what a lawyer would advise her.

"Witnesses saw you with a young man. Who is he?"

"I've answered all these questions before." Taylor forced herself to project her voice. "So I'm done. I have nothing else to say."

The detective jumped to his feet. "You're done when I say you are." He came around to her side of the table and stuck his face right next to hers. "You killed that old woman. Smashed her head with a heavy flashlight and stole her cell phone. Just fucking admit it." His breath reeked of cigarettes and bad coffee.

"No, I didn't.

He grabbed her by the chin and squeezed. "Without a plea deal, you'll do life in prison."

Taylor ignored the pain and spoke through clenched teeth. "I want to call a lawyer." She was bluffing, but as she said it, Taylor remembered one of her mother's military friends was a lawyer. Cole Ronan. But she had no idea how to reach him.

Detective Blunt plunged his hand into her hair and jerked her out of the chair.

Taylor let out a yell.

He pressed his palm over her mouth. "Quiet."

The door popped open, and Detective Miller came in. "What's going on?"

Taylor jerked away from the older man and stared hard at Miller. "I want to call a lawyer, and I need you to find his number for me. Cole Ronan. He lives at Fort Carson."

Miller's eyes darted back and forth between her and Blunt.

"I'll file a complaint if you don't." She couldn't believe she'd just said that. It was a risk! But she was in survival mode. She had to get free.

The younger detective led her into the hall. Relief washed over her. She was out of that horrible room.

They walked down an empty passage, their footsteps echoing in the quiet building. Taylor asked to use the restroom and took the opportunity to rinse the stale taste from her mouth. Her reflection in the mirror startled her. Puffy eyelids, unwashed hair, and a gray undertone to her skin. As if she'd been locked up for a week instead of twenty hours. Or however long it had been. *It's not over,* she reminded herself. Just because Miller was giving her a break didn't mean he would release her.

She stepped out of the restroom and smiled. "Thanks for intervening."

Miller silently steered her into a small office. "Tell me the name again."

"Cole Ronan." Would the lawyer even remember her? She hadn't seen him since a backyard barbecue her mother had hosted nearly six years ago. Cole had called once after the funeral, then faded away. Like everyone else. No one had known what to say to her.

After a two-minute computer search, Detective Miller jotted down a number, handed her a slip of paper, and turned his desk phone toward her. "You can make the call here."

She'd never used an old-school phone. With a shaky hand, she punched in the numbers and held her breath through five rings. The lawyer was probably asleep, and his publicly listed number was likely a business phone. Why would he pick up? A voicemail kicked in: "You've reached Cole Ronan, attorney at law. Please leave a message."

This would be a waste of time. "Mr. Ronan. This is Taylor Lopez, Mariah's daughter." She sounded like a little kid, even to herself. "I'm at the police department in Colorado Springs, being questioned about a murder I didn't commit. I need your help. Can you get me out of here?" She hung up and bit her lip to keep from crying. Two nights of minimal sleep had left her exhausted and vulnerable.

Detective Miller led her to a different room, a slightly larger version of the gray windowless walls, but with a small couch. "We're either going to let you go or book you into jail. I'm not sure yet, but you might as well rest until we decide."

That seemed like progress. Maybe just making the call had paid off. Not that she wanted to end up in jail, but at least they would feed her there. And the questions would stop. She lay on the couch and let her mind drift. Where was Jake? Had he hotwired her car and gone back to Denver? Or was he camped out at the motel, waiting to see what happened with her? She bet on the second option. For a homeless guy, he sure had locked onto her investigation with tenacity. He seemed like the kind of friend who wouldn't abandon her.

Out in the hall, raised voices made her sit up. The two detectives were arguing about what to do with her. She thought she heard Miller say they didn't have any evidence. The argument drifted down the hall. Taylor lay down, again, closed her eyes, and tried to rest.

A few minutes later, someone stepped in and shouted at her to get up. It was the older man, looking grumpier than usual. "Your lawyer isn't here, but he called. So we're letting you go."

Yes! A barrage of emotions rolled through her, but she was too tired to express them. She hurried out the door and into the hall.

"This way." Blunt grabbed her arm and tugged.

Taylor didn't care. She was getting out! They walked through a maze of hallways, the office doors closed and the building quiet. A moment later, they were in the wide lobby and she could see the glass front doors. The parking lot on the other side was dark and empty.

She pulled on the thick sweater that had been tied around her waist and turned to the detective. "I need my phone."

He hesitated, then from his pocket, pulled out her phone pouch, which also contained her Bluetooth and car key. The detective held out the pouch, but didn't let go. "This isn't over, so expect to hear from us again."

She nodded, snatched her cell phone, and hurried out the front door. In the middle of the parking lot, she stopped and checked the time: 6:07 a.m. Now what? She had to call Jake and let him know, then start walking to the motel, which was closer than her car. The frigid air made her fingers stiff as she put in her earpiece and pressed the screen. *Damn.* This sweater wasn't warm enough. After seven rings, her call went to voicemail and she left a message, sounding more frantic than she intended.

Taylor walked to the sidewalk. Left or right? Her phone rang, and it was Jake. "Hey, I was sleeping. You must be out."

"I'm in front of the jail. The motel is south, right?"

"Yes, but be careful. The assassin was at the clinic and came after me. I got away, but I suspect he'll keep coming until he kills us both."

Good god. Her whole body stiffened, and she glanced

around. A dark SUV sat across a side street, the only vehicle in sight. "Do you have my car? Can you come get me?" She started walking away from the dark vehicle, not wanting to pass by it, even though the motel was in the other direction.

"I didn't have the key, and I was afraid he was watching it. Look out for someone in dark clothes, a hooded jacket, and an androgynous face."

Was the killer one of them? "Stay on the phone with me, okay? I'm a little freaked out."

"Sorry to scare you. Just stick to the side streets. It's only a mile or so."

On the corner, she hesitated. Should she go another block before she circled back?

Sudden movement to her right. Taylor spun, but she was too late. Someone rushed her from behind a tree.

She let out a yelp just before a hand with a rag pressed into her mouth. The strong medicinal smell gagged her. *Poison!* Her pulse raced with panic. Taylor dropped her phone pouch and grabbed the assailant's wrist with both hands. But she'd lost her strength. She tried to scream, but the pressure on her mouth was too forceful. For a moment, she locked eyes with her attacker and saw no malice, only determination. So this was how she would die, in front of a police station, at the hands of someone who may have been delivered by the same doctor. Taylor's brain clouded, and she could no longer think clearly. As her knees buckled, a strong arm wrapped around her. She was dying . . . but she wasn't alone.

Chapter 18

Devin drove south, keeping her speed reasonable and her eye on the rearview mirror. Adrenaline still pumped in her veins. She'd just kidnapped someone five-hundred feet from a police station! Her boldest mission yet. Reckless, actually. But the major had called and said Lopez was being released. Devin didn't ask how he knew. Her father had connections everywhere through the military structure, officers who did what they were told, with no direct knowledge of the major or his research. Or maybe Taylor's monitor had reported it.

Devin had been taking a sleep break in a nearby motel on the assumption that they wouldn't release Lopez in the middle of the night. *Foolish!* After racing down to the police station, she'd taken a position and waited. Once she had eyes on her target, she'd moved in. Devin wouldn't risk letting Lopez disappear into the night again.

Devin checked the rearview mirror, but had no reason to believe anyone had witnessed the kidnapping or was looking for Lopez. Yet. By the time anyone realized the little troublemaker was gone, she would be deep underground, and no one would ever find her.

Devin turned off at the familiar sign for Fort Carson, showed her ID to the young soldier working the only open gate, and drove onto the base. She passed dark apartment buildings, recreation centers, and fast food restaurants. The base was its own small community of twenty-three thousand, and she'd grown up there, getting to know every numbered building and all the spaces in between. The hospital where her father had originally worked, and still commanded, was on a small rise at the back of the base. Cheyenne Mountain was behind her, towering over everything. The Rockies, the fresh air, and the dry beauty made Fort Carson the second most requested assignment for new recruits, after Fort Lewis in Washington.

When she reached the T in the road at the hospital, she turned right and passed the golf course she'd never played on. Neither had her father. His research was too important to allow much free time, and when he did leave his office or lab, he preferred the shooting range or bear hunting with a bow in the Silver Peak wilderness. She'd started hunting and shooting with him at the age of five, firing a Luger handgun at a paper target and rarely missing the body outline. She'd killed her first bear at the age of eight. They never hunted deer or any other passive animal. It wasn't sporting. Her father had treated her like a son, and all her paperwork indicated she was male. Correcting his assumption had never been an option. The major would have disowned her. Being male in the army was definitely an advantage anyway. Her female organs were on the inside, and so was her secret identity. She could live with that.

After a few miles, Devin was no longer officially on the base, and the paved road narrowed and turned to gravel. The terrain rose in gentle hills with patches of green scrub—an open wilderness with no one in sight. Fifteen minutes later, she neared the familiar butte. Another five-hundred yards, and she would enter the security area for the Stratton Research Complex, where the military conducted long-term medical studies and carried out covert operations related to its discoveries. Buried partially in the side of the butte with more levels underground, the top-secret facility was known to fewer than fifty people. Her father had been selected for the program soon after its inception, and he'd recruited her when she'd officially enlisted in the army, even though she'd been training for years before that.

A sliver of a pale moon reflected on the giant boulders lining the road, and the night was silent except for the hum of her engine. Feeling warm, Devin shut off the car heater. In the sudden quiet, she heard a scraping noise in the back of the vehicle. She slowed for the next curve and looked in the rearview mirror. Lopez was upright and next to the back car door. *Shit!* Devin slammed her brakes and reached for the master lock.

Chapter 19

Twenty minutes earlier

Taylor opened her eyes, but blackness still enveloped her. Where was she? Why couldn't she see anything? A gag cut into the corners of her mouth and her head ached. Slowly, her eyes began to focus and she realized she was in the back of a vehicle. A moving vehicle. Oh god, where were they taking her? Terror gripped her, and she almost vomited. She couldn't let that happen or she would choke. The gag wouldn't let her take deep breaths either. Her heart slammed in her chest and she willed it to slow down. Why was this happening? She'd expected to be killed, not kidnapped. Confinement—and torture or rape or whatever they had in mind—frightened her more than death.

She rolled on her side to look around. Something dug into the front of her hip. Her little knife tool! Could she get to it? Her wrists were bound by plastic handcuffs this time, but her fingers were free. Still, her arms were awkwardly bound together, and she couldn't get both hands into a front pocket. Using her fingertips on the outside of her jeans, she inched the tool upward toward the opening, then slipped it out. Getting the blade open was a struggle, but she finally managed. Now she felt almost more frustrated. Even if she could hack through the duct tape on her ankles—and that was doubtful—the vehicle was going thirty or forty miles an hour. It was also too dark to see what the terrain was like. If she jumped out, she would probably die or injure herself so badly she would wish she were dead.

Still, she had to do something! If she could get her ankles free, she would wait until the car slowed, then make a run for it. She'd rather be shot in the back than face whatever they had in mind.

Taylor brought her knees up to her chest and started cutting at the tape on her ankles. With little ability to apply pressure, she quickly grew frustrated and had to stop. But after a short break, she resumed, working until her hands ached and she had to rest again. A low voice from the front seat startled her. She glanced at the driver. Her abductor was talking softly to herself, unaware of the activity in the backseat.

Taylor resumed cutting at the layers of tape on her ankles. When she finally broke through, she had to choke back a sob of relief. With her legs free, she could run! She needed her hands free too, but at least she was functional. Should she go now? The plastic handcuffs could take forever to cut through—if she could even get the little blade into position. She needed to sit up for more leverage but couldn't take the risk. When she tried to maneuver the tool into a new position, she dropped it. *Damn!* Finding it with her fingertips on the dark floor of the backseat proved impossible.

The car slowed for a curve, and her body rolled against the back of the seat. The deceleration gave her hope that she could make a leap and survive. She just had to get into position and anticipate the next opportunity.

The driver had gone quiet again. Did that mean anything? Taylor tried to calculate her location. Considering her suspicion about the military's involvement, it seemed likely she was somewhere on Fort Carson. No, the base wasn't that far from Colorado Springs, and they were still traveling. She had no idea how long she'd been unconscious. Maybe only ten or fifteen minutes. Her body processed sedative-type drugs very quickly. She'd learned that at an early age during painful dental appointments. When her tonsils had been removed as a teenager, she'd come awake during the surgery. But none of that mattered. She needed to get out now, wherever the hell she was.

Taylor slowly sat up, planted her feet on the floor, and inched toward the door on her right. Leaping to the outside of the curve was risky, but it also gave her the best chance of getting away. With her shoulder hugged against the door, she grabbed the door latch as best she could with her bound hands and waited for the right moment.

After a few minutes, she felt the car slow down. Her pulse accelerated, but her legs felt like lead. She couldn't do this. It was too dangerous. Hitting the pavement would hurt a lot. *Shut up and go!* Taylor pulled on the door handle. Locked! She fumbled around for the mechanism and pressed it hard. The click was distinctly audible. Taylor glanced at the driver, who suddenly turned and stared at her with wide eyes.

No!

The car braked to a stop. Taylor leaned into the door to force it open and clambered out. On instinct, she turned back in the direction they'd come and ran along the road. With her hands bound, her movement was slow and awkward. She needed a place to hide before her abductor caught up. She scanned the terrain, but the near darkness was overwhelming.

Footsteps pounded behind her, moving fast.

Taylor tried to sprint, but without the use of her arms, it was pointless. She had to turn and fight and somehow overcome the assassin if she could. It was her only hope. She glanced down at the side of the road. *There!* A big rock, about ten feet ahead.

The loud footsteps were right behind her now.

Taylor scurried over, squatted, and grabbed it with both hands. The weight surprised her. She turned and lifted the rock, prepared to smash it down on the assassin's head.

Stinging pain suddenly burned into her chest and thigh. *Oh god! A stun gun.* Shock ripped through every nerve in her body, and she lost control of her muscles. The rock crashed to the ground as she sunk to her knees.

The assailant squatted next to her and grinned. "I like your spunk." Then she smashed a fist into her face.

Chapter 20

An hour earlier

Jake heard a thump, then the phone went quiet. "Taylor? What's happening?" More silence, except for the sound of footsteps moving away. *Oh shit!* The assassin had found Taylor! Jake jumped to his feet, still in his briefs. He was too far away to be any help. Panicked, he called 911.

"What's your emergency?" A male voice and not very pleasant.

"My friend is being assaulted and needs help. She's right in front of the police station."

"Is this your idea of a joke?"

What? "No! She called me because she was scared. I heard her make a startled noise, then drop the phone."

"Then what happened?"

"Nothing. I heard faint footsteps walking away." Taylor was probably dead, lying there on the sidewalk bleeding, like Zion had been. Jake's throat closed up.

"Which police station?"

"The main one on Nevada Avenue. Will you get a cop out there please?"

"I'm calling it in now. Stay on the line."

Why was that important? Jake put the phone on speaker and started getting dressed. He had to go out and see what was happening. It was stupid and dangerous, but he had to do it anyway. Taylor might still be alive, and he was only a mile or so away.

What if he got arrested? He hesitated for a moment, then pulled on his tattered athletic shoes. He would be careful. Sitting here just wasn't an option.

"Sir, are you there?"

"Yes. What's going on?"

"An officer at the department says there's no criminal activity out front. Are you sure about the location? Could it have been the station on Center Park?"

"Maybe. Did you alert them too?"

"I will."

The dispatcher should have done that already. Jake ended the call. He pulled on his jacket, grabbed the room key, and headed out. He would stick to side streets and keep a watchful eye for the killer. On the sidewalk, he changed his mind and sprinted down Nevada Avenue. He didn't have time to waste. The thought that Taylor might die in an alley or a dumpster because he'd been afraid for himself . . .

Jake pushed down the emotions that threatened to derail him and focused on what he knew. *No criminal activity?* That just meant Taylor wasn't lying in the open. Had the assassin taken her somewhere to kill her or had he just hidden her body? Were the cops even looking? The dispatcher had thought the call was a prank, so maybe the jerk had shared his skepticism with the police, and they hadn't done more than walk outside and glance around.

The night was quiet except for the sound of generators humming. A lone pair of headlights appeared in the road a few blocks ahead. Jake veered off the sidewalk and ran under the carport of a fast food drive-up. The steel-and-glass enclosure of the pick-up window stuck out just enough to offer protection. He flattened himself against the wall behind it and waited.

A moment later, a truck drove by, moving too quickly to be looking for him. Jake counted to three, and ran back out to the road. He tried to think like the assassin. Where was the man in black? Lying in wait for him near the police department? Taking Taylor someplace to torture her for information?

Jake's lungs ached with exertion, and he cursed himself for all the pot he smoked over the years. He would get back into shape after this, maybe start playing basketball again. If he survived. Jake tried to remember which cross street the department was on. Anything to distract himself from thinking about what he might find.

Seven streetlights later, he spotted the red-brick police station, the only building along the avenue with multiple lights on. Jake slowed to a walk. Time to start searching for Taylor. She might have been further away from the station than he'd thought.

He heard voices and saw two uniformed officers in the parking lot. They were walking toward the front door. He paused until they went inside, not wanting to encounter them. The way things were going, they might arrest him for making a false 911 call. If Taylor had given the detectives his name, they could have a warrant for his arrest. He wouldn't blame her. This was his fault.

He searched the side street, but other than a few parked cars, it was obviously empty. The businesses didn't have any landscaping that could hide a body either. Back at the corner, he stopped. Would the cops be watching out the window? Jake decided to cross the street and walk along the other side.

When he reached the next corner, he crossed back, hoping he was out of sight.

More cars and trees lined this side street. With a heavy heart, he began to search, even glancing in back seats of vehicles. Maybe Taylor had gotten away and was hiding somewhere. But why wouldn't she call? Because she'd dropped her phone. Yet his gut knew it was all wishful thinking. She wasn't here because the assassin had taken her. Maybe just to dump her body in the wilderness where it would never be found.

Something on the sidewalk caught his eye, and he knelt down. Taylor's phone pouch with the cell still in it. She must have dropped it when she was attacked. Now he knew for sure she was gone. His first instinct was to go inside the police department and shout at them to find her. But if he was arrested or jailed for his part at the clinic, no one might ever look for Taylor. He was on his own to figure out what the military had done to those women and why they were killing their offspring.

No, he needed help. Time to call the FBI. They had the authority and the resources to investigate everything: the deaths in Denver, the murder of the receptionist in Colorado Springs, and Taylor's abduction. They would take him seriously—and might never need to know about the incident at the obstetrics clinic.

Chapter 21

Friday, Oct. 14, 8:45 a.m., Eastern Time, Washington D.C.
Andra Bailey's phone rang soon after she sat down at her desk. She'd managed to read and respond to only one email so far. As she picked up, she glanced at who was calling. Special Agent Lennard. "What have you got for me?"

"Come to my office now please." Her boss hung up.

What the hell? This didn't sound good. Bailey stood, straightened her shoulders, and planned a diversion.

When she walked into the corner office, her boss looked chagrinned. "I think you were right about Colorado."

Of course she was. "Did something new happen?" Bailey took a seat, keeping to the edge of the chair

"A woman was kidnapped early this morning outside a police station in Colorado Springs." Lennard's broad shoulders gave a small shrug. "Or so her boyfriend claims. The victim is Taylor Lopez, a student at UC who interns at the Denver Medical Examiner's office."

The morgue where Logan Hurtz had been processed after his death. This case was definitely getting sticky. "Did the boyfriend witness the kidnapping?"

"He heard it over the phone."

"What time?'"

"Forty minutes ago. About 6:15 a.m., Denver time."

Bonnie Yost had been murdered in Colorado Springs. What if Lopez was the young woman who'd been spotted outside the victim's house? "Any idea why Lopez was at the police department at six in the morning?"

"Not yet. The message came through the front desk and went to the kidnapping unit. Someone in the monitor room noticed the Colorado connection and remembered your interest. You can follow up." Lennard handed her a printout with contact information for the witness.

"I'll get on a plane for Denver this evening." Stating her intentions was always better than asking permission.

"Great. We need to know what the hell is going on." Lennard leaned back. "Even if it's not connected to the Freedom Guardians."

Bailey was starting to doubt that too. She stood. "I might as well get going." She could have shared her new intel with Lennard, but it might be in her best interest to wait until things jelled.

"Keep me updated."

"I'll file daily reports." Bailey hurried out. She had a dozen calls to make. But first, the witness. She keyed in his number as she walked back to her office.

A young male said, "This is Jake Wilson."

She introduced herself, then launched straight in. "Tell me everything you know about Taylor Lopez's kidnapping."

"I'm sorry, but I didn't even see it. Taylor was on the phone with me, then made a startled sound, then the connection went quiet. I called 911 and ran to the police station where she'd just been released, but she was gone. I found her phone though."

"Why was she at the station?"

"They questioned her about the murder of a woman

who'd worked at a medical clinic. But Taylor didn't do it. She just wanted to talk to Bonnie."

"About?" Bailey passed another agent in the hall and nodded.

He paused, then blurted, "The intersex babies who were born twenty years ago, all delivered by doctors connected to Carson Obstetrics."

What the hell? "Intersex? You mean they have both kinds of genitals?"

"Yes, but what's important is that three of them died in the last month, and now Taylor has disappeared." He lowered his voice. "What if the military is trying to cover up something? Like an experimental drug they gave a bunch of pregnant women?"

Whoa. Definitely not related to armed militants. "Okay, slow down." She stepped into her office and closed the door. "Tell me who's dead and how." Bailey slipped into her chair and opened a file on her computer, prepared to key in notes as the informant talked.

A paper crinkled in the background. "I don't know the dates because Taylor's the one who noticed the bodies. She works in the morgue." A catch in Wilson's voice. "Adrian Warsaw and Logan Hurtz both died accidentally in the last three weeks. One of them drowned and one fell off a balcony."

Bailey took a moment to note the information. "And the third?"

"I found his body in an alley where he'd been shot. Taylor had left a message on his phone. That's how I connected with her and learned the rest." The information came out in a fast gush, and she suspected he'd left out some details.

But they could wait. "The dead man's name?"

"Zion Tumara."

"Give me a second." Bailey had caught up with her notes and keyed the victim's name into the database. She learned that Tumara had been questioned about an arson but had no criminal record. So his homicide wasn't gang or drug related. Three men were dead, possibly all murdered, and the woman who'd connected their deaths was missing. The abducted woman had also talked to the clinic receptionist, who'd later been murdered. Some kind of cover-up was definitely going on. In addition, the young victims were all intersex and born around the same time. Adrenaline surged in her chest. This case was so much more interesting than anti-government, militia cowboys!

Bailey turned back to her phone call. "Any idea who kidnapped Lopez?"

"No, but he came after me too."

An aggressive, deadly unsub. "Describe him."

"About five ten, slender but buff. With pale skin. That's all I've got. He wore a hood, and I was running away." A nervous laugh. "I hid in a grocery store."

"Was the man armed?" Bailey logged into the bureau's travel site. She needed to fly out to Denver ASAP.

"Yes. This is Colorado and near an army base."

"Did you call the police?"

"Not that time." He was silent for a long moment. "I had just seen Taylor get handcuffed and shoved into a police car, so I was afraid of getting arrested."

"What are you not telling me?"

Another hesitation. "We were at the clinic earlier trying to get information about the doctors." His tone grew impassioned. "Bonnie, the receptionist, was there in 1996 when Taylor and the other subjects were born. She sent Taylor a list of all the intersex babies. Five names were marked. Three are dead, and Taylor has been kidnapped." He choked up. "She's probably dead now too."

Subjects? Was this guy a conspiracy theorist feeding her a line of bull? "Tell me about yourself, Jake."

He let out a bitter laugh. "I'm an unemployed journalist and perfectly rational. I'll email you the list, and you can see it for yourself."

A reporter. Interesting. Bailey gave him her digital contact info. She had more questions, but they could wait. She needed to buy a plane ticket right now. The killer/kidnapper—if they were the same person—already had a head start. "Why didn't you contact the Denver FBI field office?"

"I didn't think about it. I'm new to Colorado."

Not everyone knew the field offices existed. "Some of these events were already on my radar, and I'll get out there as quickly as I can. Meanwhile, you should go to the Denver bureau and ask for protection."

"I can't do that. Taylor was abducted from Colorado Springs, and I have to stay here until I find her . . .or hear otherwise."

Empaths could be such idiots. "Stay inside. I need you alive to answer questions when I arrive. Call me if anything changes. I have to get going." She clicked off, called the bureau's contact person at United Airlines, and booked an evening flight. If her travel went well, she would be in Denver by midnight.

Chapter 22

Friday, Oct. 14, 6:52 a.m., Stratten Research Complex
The car slowed, and Taylor braced for what might come next. She stared out the window, and in the trickle of new daylight spotted a low-to-the-ground building about the size of a grocery store. It didn't seem big enough to be a military facility, but the fact that she wasn't wearing a blindfold meant her captor had no intention of letting her ever leave this place. *Oh god.* What if they water-boarded her? If the torture became unbearable, could she find the means and the courage to kill herself? Her mother had made that choice.

They drove up to the building, and her abductor flashed a badge at a small, automated security post. An overhead door opened, and they drove into a parking garage, coming to a stop between an oversized SUV and an open-style jeep. The kidnapper turned to her. "No more fucking around. I don't want to drag you in there unconscious and bleeding. Your stay here will be more pleasant if you just accept—better yet, embrace—your fate." Her captor stepped out of the car and opened the back door. "My name is Devin, by the way. And you should consider yourself privileged to have the opportunity to serve your country and make the world safer." The man leaned in and cut the new tape on Taylor's ankles.

What the hell was he talking about? Taylor's chest tightened, and she struggled to breathe. Much to her mother's dismay, she'd never wanted to serve in the military. "What is this about? Please just tell me." The strength of her own voice surprised her. She was terrified.

"Soon. For now, just be quiet and come peacefully."

Devin grabbed her arm, tugged her out of the vehicle, and led her to the back of the building. A single guard sat by the door, a rifle strapped to his chest, watching something on a tablet computer. He looked up, nodded at Devin, and went back to his entertainment. After Devin flashed his ID at the security camera, a steel door slid open, and they entered a wide hallway. The scent and feel of the air reminded her of a mechanic's shop, heavy with the stink of oil, exhaust, and grinding metal parts. What was going on here? The obstetrics office and the possible pregnancy drug had made the experiment seem medical, and Taylor had expected a clinical setting. Her legs trembled as she walked down a long, sloped hall past closed doors. Were they headed underground? At the end, more doors opened, and they entered a cavernous room with concrete walls. The temperature was noticeably cooler. A shiver ran up her spine.

Devin pointed at one of several golf carts. "Get in."

Taylor complied. Her face still hurt from the last punch, and her chest burned from the stun gun. "Are we underground?"

"Yes." Devin climbed in and push-started the engine, which barely made a sound. "Don't ask any more questions. The major will tell you what he wants you to know."

The major. Another tremor ran through her body. Taylor hated him already.

They drove through a room stuffed with equipment she

didn't recognize, then passed into a dark tunnel. The hum of another electric cart filled the silence ahead. Devin pulled off to the side and let the other cart pass, saluting the driver as he went by. The man was middle-aged and wearing civilian clothes. Did people both live and work in this hidden complex? How unhealthy to live underground. She and Devin traveled for another few minutes, and Taylor's dread deepened. Even if she escaped, could she find her way out?

Abruptly, the tunnel branched, and bright lights appeared along the ceiling. Devin turned left and stopped at the second door. The only marking was the numeral two near the knob. Devin hopped out, pushed a button on the wall, and said, "Lieutenant Blackburn to see you, sir. I have Lopez."

At least she was still human to them, not just a target or package. After a moment, Devin motioned for her to get out. Taylor glanced at her unbound feet. Last chance to run. But where? No, the parking lot had been her last chance, but the guard with a rifle had discouraged her. She had no choice but to face this. If she ever got lucky and saw daylight again, she might be able to make a real break. Probably wishful thinking. Her life as she knew it was over. She'd never work in the morgue again or find her father. Her poor fish would die, if they hadn't already. Sadness and guilt washed over her. Taylor bit her lip, refusing to cry.

The metal door slid open into a pocket in the cement, and they entered an office. The walls were white and covered with plaques, photos, and awards. Papers cluttered the big oak desk, and the leather chairs looked comfortable. The normalcy of everything surprised Taylor.

Devin stood near a chair and waited. "Don't sit until the major does."

Not quite normal.

A side door opened, and a man walked in. Six feet of lean, rigid muscle and short-cropped blondish-silver hair. His chiseled face would have been attractive under other circumstances, but he wasn't smiling. His unlined skin looked younger than the graying hair indicated, but maybe that was because he never went out in the sun. The mud-brown button up shirt made him seem even paler. It wasn't exactly a uniform, but no civilian would ever wear it.

"Why is she bleeding?" The major's voice wasn't deep, but it commanded attention.

"She tried to escape, sir, and an altercation ensued." Devin was still rigidly upright.

"You must have failed to secure her properly. Fifty pushups."

Devin dropped to the ground and started cranking them out. Taylor watched in astonishment for a moment, then turned to the major. "Why am I here? Why didn't you just kill me like the others?" She couldn't believe she'd just asked that.

"We think you're suited to our infiltration program. It's an opportunity to serve the goal of global peace."

Infiltration? "You mean spy? I can't do that." She glanced away from his steely expression. "I don't have the courage. I'm not like that."

"I think you're wrong. You infiltrated my clinic and asked questions about the experiment." His mouth relaxed.

His version of a smile? "What did you do to those pregnant women? And why?"

"If you excel in our program, you'll earn the clearance to know about our research. For now, I'll ask the questions." He gestured for her to sit.

Taylor glanced at Devin, who was still doing pushups.

"Now." The major didn't raise his voice, but his glacial

tone unnerved her.

Taylor eased into a chair, and a moment later, Devin took the seat beside her, making an effort to control his breathing.

"All you need to know at this point is that you're part of our program. You can work with us to serve your country—" The major paused and locked eyes with her. "Or not."

Cooperate or die. Taylor shuddered and cried out, "Why me? I'm not a soldier. Or a spy. I have no skills and I can't help you."

A flash of frustration in the major's eyes. "You're an investigator. You're the first person to realize that numerous intersex people had been born at the same time." The older man nodded at Devin. "The first thing we need to teach her is confidence. Start with body awareness and defense sessions. Then Marissa will teach her to blend, adapt, and seduce."

Taylor's heart accelerated with each casual word. This was insane. Whatever it was, she couldn't do it. Sobs threatened to take over her exhausted body.

A phone on the desk rang. A landline. Two cell phones sat next to it. The major picked up the landline receiver. "Blackburn speaking."

A long pause while he listened. Then he placed his hand over the mouthpiece, looked at Devin, and said, "It's time. The last operative is in place." One corner of his mouth turned up. "Phase Two of the Peace Project is about to begin."

Devin shot out of his chair. "Excellent news."

The major nodded at Taylor. "Get her out of here. We have details to discuss."

Chapter 23

A surge of pleasure ran through Blackburn's body. He'd been working on this project for decades, and it was about to payoff. Not in an immediate way such as winning a battle, but he would see the incredible results in his lifetime. He wanted to pump his fist in the air and shout "Huzzuh!"—but not in front of his son. The boy tended to be too emotional and needed a strong male role model. Training him as a sniper and covert assassin had gone a long way toward suppressing Devin's girly side. Blackburn would make a man of him yet.

"Which quarters do you want her in?" Devin's weak voice never failed to annoy him.

"The A block. Get her settled and come right back. I want to discuss your assignment." Devin hadn't reported the journalist as dead yet, so his son had obviously failed that part of his mission.

"Yes, sir." Devin grabbed the new recruit's arm and steered her toward the door.

The girl looked terrified. Blackburn hoped he wasn't wrong about Lopez's potential. Even more, he hoped he didn't have to terminate her. He'd been startled when he'd scanned her file and realized who her father was. Taylor had been born a soldier, she just hadn't accepted it yet. Out of respect for Officer Lopez, Blackburn had brought Taylor into the program rather than eliminate her. When she was ready, he would tell her father she was here.

When Devin and Lopez had left, Blackburn picked up his work cell phone and called his most frequent contact. The project's designer answered before it rang a second time. "Good morning, major."

The peacekeepers of the free world were all light sleepers.

"Rashaud. It's time. The last operative is ready."

"On my way." The phone went dead.

Captain Ahmed Rashaud was the only lower-ranking personnel who didn't have to call him "sir." They'd been working together on this project, and others, for so long, the formality had dropped away, and neither had ever commented on it. As a psychologist, Rashaud had probably noticed and analyzed the trend, but out of respect, never brought it up. Blackburn opened a bottom desk drawer and pulled out a half empty bottle of Glenfiddich and two shot glasses. Regardless of the hour, this called for a celebration.

Moments later, Rashaud stepped in. A compact man with black hair that had gone silver at the temples and brown skin that had lightened after years of working underground. Rashaud gave a victory salute but didn't sit down. His eyes flashed with excitement. The psychologist had been born in Syria, but had moved to the states with his parents when he was twelve. Rashaud understood the root problem better than anyone else in the research complex. In fact, he'd been the one to suggest the long-term mission when Blackburn had shown him the powerful pacification effects of the drug, especially on male lab animals. What an exciting day that had been! The mixed gender issue that affected some of the subjects was a side effect, but one that would ultimately enhance their peace goal, since most hermaphrodites couldn't reproduce. Still, proving ImmuNatal could work in humans had taken another twenty years.

"This deserves a toast." Blackburn poured two shots and handed one to his project partner. They lifted them in silence.

"Congratulations," Rashaud said. "Placing the operatives and manipulating them into position was the most challenging component. Well done."

"The CIA did their part, and the original idea was yours. This is your celebration."

They downed the scotch and eased into their chairs.

"Waiting has been the hardest part," Blackburn said. "Remember the day we realized some of the mixed-gender kids were pyromaniacs? You wanted to give up."

Rashaud laughed politely. "You were pretty stressed too."

Blackburn shook his head. "I still don't know for sure what caused the pyromania and hyper-sexuality in that first group, but the hormone somehow affected their mesolimbic pathways and allowed for high levels of dopamine." He straightened his shoulders, not wanting to focus on their setbacks. "I never doubted the mission. Any synthetic drug can be modified."

Rashaud raised his glass again. "You succeeded. "So far, the second set of subjects has shown no signs of either issue." He rapped his knuckles on the desk for luck. "At fifteen years old, we would be seeing the problems if they existed."

"What's the latest on the third group of subjects?" They were only ten years old, but their personalities had developed enough by then to know their true nature.

Rashaud raised a hand in victory. "A perfect score, so far. Not one incidence of violence or aggression. Not even a single fist fight."

"And the gender-neutral rate?"

"It has stayed consistent at thirty to thirty-five percent."

Blackburn nodded. Not only had they refined the pharmaceuticals to make them water-soluble, they'd also tested the hormone in non-military mothers in the second trial and third trials. There was growing evidence that soldiers with PTSD passed the trauma to their children through their DNA. But the entire Middle East was experiencing the devastating emotional effects of war, so they couldn't control for that.

Blackburn was ready to move forward, even if the new version of ImmuNatal still had moisture concerns related to the packaging. Rashaud was the cautious one. But the future of his people was on the line, which was why they'd never developed a pure infertility drug. They wanted peace, not annihilation.

"Phase Two will take even more patience," Blackburn added.

"Another two decades." The psychologist let out a small sigh.

"We'll see the difference in fifteen years," Blackburn countered. "The terrorists are recruiting them younger than ever, so their ranks will thin as the last of the violent generation takes casualties." Between the coalition air strikes and supporting tenacious Kurdish fighters, the frontline managed to keep the terrorists in check. But it wasn't enough to ever declare victory. Blackburn continued. "Their recruitment efforts will start to collapse in twelve or thirteen years. Twenty years from now, all the extremist cells could be gone."

Rashaud nodded. "Is it time to conference with General Northup and Director O'Brian to launch the peace drug?"

They had needed help from the CIA to place and monitor the young operatives, and only one out of the twenty they sent out had gone dark. They still didn't know what had happened to him. He could have been killed and his body never found, or he could have joined the enemy. Was it time to inform the higher command that Phase 2 was about to launch? As eager as he was to move forward, Blackburn hesitated. "Let's check with the lab and make sure the scale-up batch is ready. We have to hit every source at the same time."

"They'll never detect it," Rashaud assured him. "We've designed it that way." The psychologist paused, then asked. "Did Devin complete his mission?"

"Not yet, but he will." Blackburn stood, ready to move on.

"The journalist has to be the priority." Rashaud got up too. He cocked his head and quietly asked, "Can Devin handle it, or do we need to send a more-experienced clean-up man?"

Blackburn bristled. Only Rashaud could suggest his son was incompetent and not suffer a demotion—or worse. "Devin will take care of both remaining targets today. I assure you."

Blackburn reached for his work-only cell phone, and it rang in his hand. The ID said *Bohmer.* The monitor assigned to Seth Wozac. Blackburn snapped, "What is it?"

"It's Bohmer, sir. We have a problem."

Chapter 24

Three hours earlier, Colorado Springs

Seth Wozac paced his apartment. Fourteen steps and turn. Fourteen steps and turn. The space was too damn small, and his body felt like it would explode. Being outside had been even worse. In public, he'd felt exposed, like people could see right through him and know he had a foreign thing inside. *A uterus!* How the hell had he ended up with a fucking uterus? A doctor had discovered it the day before when they'd done an MRI at the emergency room. Seth still couldn't believe it. But he'd seen the image, and the doctor had even showed him how to feel for it under his skin.

Repulsive! Seth punched himself in the gut. The blow didn't faze him. Meth dulled his pain. But not yesterday. He'd crashed into a tree at the skate park and ended up with a branch sticking into his gut. He'd been straight at the time, and it hurt like a motherfucker! But if it hadn't happened, he wouldn't know about the damn uterus. Now that he knew, he had to take action.

Seth curled his hand into a fist again. He wanted to punch that smug doctor in the face! "It happens sometimes," the bitch had said with a shrug, as though the uterus was a third nipple or something sick-cool. When Seth had demanded she remove it, the doc had given him a snotty smile and jabbered on about the expense of elective surgery, especially for the uninsured. Then she'd suggested he simply forget about it.

Like that was possible. The rage brewing in his body burned with a new intensity. The uterus had to go. It was that simple. He was a man, for fucks sake! He had chest hair, an eight-inch cock, and a hard-on for girls. How the hell was it even possible to have female junk inside him? But not for long. Seth pulled his stash from the canister in the kitchen and laid out another line of meth. He preferred the needle, but he didn't have the time or patience to cook a hit right now. He'd been up all night and he wanted to act now. With a short, plastic tube, he snorted the meth, half in each nostril. The burning sensation was soon overtaken by a joyous energy. He could do anything! Including operate on himself. He'd been thinking about it all day. He'd even watched a video of a doctor performing an appendectomy on himself. The dude rocked. Balls the size of fists.

What did he need? Towels to put pressure on the bleeding, a mirror, and his suture kit. He'd been doing his own minor skin repair since he was fifteen. As a skateboarder, he'd scraped the pavement a few times, but he hated doctors and refused to see them unless the damage was beyond his skills. Like a broken arm or a branch broken off in his gut.

Seth raced around his studio apartment and gathered everything he thought he would need. His mind kept jumping ahead to the surgery—watching it play out in bloody technicolor. He had to cut quickly and not be timid. And to be careful and not hit his aorta. The thoughts were coming so fast he could hardly process them.

Plunge the blade all the way through the skin and fat and

make one clean cut. The meth would override most of the pain, and he could ignore the rest. What if he bled to death? So what if he did? A life of mental illness, anxiety, and self-loathing was far worse. This could be his final act. Cut out the alien thing and die a real man. At least now he understood all those girlish impulses he'd had as a kid. Once this thing was gone, he might find some peace. Maybe call his mother. His parents had divorced because of him and his weirdness. But his father was a fuckwad and could rot in hell.

He didn't really want to die. He had a long-board competition this weekend. Maybe he should call 911 right after he made the cut, just in case. As long as he got the damn uterus out before the paramedics arrived, the hospital doctors could put him back together and he'd be fine. Maybe he would do this in the bathtub so he didn't have to clean up afterward. And he had to hide his stash, in case things went wrong.

Fire! He needed to see and feel a flame to calm himself enough to make the cut. Seth lit a candle and his body inhaled the beauty of the flickering light as he passed it under his palms. Better, for now. He would go out and light a real fire as soon as he could. That was another thing that was wrong with this apartment—no fireplace! How was a person supposed to live this way?

Focus!

He ran his knife blade over the flame to purify it, then gathered his supplies and rushed back to the bathroom. He stripped off his T-shirt, climbed into the tub, and lay back against the cold porcelain. With his fingertips, he located the area where the foreign lump of tissue lay under his skin. The medical image of the thing was burned in his brain. He would start on the outside and cut toward the middle, making a three-inch incision. The uterus was only connected by a few small arteries. He would just yank it out and shove a small towel into the hole to stop the bleeding.

But first, he'd call the paramedics. He grabbed his cell phone from the floor and hit 911.

"What's your emergency?"

"My belly is bleeding. I was in the ER yesterday after crashing into a tree branch, and the wound is bleeding badly." True enough. Yesterday's stitches were in the same general location. Maybe he should pull them out so it looked . . . Never mind.

"No need to shout," the dispatcher said. "What's your name and address?"

Was he shouting? Too bad. Seth gave her the information and shut down the call. No more stalling. No more distractions. *Goodbye, girly parts.* Seth brought the blade to his abdomen and plunged it in.

Chapter 25

Friday, Oct. 14, 9:30 a.m.

Jake woke to the sound of his phone alarm and sat up, feeling groggy. He grabbed the cell and checked the time. Oh right, late morning. His body clock was totally messed up. He forced himself to get up and take a shower. Clean clothes would have been nice, but they weren't a priority, so he dressed in what he had, ignoring the smell. Finding Taylor was still his focus. After he had called the FBI earlier and talked to Agent Bailey, he'd felt calmer, like he'd done everything he could for Taylor. So he'd called Seth Wozac's number and left a message, then stretched out to get some overdue sleep.

But only a few hours. Guilt about Taylor would keep him from any kind of normal life until he knew what the hell had happened. It would be easy to assume she was dead, and he winced at the thought. But why wouldn't the assassin leave her body like he had with Zion? The fact that she'd been taken made Jake believe she was still alive. Why did they want her? He shuddered to think of her in captivity, possibly being experimented on. He hoped like hell the FBI would find her.

His stomach growled, and he looked around the room.

The pizza he'd ordered the night before was gone. His mouth was dry, and the stink of his own breath was toxic. Time to brush his teeth and get back to his investigation. He couldn't do much else. If he left the motel, the assassin might shoot him. Agent Bailey's suggestion that he seek protection from the Denver field office sounded good in theory, but he was in Colorado Springs. Anything could happen in the hour it would take to drive to the city.

More important, he wanted to find Charles Metzler. The doctor had delivered many of the experiment babies and was probably key to this whole thing. Or maybe not. Still, Metzler had to know something, and Jake needed to interview him for the article he planned to write.

First, he needed food, so he hurried down the covered walkway to the lobby and raided the vending machine for snack packs of nuts and cookies. The clerk glanced over and tried to catch his eye, but he ignored her. He wouldn't pay for another night until he had to. While scarfing cashews, he searched the online white pages for the doctor, but didn't find him. A broad internet search didn't produce usable results either. Metzler had probably retired. Jake opened the clinic files again, scanned for the second doctor he'd noticed, and found the name David Novak. The doctor came up quickly in an internet search as an obstetrician at St. Paul's Medical Center.

Novak might have known about ImmuNatal too, or could help him find Dr. Metzler. Calling to set up an interview seemed like a waste of time. Doctors were notoriously hard to reach, even when you were their patient. Jake called the hospital anyway just to see if Novak was in the building. The receptionist transferred him to the maternity unit.

"Third floor nurse's desk. How can I help you?"

"I'd like to speak with Dr. David Novak."

"He's in the delivery room. Can I take your name and number?"

"Sure." Jake gave them to her. Why not? There was a one-in-a-million chance Novak would call back. "Thanks." He clicked off, grabbed his backpack, and headed for the door. He knew where Novak was right at this moment, so he shouldn't waste this opportunity. Even if he hung around the hospital for hours and didn't get to question the doctor, it was still better than being cooped up in this motel room, feeling helpless. He could search online and make calls from anywhere.

He stopped at the door, his chest tightening. The assassin could be out there, waiting and watching. Maybe not the one who'd taken Taylor, but another one. The military had a million people.

Man up!

Jake yanked open the door and charged across the parking lot to Taylor's car. He'd picked it up after finding Taylor's phone pouch with the key near the police station. Inside the vehicle, he locked the doors, started the engine, and let out his breath. Good so far. No one seemed to be sitting on a nearby rooftop with a rifle trained on him. But an assassin could be waiting for a better opportunity. Or maybe the military wanted to abduct him too. No, he wasn't one of the subjects. They just wanted him silent. He raced out of the parking lot, past a young family getting out of their car. Around him, people were working their jobs, going out to lunch, or strolling in the crisp fall sunshine. He envied their peace of mind, but not their lives. He craved stimulation and puzzles and uncertainty. He'd just never thought it would actually get him killed.

He watched the rearview mirror obsessively for the first five minutes on the road but didn't see a car following. After almost rear-ending a truck, he settled on occasional checks behind him. But he couldn't let down his guard. Until when? Until his article hit the national media. When everyone knew about the gender experiment, there would be no point in killing him to keep it quiet. Unless, they simply wanted revenge. Even if the FBI caught the man who'd taken Taylor, the military had thousands of trained killers. He might never be safe. Jake's throat dried up, and he gripped the wheel so hard his knuckles hurt. What the hell had he gotten into?

St. Paul's Medical Center sat on the edge of a massive city park. Jake glanced up at the third floor and thought the patients must have a nice view. Not that women in labor cared much about that. He entered the parking garage, stopped at the ticketed gate, then circled his way up to the third level. As he shut off the car, his reporter routine kicked in, and he reached in his backpack for a notepad. But he couldn't find it. Had he left it at the hotel? No worries. He would record the conversation on his phone. He checked his face and hair in the mirror. *Shit!* He hadn't shaved in days, and his T-shirt was wrinkled. He looked like a homeless man. Jake's gut contracted. He was homeless. But not for long. He pulled on his sweatshirt to cover the ugly T-shirt and climbed out of the car. Straightening his shoulders, he walked toward the building. As long as he looked confident and friendly, people would trust him. Or so his dad used to say. But the world today was different. People were more suspicious, especially here in Colorado where they'd had four mass shootings.

An engine rumbled in the dark concrete space, and he

spun around. A middle-aged woman with several kids in a minivan. No one had followed him.

Once inside, the pinkish hospital walls and narrow, windowless corridors unnerved him. This probably wouldn't go well. At the main desk, he approached a woman in scrubs. Her short hair was cobalt blue. *Interesting choice.* "I'm Jake Wilson. I called about meeting with Dr. Novak."

She gave him a once over. "Uuhh, right. He's still in the delivery room, but when he's out, I'll let him know you're here." She pointed down the hall. "There's a family lounge you can wait in."

Jake thanked her and strode toward the waiting room. Maybe there would be some free food, like a tray of donuts, or at least coffee.

The little space had a couch, three padded chairs, and a table with a coffee urn. *Thank god.* He filled a disposal cup, sat down, and turned on Taylor's laptop. But before he delved back into the patient data, he would try Seth again. His third call since last night.

After five rings, a pleasant female voice answered. "This is a nurse at St. Paul's. The person you're trying to reach is a patient here. I hope you're a friend or family member."

Seth was in this hospital! "Uh, I'm a friend. What's wrong with Seth?"

"I can't give you any information without his permission, but you should come see him. Oh." She sounded surprised. "He's waking up. I have to go." The connection went dead.

What the hell? Had Seth been shot by the assassin but somehow survived? Did the killer know his victim was here? Jake shut off the laptop and jumped to his feet. He had to find Seth, but this was the wrong floor. Jake rushed to the nurses' desk. "Can you tell me what room Seth Wozac is in? He's a friend, and I just heard he was here. I might as well visit him while I wait."

"How do you spell that?"

Jake rattled it off. "If I give you my phone number, will you call me when Dr. Novak is available?"

"Sure." She didn't sound sincere. "Your friend is in room two-seventeen. That's intensive care. They may not let you in." The nurse handed him a small sticky note. "Write your name and number for me, and I'll give it to Dr. Novak."

Jake made himself write neatly, then rushed down the hall to the elevator. Seth was in critical condition, and the nurse had answered his phone. That was bad news. She must think Seth might die. The reality of it hit him hard, and Jake slowed down. Warning Seth now seemed almost pointless and cruel. But he had to see him anyway. Seth might be able to describe his attacker. He might even know something about the experiment he'd been part of.

Jake took the elevator down one floor, followed the signs to the ICU, and pressed the buzzer. A young male voice asked who he wanted to see, then let him in. They obviously weren't worried about Seth's safety. After Jake entered the ward, the young man in lavender scrubs reported, "Seth is recovering nicely, but we're concerned about his mental health. Will you help him understand that he needs to talk to our staff psychiatrist?"

They thought Seth was crazy. Because he'd talked about the experiment? "What happened to him?" They walked down a wide corridor with glass walls defining the patient rooms. When they entered Seth's area, he was sitting up on the edge of his bed. He stared at Jake with wild eyes. Seth didn't know him and didn't look happy to see him. Jake turned to the guy in scrubs. "Will you give us some privacy?"

"All right." The nurse stepped out and closed the sliding glass door.

"Who the fuck are you?" Even seated and wearing a hospital gown, Seth was a big man. About the same height as Jake, but broader with thick arms and legs. He had short facial hair and a wide jaw and didn't look androgynous like Zion and Taylor.

"I'm Jake Wilson. Sorry to barge in here, but I have to talk to you about Carson Obstetrics and the circumstances of your birth."

Curiosity flickered in Seth's gray eyes, but anger took over. "Whatever the hell happened, I fixed it. So fuck that. I'm getting out of here." Seth stood on wobbly legs. "If you want to help me, find my pants!"

He didn't look ready to leave the hospital, but maybe it was the safest thing for him. "They're probably in a plastic bag somewhere." Jake strode across the room and started opening cabinets. "What happened? Did someone assault you?" Jake looked over his shoulder as he talked.

Seth laughed, a harsh sound. "I assaulted myself and yanked out a little extra something I had in my gut."

What the hell was he talking about? "You did some kind of self-surgery?"

"None of your fucking business. Hand me my clothes."

Jake found the bag and passed it to the patient. "I came here to warn you. I think someone might try to kill you."

Seth's brow wrinkled. "No shit? I almost beat them to it." Another mocking laugh, then he turned serious. "What does this have to do with my birth?" He pulled on his pants under the hospital gown.

"I think the military conducted an experiment with pregnant women in 1995." Jake paused. Seth didn't look gender-fluid and might resent being lumped in with people who were. "Many of the babies born to those women have gender issues."

Seth's eyes narrowed. "You mean like having a uterus inside your male body?"

Poor dude. "Yes, stuff like that."

"Are you fucking for real? They did this to me on purpose?" His cheeks puffed and turned bright red.

"I think they were testing a drug, and it had unexpected consequences."

"Those motherfuckers!" Seth slammed a hand down on the tray by his bed.

"I'm sorry, but I think you're on a list to be terminated as well."

"Are you fucking serious? It's not enough to ruin my life? Now they want to end it too? Why?"

Taylor had suspected it was because of his fascination with fire, but Jake wouldn't share that yet. "I don't know, but I'm working on it."

Seth suddenly sucked in a sharp breath and flopped back on the bed. The flush in his cheeks faded and he blinked rapidly. "I need some pain meds."

"Should I get your nurse?"

"Not yet. Tell me more about this experiment."

"I'm still investigating, but the women who had intersex babies were given a drug called ImmuNatal. They were all patients at Carson Obstetrics, which is connected to the military hospital inside the Fort Carson base."

"My father was stationed at Fort Carson when I was born." Seth rolled his eyes. "He's a military asshole."

"I have a list of the intersex babies born in 1996." Jake had to tell him. "Four names are marked, including yours.

The other three people are dead."

Seth stared, opened-mouthed. "First, I'm not intersex, so don't ever say that again. But if I am on the list, I'm not going down easy. Now that I finally know what was wrong with me and got it the hell out of my body, I'm ready to really live."

What a strange, brave man. "How are you feeling? I'm not sure the hospital is a safe place for you." Jake was thinking of Dr. Novak. If he was involved in the experiment and reported Jake's presence—

"I'm good. And I was leaving anyway." Seth pulled shoes and socks out of the plastic bag. "No shirt, huh?"

The ER docs had probably cut if off him. Jake was curious about Seth's self-surgery and how he ended up in the hospital, but that conversation could wait. He had a sudden sense of urgency. "Here, take my sweatshirt. It might be small, but it's better than nothing." Jake pulled it off. "Can I give you a ride somewhere?"

"I'd like to go home."

"It may not be safe there."

"Don't worry. I'm off the grid. I don't even get mail there."

Was he paranoid? "Ok. But be careful. Do you still need the pain meds?"

"Nah. I've got medication at home."

Whatever that meant. A drug addiction?

Seth, fully dressed now, stood again. "Where are you parked? I don't know how far I can walk."

"On the third floor of the garage. I'll go get a wheelchair." Jake stepped out of the room, remembering his quest to interview Dr. Novak. He would take Seth home and come back. He stopped a nurse walking by. "Can I get a wheelchair for my friend?"

She looked startled. "For Seth? He's not ready to go

anywhere."

"He's dressed and anxious to leave." Jake gave her a charming smile. "I don't think I can stop him, so I might as well keep him from hurting himself again."

She rolled her eyes. "I'll talk to him." The nurse turned toward Seth's room.

He stood in the doorway, looking pained and angry. "Fuck the wheelchair. Let's just go."

Jake didn't know if he should offer an arm for the guy to lean on or not. Seth seemed a bit macho, even defensive. But discovering a uterus inside your body could do that to a guy. Jake wondered again about Taylor's body. He really hoped she didn't have a penis. It was stupid that it mattered to him, since they'd already decided they would just be friends. But still, he was attracted to her, so the idea of her having male body parts kind of freaked him out. He would just have to get over it.

Jake stepped next to Seth and held out his arm. The injured man made a grunting noise, but after two steps, grabbed onto Jake's elbow. They moved slowly toward the elevator. As they reached it, the nurse jogged up behind them with a wheelchair. "Please take it easy," she implored.

Seth flopped down into the chair and mumbled, "Just until I get some pain relief."

The nurse handed him a white pill. "I was on my way to bring you this."

Seth swallowed it dry, the elevator doors opened, and Jake rolled him in.

In Taylor's car, Jake turned to his wounded passenger. "Where do you live?"

"I'll direct you as we go. And you can't ever tell anyone!"

"No problem." Jake started the car and backed out. "Can I ask why it matters?"

"I don't want my parents bugging me."

"They're looking for you?"

"My mother has searched for me." Seth glanced around. "But she's not the only one."

He was paranoid! "Who else is looking for you?"

"I don't know, but someone's been watching me since I was thirteen."

"That seems unusual. How do you know?"

"It's mostly a feeling, but there's little stuff too. Like seeing the same dude in completely different places, like at the school, then two years later near the skate park." Seth laughed, with less bitterness. "I walked over to confront him, but the chickenshit drove away in a hurry."

Maybe Seth wasn't paranoid. "I wonder if watching you is part of the experiment. Maybe they're keeping tabs on the kids as they become adults. That might be why your name was marked. They think you're a problem somehow."

"Yeah, everybody does." Seth dropped his seat back and stretched out. "But stuff will calm down for me now. Discovering that thing in my body was pretty fucked up. Then I realized it explained my confusion and self-loathing, and it was a relief to know. I'm in hella pain, but my brain feels better."

"Good to hear." Jake cleared his throat. "But why take it out yourself? Wouldn't a doctor remove it?"

"The bitch said it was harmless. When I pushed for the surgery, the consultant said I needed seventeen thousand cash up front. And that's just the surgeon's fee, not including the hospital." The bitterness was back.

"Well, I guess you got it done."

"Damn straight." Seth sat up for a moment. "Head toward the old part of town. I live in the basement of a friend's house."

Jake made a left out of the parking garage. "I have to drop you off and come back to the hospital. There's a doctor I need to talk to. In fact, he delivered you."

Seth snapped his head toward Jake. "The one who gave my mother the drug? I'll fucking kill him."

Oh boy, this guy was a hothead. "The doctors at the clinic may not have known what was going on. They have been told the drug was beneficial. I hope to get more details soon."

"You have to tell me, man. I want to know."

"I will." Jake made another left and glanced in the rearview mirror. Was that a black SUV? Yes, but the vehicle pulled off the street and he lost sight of it. He decided to tell Seth about Taylor and the others. "I know about all of this because I found one of the dead subjects. Zion was on the hit list too. So was Taylor. She works in the morgue and figured out what was going on." Jake choked up and could hardly continue. "They abducted her yesterday."

"No shit? People are dead and missing?" Seth's macho receded a little.

"I called the FBI, and they're sending an agent, maybe even a team, from headquarters."

Seth crossed his arms. "I'm not talking to the feds. Count me out."

Jake tried to ease the troubled man's mind. "I won't tell them where to find you. Hopefully, they'll be focused on locating Taylor and the assassin."

"This shit is too weird."

Jake kept quiet. He was plotting his next move. If Dr. Novak wouldn't talk to him, then it might make sense to leak some of the story to a friend at the Denver Post. If the media reported certain events—like Taylor's disappearance and Seth's self-surgery—it might actually protect all of them. Media coverage could backfire too. The people who'd conducted the experiment might panic and destroy all the evidence—including Taylor.

Chapter 26

An hour earlier, Stratton Research Complex

Devin stepped into the major's office and tensed. Something was wrong. He had that stiff, flushed look she knew so well. "What happened, sir?"

"Seth Wozac is in the hospital. Paramedics carried him out of his house after he cut open his abdomen. His monitor thinks he tried to commit suicide."

That would be convenient. "Did he succeed?"

"Don't be a smart ass. He's in the ICU at St. Paul's, and I don't think it was a suicide attempt." The major was still standing. "Maybe Wozac is mixed gender too. Some hermaphrodites have extra sex organs on the inside, so maybe he tried to remove something. As fucked up as he is, that wouldn't surprise me. We need to silence him and keep this out of the press."

"Yes, sir, I'll get it done." Devin recalled the discussion about the need for the terminations. "You knew the pyromaniacs couldn't be trusted not to bring media attention to themselves and the clinic."

"I was worried about a major arson fire, not a damn self-surgery." The major scowled. "The hospital will probably insist that Wozac undergo a psychological evaluation. If he discusses his gender issues or his birth circumstances, we could have trouble." Her father poured a shot and downed it. "Others in the first group have undergone counseling and two committed suicide. Colorado Springs is a small town, and some shrink or physician will start putting it together. Sometimes, I think we should shut down all the original subjects."

Kill thirty more people? The thought horrified Devin. "But most of them moved away. I don't think that will be necessary, sir." She also had to reassure the major that she would handle the last two targets and that things would smooth over. The hospital setting was challenging though. What about an overdose? Could she slip in and out without being seen? Patients in the ICU were closely watched. *Show no weakness!* "People die in the hospital all the time," she finally said. "I'll get it done."

"Today!" The major's expression shifted, and Devin couldn't read it. The old man paced as he talked. "We need to silence Jake Wilson immediately too. Can you handle both, or do I need to bring in someone else? The CIA director has offered one of his operatives."

Devin flinched. Why did he doubt her? She'd taken care of all the other pyro subjects and brought in Lopez without incident. "I can handle it, as I have the others."

The major nodded. "You've done well, son. But now it's about timing. We no longer have the luxury of carefully planned terminations."

The praise surprised her, and Devin took a moment to savor it. "I can act quickly. I believe the reporter is staying in a motel near the clinic and driving Lopez's car, so he'll be easy to locate. The ICU will be more challenging, but a diversion might be a successful tactic."

"The director thinks Wilson downloaded files from the

clinic, so search and destroy."

He was dismissing her. "Yes, sir." Devin saluted and strode out. Every minute counted now. But it wasn't her fault that Seth Wozac had finally spiraled out of control. When the major had assigned her to terminate the four subjects who'd become obsessed with fire, she'd been given a flexible deadline. A secondary objective was to make them look like accidents so no one ever linked their deaths or their bodies. But Taylor Lopez had made the connection and shared her findings, so now expediency was critical.

Devin doubted that Lopez would make a good operative. She was too old to start the training. Most of the other Peace Project operatives had been conditioned and placed in their respective countries as teenagers. Devin was grateful to be stateside. She didn't know if it was because her father hadn't wanted to risk her life in a foreign country or because he liked having her around. Or maybe she just wouldn't have blended in well enough. The major had talked about the operatives and their long-term mission a few times when he was drinking heavily and it was just the two of them having a late dinner. Devin loved those moments when she felt like his confidant. They almost made up for the commander-subordinate way he treated her most of the time.

She stopped in the mess hall, grabbed some rations, and headed out of the compound. She needed a shower and some sleep, but both would have to wait.

After a dozen phone calls, she located the motel where Wilson had stayed the day before. The Jetta wasn't in the parking lot, and a stop in the office revealed that Wilson hadn't paid for another night. He was moving around. Smart. But not good for her. She decided to check out Wozac's situation in the hospital before she spent more time looking for the reporter. Wilson might have fled back to Denver.

The biggest concern was that Wilson would go to his friends at the Post—or write and publish an exposé himself. He had to be stopped. Devin still didn't understand how the morgue attendant and the reporter had connected. Unless they were old friends. The staff that monitored the subjects kept only intermittent track of them, unless they displayed problematic behavior like the fire-starting tendency. The four pyros had been under close supervision for a year before the major had decided to shut them down. The monitors, desk clerks mostly, were not privy to that order or suited to carry it out.

At a traffic light, Devin keyed the hospital's name into her GPS and promptly circled back. Located near a big city park, St. Paul's was easy to find. As she drove, daylight faded in the cloudy western sky. Devin welcomed the coming darkness. She would need all the cover she could get for the hospital mission. *So risky!* Waiting for Wozac to be released would make the termination so much cleaner. Could they afford the time? She pulled over, found the number, and called the medical facility. Pitching her voice lower, Devin said, "This is Detective Miller with the Colorado Springs Police Department. I need to question a patient, Seth Wozac. Is he still in the ICU?"

"Just a moment." The woman put her on hold for a second, then said, "Yes, but he's stable, and they'll probably move him to another floor tomorrow."

"Thanks."

"I can transfer you to the second-floor desk, so you can ask about talking to him." The hospital clerk lowered her voice to a whisper. "You should know there's a psych consult requested for him."

"Why? What did he do?" Devin wanted details.

The clerk cleared her throat. "As strange as this sounds, he operated on himself to cut out a uterus."

"That is strange," Devin said, reacting how she thought a cop might. But it wasn't strange to her. She thought about the ovaries in her otherwise mostly male body. She'd never give them up. They made her who she really was. "Don't bother transferring my call. I'll come in." Devin clicked off. Now that she knew Wozac's injuries would keep him in the hospital for days, she had no choice but to move forward immediately. An idea began to form, and her shoulders relaxed. She might just pull this off—without getting arrested. But if she were detained, she would go silent. Her father's secrets were safe with her, even if she were convicted and sentenced.

The tension returned to her body. She was about to take two more lives. She would honor them, like she had the others, with tattoos that represented their souls. As a fire-starter like the other three subjects, Wozac would be another flame added to the fire inked on her forearm. She would have to think about a new design for the reporter. But not now. Devin got back on the road and worked through her plan. She needed a jacket like a detective would wear and a needle full of dope. A stop at the Goodwill, followed by a smash-and-grab in Heroin Alley. This might even be fun.

The short block near Highland Park where many of the city's heroin addicts hung out was strangely empty. *Fuck.* Now she needed a new plan. Devin cruised the street slowly, just in case a druggie emerged. No luck. As she was about to drive off, a silver Toyota turned down the block. After it passed, Devin parked and watched the vehicle in her rearview mirror.

Two shaved-head thugs in baggy jeans got out and walked toward a seedy apartment building. *Go now!*

Devin shot out of her SUV and sprinted down the sidewalk, closing the gap in seconds. They heard her coming at the last moment and turned, with startled expressions. She punched the taller guy first, coming from underneath to break his nose. The second thug started to run, so she slammed a foot into his back and knocked him to the ground. The first guy swung at her, his other hand gripping his bloody nose. But he was dazed and slow. She easily blocked the punch, snapping a bone near his elbow. The sound echoed in the empty street. The pussy bellowed like a steer on its way to slaughter and dropped to his knees. The second guy, already on the ground, rolled over to face her. Eyes wide with terror, he shouted, "What the fuck?"

"Give me your stash. All of it! Or I'll break your face too." While the thug scrambled for an inner pocket, she pulled out her Beretta. "If I see a gun, you're dead." She glanced sideways and slapped the tall guy's face. "Shut up and give me your stash too."

Still moaning, he didn't comply.

The prone man shouted, "He's not carrying! Just me. Here, take it." He shoved a pocket-sized leather pouch at her.

Devin grabbed it and ran back to her SUV. The druggies weren't likely to call the police, but addicts and criminals were often too stupid to know better. Inside the car, she pulled on the used business jacket she'd purchased and removed her sunglasses and baseball hat. A peek in the leather pouch revealed about three grams of H, five needles, and a spoon. They'd planned a little party. Perfect. Devin started the engine and drove off. She would stop in a few blocks and prep the heroin overdose somewhere safer. She'd done her homework and knew a hundred ways to end a life.

Fifteen minutes later she pulled into the parking lot at the hospital. When she didn't find a space in front, she drove into the garage and ended up on the third floor. Despite the full lot, no people were around. She grabbed her bag of disguises from under the seat and applied a layer of dark bronze foundation, then popped in brown contacts. After she used the touch-up gray hair color, the hospital staff would describe her as "older" and "brown-skinned." And male, of course.

Voices caught her attention and she looked over at the entrance. A young man pushing another young man in a wheelchair. *Holy shit!* Jake Wilson was taking Seth Wozac out of the hospital. Devin shoved her supply bag under the seat and slouched down. *Yes!* She was finally catching a break. This whole clean-up assignment had gone sour for her when the old woman at the clinic had been added as a rush job. One more mission, and she would be done. Too bad the targets weren't likely to take a drive up into the canyons where she could run them off the road and not have to see them die.

When their engine rumbled, Devin started hers in unison. She hoped Wilson was still driving the ugly Jetta. So easy to follow and spot. She heard the car pass behind her, waited ten seconds then pulled out. An extended family crossed the space in front of the entrance, and she had to wait for the old man bringing up the rear. *Move!* Her targets were already leaving the parking garage.

Once the family had cleared, Devin pressed the accelerator and squealed around the corner. Someone yelled at her to slow down and she did. Hitting a pedestrian would derail her mission. Besides, she could guess where the targets were heading. Either to a motel on Nevada Avenue or Wozac's house. The man had nearly bled to death twelve hours earlier, so he probably needed to be in bed. The two men might stop at a pharmacy for a prescription or at a burger place, but they weren't going far.

At the bottom of the exit ramp, she went right toward Fillmore Street and was rewarded with the sight of the Jetta moving toward the main intersection. But she was too close! Devin pulled off and tucked in between two parked vehicles. Wozac's monitor had sent the subject's home address earlier, so if she lost them, she could drive straight there and wait. Unless they were headed for Denver, where they could disappear into the city. Now that Wilson possessed clinic files and his little girlfriend was gone, he might not stay in Colorado Springs. He had worked for the Denver Post, so he could be headed there to share his findings.

Devin got back on the street, wishing she'd taken a different vehicle from the compound. Hers was too big and black and noticeable. But the reporter had probably never seen her SUV, so she just had to hang back and be careful. As she drove, she watched ahead to the intersections. The important thing in tailing a car was spotting when it turned.

The boulevard suddenly split, and the van in front of her blocked her from seeing which way the Jetta went. Devin swore out loud and guessed left. Even if they were planning to travel to Denver, they would likely stop at Wozac's first to get clothes or his cell phone or whatever. Wozac had left his place in an ambulance the night before, so he wasn't prepared for an extended stay anywhere.

Her guess was correct, and ten minutes later she spotted the Jetta headed up Hagerman Street, where Wozac lived. Even from a distance, the small brick house looked old. Wilson parked on the side lawn under a tree, and the two men walked around to the back. Devin parked two houses down and studied the home. Windows near the bottom of the wall indicated a basement. Wozac probably lived in that space. She had perused his file, and he didn't seem to be employed. He'd been on her termination list all along, but she'd saved him for last, wanting to get all three Denver hits done first. She knew his basic info, but hadn't cased his house or habits yet. Having to rush the job annoyed her, but nailing the two men together was a plus. This could be ideal. She could make it look like a drug deal gone bad. Shoot the first one she encountered, then give the second one an overdose and wrap his hand around the weapon. Or maybe the other way around. She would be prepared for both scenarios.

Devin crawled into the back seat, opened the locked weapons case, and extracted an untraceable handgun. She preferred to use her Berretta or Remington rifle, but the little Colt would seem more appropriate for a small-time addict. Although considering Wozac's self-surgery, maybe a straight suicide would be best for him. Either an overdose or a gun to the head would be effective, and a flash-bang would stun both guys long enough to get needles into them. Did she still have one? Devin leaned into the cargo area, rummaged through her toolbox, and didn't find one. *Crap.* She'd used her last flash-bang on Hurtz to subdue him before throwing him off the balcony. Devin took off the blazer she'd planned to wear into the hospital, put on a baseball cap, and jumped from the vehicle. Time to just go for it. The targets might be stopping in the house for only a few minutes.

The neighborhood was surprisingly quiet. A young girl on a bike rode past Devin without looking—hell bent on getting home before dark. Devin strode across the street and covered the distance to the brick house in a few seconds. At the last moment, she readied her handgun and loaded needle. Soon, this phase of the project would be over, and she could ask for a different assignment, maybe relocate to Washington State to help monitor the second generation of subjects. She'd had enough killing. And maybe it was time to get away from her father.

Chapter 27

A few minutes earlier

Jake stepped into the basement apartment and glanced around. Seth's living space was stark—a couch that he obviously slept on, a TV, and a game console. Two brown boxes with clothes draped over the edges occupied a corner near the tiny kitchen. The only natural light came from two rectangular windows at the top of the front wall.

"Hey, I'm fine. You can go." Seth stood near the door, looking embarrassed.

Jake was ready to get the hell out. The place was depressing, and Seth wasn't exactly Mr. Friendly. Still, the man had fresh stitches and a killer after him. "Do you have enough food for a few days? Or a fresh bandage for your, uh, incision?"

"Dude, you sound like my mom. Just go."

"Okay. My number's in your phone if you change your mind." Jake walked out into the narrow subterranean walkway. Concrete walls held back the dirt of the side yard, and the steps led up to a patio. A shadow crossed the grass above him. Instinctively, Jake bolted back inside. Seth hadn't moved, and his mouth dropped open.

"I think the assassin is here." The words came out in a rush of panic. He turned to lock the door but didn't see an obvious mechanism. A thud sounded on the other side, as though the killer had jumped down into the entrance rather than take the steps. *Shit!* He needed a weapon. The only thing in Jake's line of sight was a long skateboard leaning against the wall next to the door. He grabbed it with both hands, stepped off to the side, and prepared to swing it hard.

The door flew open and barking suddenly filled the space outside. The man in the dark jacket crossed the threshold, and Jake brought the skateboard down hard, striking the side of his face and arm that held the gun. The killer made a soft grunting sound, shook his head, and spun toward Jake. The barking ceased as a dog latched onto the back of the intruder's lower leg and sunk in his teeth.

The assassin cursed loudly and twisted around. He jerked up his gun and fired point blank at the dog. The loud crack boomed off the walkway's concrete walls. Seth, already in motion, rushed straight at the assassin, who was still turned toward the dying dog. Before Jake could jump in, Seth shoved the killer out, slammed the door shut, and locked the bolt at the top.

The assassin still had a gun. "Get down!" Jake dropped to the floor and began crawling toward the corner.

New voices outside—a woman crying and a man shouting for someone to call 911. Footsteps retreated rapidly up the concrete stairs. The killer was fleeing! Jake stopped crawling and turned back. Seth was flat on the carpeted floor in front of the entry—not moving. Jake's heart skipped a beat. Was Seth dead? "Dude! You okay?"

Seth held up a hand but didn't lift his head or make a sound.

Had he been shot? Not likely. The door was intact, and Jake had heard only one round of gunfire. Still, Seth could

169

have pulled out his stitches and might be bleeding internally. Staying low, Jake hurried over to the prone man. "Hey, are you bleeding?"

Seth finally raised his head. "I think I just blacked out for a moment."

Jake didn't know what to do next. The police were likely on the way. And if he stuck around, they would probably take him to the department for questioning. And if the obstetrics clinic had video surveillance of his data theft, he could end up in jail. Avoiding all that was in his best interest.

Jake stood. "I have to get out of here before the cops arrive. You should probably leave before the killer comes back." Jake didn't want to take Seth with him, but he would if the injured man needed a ride.

"Just go. I'll be fine."

Jake didn't buy it, but he had to get moving. The FBI agent would be arriving soon, and he needed to give her the clinic data. He couldn't do that from a jail cell, and she might not bother to find him there. "Should I call an ambulance for you?"

Seth sat up. "Hell no. I'll grab my backpack and go out the back gate. I have a friend down the street."

The back gate sounded good to Jake too. But he needed the car and leaving now was the only option. Jake patted Seth's arm. "Stay safe." Heart still pounding like he'd run a mile, Jake bolted out the door and almost plowed into a woman kneeling next to the dead dog. "Sorry." He pushed past her and jogged up the steps. "The shooter's gone!" she called through sobs.

After a look around, Jake charged across the short strip of lawn to Taylor's car. A few neighbors stood along the street, and an elderly man paced next to the home's front porch, talking excitedly into a cell phone. Jake climbed in the Jetta and backed out to the street. He hoped no one would take down the license number. He drove away, trying to look casual and not like someone fleeing a crime. Still, he glanced at every vehicle on the street and checked his rearview mirror. The assassin could be waiting to follow him again. Or the killer might go after Seth. As the fourth name on the hit list, Seth might be a priority for the researchers, which would explain why the man in black had been at the hospital and picked up their tail.

Relief washed over Jake. Maybe now that he wasn't with Taylor or Seth, he might not be a target. That would leave him free to investigate. He drove toward Nevada Avenue. He needed to move to a new motel, but that might not be enough. Maybe he should buy new clothes and some dark hair dye and scissors—change his whole appearance. He checked the time on the dashboard: 6:35 p.m. When was Agent Bailey supposed to arrive?

A paranoid thought hit him. Maybe he couldn't trust her. She might be tracking his phone right now and be somewhere on standby with a team of men in black suits, ready to swoop in and arrest him. Maybe it was time to get the hell out of town and forget this whole crazy mess.

Chapter 28

Saturday, Oct. 15, 5:15 a.m., Denver

Bailey climbed into the rental car, weary but relieved to finally be on the ground and mobile. Her flight had been delayed for five hours because of weather, so she'd napped on the plane instead of getting a decent sleep in a hotel near the airport. *Maddening!* Now she was even further behind in tracking the kidnapper.

After keying Carson Obstetrics into the GPS for later, Bailey added a street address in Denver. Her first stop would be the bureau's Rocky Mountain Safe Streets Task Force, where she would enlist local agents to investigate the three deaths that were reportedly all young intersex people. Plus Bonnie Yost in Colorado Springs. Bailey wanted to do the legwork herself—no one else could be as thorough—but a woman was missing, and that had to be her priority. If the witness' story checked out, she would ask the bureau to send backup to Colorado Springs as well.

Bailey found the vehicle's push-button starter and rolled out of the lot, relieved that she knew the area well. But she'd never been to this particular FBI location, a secondary field office in Northeast Denver, and the route took her away from downtown where the main bureau was located. The turns led under a highway, to an old, four-story structure that looked like it had once been a hotel. In the early morning darkness, the signs were hard to read, but it seemed that a livestock business occupied most of the space. She drove around to the back, parked next to a row of new sedans, and entered the quiet, century-old building. Was the bureau trying to be discreet about the location or just saving money?

Based on the instructions she'd been given, she took the elevator to the fourth floor and found a familiar-looking steel door with an intercom and coded entry. She pressed the Call button, waited for a response, then gave her name and badge number. Every field office had that level of security, and many were located in buildings with metal detectors. A tall man with a smooth, bald head greeted her. "Special Agent Harley Zane."

A cowboy name fitting for the Colorado location. "Special Agent Andra Bailey. This is an unusual location."

"I know. Long story."

She wasn't interested and didn't ask.

He started down the hall. "Let's get some coffee and talk in the conference room."

Caffeine would be essential. The few hours on the plane might be the last shut-eye she got for the next couple of days. With mugs of dark coffee from a small kitchen, they entered a windowless interior room with a long table. Another man stood as they entered. Shorter and older, he looked sunburned, as if he'd been skiing. "Special Agent Dennis Pritchard."

"Thanks for meeting me." Bailey took a seat, realizing that she probably appeared disheveled and her makeup was long gone. She didn't care what they thought, but physical attractiveness gave her power. "I need help investigating a group of suspicious deaths." She cited the names and circumstances of the clinic victims. "All three men were born the same year and delivered by the same doctor, Charles Metzler."

"And they all died recently?"

"In the last three weeks." Bailey passed Agent Zane a printed file of what little intel they had on the victims. "A source tells me these men were all intersex, meaning they were of mixed gender and all born to women who were patients of Carson Obstetrics in Colorado Springs."

Agent Zane's thick brows arched. "Is this about a problematic medication? Is the FDA involved?"

The older agent added. "Why just the one clinic?"

"I don't have answers yet. Just more crimes. A receptionist at the clinic was murdered, and the Denver morgue attendant who discovered the similarities in the dead men is now missing." Bailey downed the second half of her coffee. "My source says the woman disappeared about twenty-four hours ago, right in front of the Colorado Springs Police Department."

Both agents shifted forward in their chairs. Zane offered, "We'll get a full team on this as soon as we can." He glanced at the older man. "We have a huge sex trafficking operation going on right now, and we're about to raid multiple locations, but I'll personally start on this. When are you traveling to Colorado Springs?"

"Soon after I leave here." Bailey gave them her contact information. "First, I'll stop at the morgue and look at the bodies—if they're still there."

"What's the missing woman's name?" Zane asked.

"Taylor Lopez. Headquarters already has a nationwide alert out for her." Bailey paused, searching her memory for a misplaced piece of intel. This wasn't like her. *Oh, yes.* "Lopez is also intersex and was born in the same year, same doctor. I suspect there are more, but I haven't seen the supposed list yet."

"What year? How old are the victims?"

"Most were born in 1996 and are twenty years old." She felt the coffee kick in and a new urgency about the investigation. "My priority is to locate and question the doctor if he's still in Colorado Springs. I hope he'll lead me to the missing woman." She stood, ready to leave.

"Who's your source?" Agent Pritchard got up too.

"A reporter that Lopez contacted." She wanted to keep Wilson's name confidential for now.

Pritchard's eyes widened in alarm. "I wouldn't trust him. Or her."

Reporters were tools, like any other informant or source. *Would Pritchard have warned a male agent about working with a journalist?* Probably not. With her successful track record, she could afford to ignore doubts about her ability. She glanced at Zane. "Update me about the Denver deaths as soon as you have something." Bailey strode out, eager to get down to Colorado Springs and see what the hell the military was up to.

An hour later she was on the highway headed south, watching the sunrise over a familiar countryside. Images from her childhood surfaced, but she pushed them aside. Her ability to lie extended even to herself, so she often didn't trust her own memories. She knew for sure that her mother had left when Bailey was young because she couldn't face a child with sociopathic tendencies, but beyond that, her past didn't matter. The present was all that existed. She planned for a long life, but didn't count on it.

Bailey focused on the investigation. Viewing the bodies at the morgue had felt like a waste of time. The two she'd seen hadn't looked all that similar. Zion Tumara's lower torso had been torn up by bullets, and Logan Hurtz's corpse was almost a month old and so shriveled, he looked more like a horror-movie prop. Adrian Warsaw, the drowning victim whose body would have been the most helpful to see, had been shipped to his parents. When she'd asked why Hurtz was still in the morgue, the attendant had said that the victim's family had called him an abomination and refused to claim him.

Most people weren't geared to deal with human abnormalities. But who decided what was acceptable? Bailey felt perfectly normal. No, correct that. She was obviously different from most people, who made their decisions based on emotions. But she didn't hate herself or feel inferior. In fact, it seemed smarter and more honest to function according to analysis and self-interest—within limits. Her dad had tried to teach her reasonable boundaries from an early age, but she hadn't developed good impulse control until late in her teens.

Thinking about her father made her realize Garrett might be right. It seemed logical to visit the old man while she was in the state. In her own way, she loved him and enjoyed his company. He was the one person she could really be herself around. Too bad his circumstances made contact with him inconvenient. If she wasn't too burned out after the investigation, she would call the jail and ask about visiting him. He might do the same for her if she were ever incarcerated. She worked hard to ensure that never happened, but the possibility was real. She'd realized that the day a police officer visited her high school civics class and announced that at least one student would end up in prison.

She'd known in her gut it would be her if she didn't learn some control.

As she approached Colorado Springs, she took the first Nevada Avenue exit. The landscape was familiar, yet changed. New stores had been constructed, and the sidewalk widened. The farther she drove though, the more it looked like the same old route to the army base. A big brick building on the left came into view. The police department, where Taylor Lopez had last been seen. According to Jake Wilson, the abduction had happened before dawn, so finding a witness seemed unlikely. Bailey kept driving, watching for the first decent motel. According to the GPS, the obstetrics clinic was just down the road, and her source was staying nearby.

The Desert Manor didn't look up to her standards, but it would suffice. She pulled in, registered in the dinky front office, and paid for two nights. She'd likely be in town much longer, but not necessarily this motel. Bailey grabbed her luggage out of the rental car and stepped inside her temporary workspace. The carpet had a slight funk smell, but the room was decorated in shades of beige and sky blue, so at least it wasn't visually offensive. She set her shoulder bag on the desk and pulled out the copies of the Denver death investigations she'd picked up at the morgue. Eager to read them, she brewed a cup of coffee and took a fast shower. The morning routine and clean clothes tricked her brain into feeling like she was starting the day fresh, instead of just arriving after a red-eye flight.

Now that she'd recharged, she decided to skip the reports and jump right into the fieldwork. She called Wilson on the burner phone she'd picked up at the bureau, and he answered with a timid hello.

"Agent Bailey. Let's meet. Where are you?"

"The Rocky Ridge Motel, near the clinic."

"What cross street? What room?"

He gave her the information, then asked, "Have you learned anything new? Is Taylor on a national search list now?'

His raw emotions were annoying. "Yes and yes. I'll see you soon." Bailey hung up, put on a dark-green suit jacket, and headed out.

At her car, she glanced back in the direction she'd come in. At some point, she wanted to retrace the abducted woman's footsteps in front of the police station, but getting the list of subjects and questioning the doctor were more important. Taylor Lopez could be dead already, so finding the killer had to be her priority now, especially if more of the subjects were targeted. How many were there? If she uncovered solid evidence, the bureau would send a full team to confiscate computers and interrogate suspects.

The reporter's motel proved to be only a few blocks away—an even cheaper version of the one she was staying in. She stopped in front of the office and glanced around the parking lot. No one was sitting in a dark car, and no vehicle had followed her. She stepped out and scanned the surrounding rooftops. No armed unsubs that she could see. Wilson claimed the killer had come after him in broad daylight in a public place, so the caution seemed necessary. Bailey checked her Glock just for security, then hurried to room seven and rapped on the door. The young man who answered had a three-day stubble on his chin, and a musty smell wafted from his dirty clothes. *Oh hell.* Had she been lured here by a crackpot?

Chapter 29

"Who are you?" Bailey shoved her hand under her jacket, ready to pull her weapon.

"Jake Wilson." His eyes were clear and his voice steady.

"Special Agent Andra Bailey."

He motioned her in. After another glance over her shoulder, she stepped into the narrow room. A small table near the window had two chairs. Good. Somewhere they could sit and talk. A laptop on the bed reassured her that Jake might actually be a reporter—and not some homeless guy with paranoid delusions about conspiracy theories.

"Do you want some coffee or something?"

"No thanks." She headed for the table. "I want to see the list you mentioned. The email you received too."

Jake grabbed the laptop and sat down across from her. "This is Taylor's email. She's the one who heard from Bonnie at the clinic." He turned the computer screen toward her.

The email was brief and from a Hotmail server. Her bureau analyst, Gunter Havi, could probably trace it. She forwarded it to him before opening the attachment. The list of names looked as though it had been copied and pasted out of a database and into a text-only document. She scanned down, noticing four checkmarks, three that corresponded to the men in the morgue. An asterisk floated next to Taylor Lopez's name. If this was a scam, it was elaborate and inexplicable.

"Thirty-three," Jake offered.

"Any idea why these men were targeted?"

"They seem to have an obsession with fire. That's the only common trait we could find."

Pyromaniacs? Was that an unexpected side effect of the medication? This case grew stranger by the minute. A wild thought hit her. If the military was involved, the project could be nationwide, making it nearly impossible to uncover or halt. Their goals might even be in the best interest of the country. They probably thought they were. If not for the murdered receptionist and the missing woman, Bailey might be tempted to walk away from this investigation. But this case was more challenging and complex than anything she'd encountered in the bureau yet, and she rarely backed down. Ego wouldn't let her. The worst that could happen was a bullet to her head, and she didn't fear death. Once she was gone, she wouldn't know. All she had was this moment, and a burning need to know what was so important the army had invested twenty-one years in the project.

The fourth marked name was a priority too. "Seth Wozac," she read, looking up at Wilson. "Do you know anything about him?"

"I located Seth yesterday in the hospital. He had hurt himself, but that's another story." Jake ran his hands through his shaggy hair, face tightening. "The assassin followed us from the hospital and came to Seth's door. We got lucky and a dog attacked him." Wilson let out a harsh laugh. "Saved by an ugly boxer. Plus the neighbor who called the police. The assassin fled, but I'm sure he's still out there, waiting for me or Seth to surface."

"Where is Wozac?"

"I'm not sure. He went to stay with a friend who lived nearby." Wilson gave a sympathetic shake of his head. "I don't think Seth is rational. He performed surgery on himself to remove a uterus from his body."

Holy shit. "And he's walking around?"

"He shouldn't be."

An addict? Sometimes meth or PCP users did insane things that might kill a normal person. Maybe Wozac was just mentally ill. She would ask the bureau to locate and protect him if they could. The uterus inside the man's body was intriguing, and she hoped to question Wozac before this was over. "Any word from Lopez?"

Wilson shook his head. "What's your plan?"

Bailey knew he was asking about how she intended to find his girlfriend, but that effort was a long shot. She couldn't offer false comfort. "You said you went to the clinic. What else did you discover?"

The reporter stared at her for a long moment, and she realized he was attractive in a scruffy way. He was also holding back. "Did you steal files?"

A lengthy pause. "I downloaded information."

"Show me." Why wait for a subpoena if this guy already had what she needed?

Wilson turned the computer back to himself, pressed a couple of keys, then showed her the monitor again. "These are women who went to the clinic for prenatal care in 1995. Their files are coded, and there's a reference to ImmuNatal. I think it's a drug. Taylor's mother took it, and so did the others. But I can't find any information about the drug online."

Intriguing. Bailey scanned through several files, noting

the coding. NPIN, NPST, and APST. The meaning of the last two groups of letters seemed obvious. IN meant ImmuNatal, and ST indicated Standard. A group that received the test drug versus a control group that got standard care. The NP/AP reference came to her a moment later. Normal pregnancy and abnormal pregnancy. More important, Charles Metzler, appeared consistently as the physician for women who took ImmuNatal.

"I want a copy of these files and the list." She dug a flash drive out of her bag and handed it to Wilson. "Any idea where to locate Dr. Metzler?" It was worth asking. Wilson seemed resourceful.

"He's no longer at the clinic, and I can't find him online. He may have retired or moved."

Time to call Havi. Bailey stood and walked away. In the privacy of the cramped motel bathroom, she called the bureau analyst she worked with. Gunter Havi sounded happy to hear from her. "Bailey. What have you got for me? I'm sick of crunching financial data."

"Did you get the email I sent? I need it traced."

"It hasn't landed yet. But if it has a file attached, you know how long it takes to get through the spam software. What are you working on?"

"A strange case of pregnancy drug testing—and murder—in Colorado. I need you to locate a Doctor Charles Metzler. He used to practice at Carson Obstetrics."

"Got it. I'll get back to you when I have something."

"Thanks." Her relationship with Havi was worth cultivating. Bailey pressed her earpiece and stepped out of the bathroom. The sight of the dingy motel room repulsed her. Time to get out in the field. She gave Wilson her burner phone's number. "Call me if anything develops."

"I hope you'll do the same. Especially if you get any word about Taylor."

"I will. But don't get your hopes up."

His eyes flashed with grief and guilt.

Grief, she understood, but she wasn't the comforting type. "You'll stay here, in this motel, for now?"

"Yes. I'm writing a draft of this story and hope to sell it to my old paper."

That could be a problem. "Not yet! Media coverage could drive the conspirators underground or inspire them to destroy evidence."

"I meant later."

"Ask me first." She remembered his file download. "You could still be prosecuted for data theft."

"Please don't," he pleaded. "I was trying to keep more people from being murdered."

"Then hold your story until I'm ready. And come up with a plausible way you ended up with the files." She liked Wilson and didn't want to see him go to jail, but more important, she might need this evidence in court someday. "Maybe Bonnie gave you the data?"

Bailey grabbed her shoulder bag and walked out. Carson Obstetrics was her next stop. They might even tell her where to find Dr. Metzler.

The clinic receptionist scowled at Bailey's badge. "I can take you to the director, but I'm sure she won't tell you anything. We have to protect our patients' confidentiality." The blonde bun on the top of the girl's head was so tight Bailey was surprised she could think straight.

"Just show me the way."

The girl glanced at the waiting room, which was nearly

empty, then rounded the tall counter and walked down the center hall. Bailey followed her to an office in the back. The receptionist introduced her as "someone from the FBI" and left.

"Special Agent Andra Bailey."

"Clinic Director Karen Thayer." The woman was tall and thin with an oversized head and sleek black hair. "How can I help you?"

"Tell me where to locate Dr. Charles Metzler."

"He retired two years ago."

"I know, but I'm sure you have an address for him."

"I don't." The director stayed on her feet, indicating the meeting would be over before it started.

Turn on the charm or try to intimidate her? "I understand your position, but four people have been murdered, including a receptionist who worked here for twenty-some years. In addition, a young woman has been abducted. Your cooperation is essential to preventing more deaths."

The director blanched and clenched her teeth. "I don't see how this clinic is involved. My understanding is that Bonnie's death was a burglary that got violent."

"The three other dead people are all twenty years old, and their mothers were patients of the clinic when they were born. I need to talk to Dr. Metzler, and I need to see the files from 1995 and '96."

Thayer's eyes flashed with shock, and she finally sat down. "I can't give you the files without a court order, but I'll see if I can find Charles' address." The director began a computer search.

Bailey stayed on her feet. "Were you at the clinic in 1995?"

"No, I took the job five years ago."

"Are you military?"

"Yes." The director peered around the monitor, her face hardened. "Why?"

"The clinic is operated by Fort Carson's hospital, and I'm wondering about the staff."

"Most of us have a connection to the army, and Dr. Metzler was a career officer." She sounded defensive.

"Is there anyone else still working here who was on staff back then?"

The director shook her head. "No, Bonnie was the longest-term employee, then Dr. Metzler. Dr. Novak worked here in '95, but he left five years ago for his own part-time private practice."

Bailey made a mental note of the name. She would locate and question Novak as well.

"Got it." The director scribbled on the back of a business card and handed it to Bailey. "This is the last known address we have for Charles. But he could have moved to Florida for all I know."

Bailey thanked her and walked out, wondering how Jake Wilson had managed to download clinic files without getting caught. *Sneaky.* The reporter might prove to be useful.

Outside, a brisk wind made her hurry to her car. Thick gray clouds had formed, and she recognized the threat of snow, one of the main reasons she'd been happy to move away from Colorado after college. Her training made her automatically scan the parking lot, rooftops, and businesses across the street. If someone was tailing her, they were very good at staying concealed. Inside the car, she cranked up the heater and keyed the doctor's address into her phone. The map showed a location south of town, near the Cheyenne Mountain State Park. The Broadmoor Bluffs neighborhood was new since she'd visited the wilderness area as a kid.

Dr. Metzler's house, assuming he still lived there, was the smallest along the bluff, an impressive two-story stone structure with ornate, tiered landscaping. The driveway sloped at a sharp incline, so she parked on the street and climbed out. The clang of a garage door opening made her look up. Bailey jogged to the bottom of the driveway to block the person exiting. An older man in a golf cart rolled downhill toward her. Bailey held out her badge.

The driver hit reverse and backed up. He was avoiding her! Bailey sprinted up the concrete slope and ducked inside the garage before the door came down. The man jumped out of his cart—which was parked next to a Mercedes—and shouted, "You're trespassing!"

"Special Agent Bailey with the FBI." She walked toward him, still holding her badge. "Dr. Charles Metzler?"

He nodded.

"You can talk to me here or take a handcuffed ride to the Denver field office for a session in our interrogation room."

The doctor clenched his jaw and swallowed hard. "What is this about?" Metzler was her height, with short steel-gray hair, a weak chin, and a potbelly.

"A drug called ImmuNatal." She gestured toward the house. "Let's go get comfortable."

"I have nothing to say. Those patient files are confidential."

Bailey stepped toward him and took out handcuffs. "Four people are dead, and you're a material witness. Turn around so I can cuff you. You don't want me to take you down on the cement floor." She looked him over, unimpressed. Metzler was in his sixties and soft everywhere. Golf wasn't real exercise.

His mouth dropped open. "Who's dead?"

"Bonnie Yost for starters. You worked with her for two decades, correct?"

He nodded again. "How did she die?"

"She was murdered, and you might be next if you don't help me." Bailey grabbed his arm. "Let's go inside, and I'll ask the questions."

The doctor's shoulders slumped, and he dropped his golf bag on the floor. "This secret has been a burden for two decades, and I think . . . I think I'm relieved to finally let it out."

Chapter 30

Saturday, Oct. 15, 2:30 p.m.

Seth Wozac made a new bandage out of toilet paper, then pulled off the bloody gauze the hospital had applied. A real, sterile pad would have been better but he didn't have one and neither did his friend. Seth glanced at the clock. Ray had gone out to score some crank and should have been back already. Seth pressed his makeshift bandage against the incision and duct-taped it into place. Ray didn't keep medical supplies around—which was just stupid. Seth had everything he needed in his apartment, but he couldn't go back there. He couldn't stay here either. This shithole was depressing and only a few blocks from his place. The crazy killer might find him here. But he didn't want to leave town or go into hiding. He didn't run from things. Not anymore.

The pain in his gut overwhelmed him for a moment, so he lay down on the couch. Ray's dog took that as a sign and padded over for attention. The pit bull was ugly, and Seth didn't want anything to do with it. But a dog had just saved his life, so he petted the poor thing. "That's it. Go away now."

The rage surfaced again, more intense this time, almost blinding. Some asshole military doctor had done this to his body on purpose! Some fucked-up experiment, for what? Seth had lived a tortured life, feeling betrayed by his body and hormones and never knowing why. At least now he understood why he'd sometimes been turned on by other men. The fucking uterus in his body! Now that it was gone, those feelings would go away, and he could try to have a normal life.

But first, he had to burn something. The rage would keep growing and only a fire could soothe it. He had tried to keep his therapy burns small and controlled. Trashcan fires were safe, so he usually stuck to them, but he'd once torched a shed on an abandoned lot. God, that had been beautiful. Almost orgasmic. This fire would be even more special. A celebration! Bigger than any of the others. Too bad he couldn't burn down the damn clinic where a military fuckwad had given his mother a pill that ruined his life.

Seth sat up, the pain displaced by the sudden joy in his heart. Why not set fire to the clinic? It needed to go. How many other freaky babies had been conceived there? How many other tortured, ruined lives? They all needed revenge, and he would get it for them. Hell, it wasn't even revenge. It would be justice. The evil place would no longer exist, and the world would be better for it.

The door opened, and Ray rushed in. "Sorry it took so long, but we're set. I owe the dude another fifty, but I got enough to keep us flying for a couple days."

Sweet! Time to rev up, then make some Molotov cocktails.

Chapter 31

Saturday, Oct. 15, 3:45 p.m.

Bailey sat on the edge of an oversized chair and waited for the doctor to settle into the couch across from her. Her body wanted to lean back and rest while Metzler told his story, but her mind was too keyed up. Adrenaline had started flowing the moment the doctor indicated he would tell her everything. As much as she wanted to know about the experimental drug and the gender mixed-up offspring, she had to ask about the missing woman first—in case she was still alive.

"Do you know where Taylor Lopez is?"

"Who?" The doctor looked confused.

"She's one of the babies you delivered back then, and now she's missing. Abducted. Where is she being held?"

Metzler blinked, and his old-man lips trembled.

Repulsed, Bailey leaned forward. "This is critical. Do you want another death on your hands?"

"I don't know anything about an abduction." His eyes pleaded with her to believe him. "I only know that I was paid good money to test an experimental drug on a large group of pregnant women. One time, long ago."

"Who paid you? And who developed the drug?"

"I assume it was a military researcher, but I don't know

who or even why." The doctor's hands shook as he brought them to his face in distress. "I was devastated when so many of those babies were born with abnormalities. I tried to question my commander, but he threatened to have me court-martialed. They knew things about me."

"Blackmail?"

"Yes, but in the military it's not called that."

"Your commander gave you the drug? And the orders for the research?"

"Yes."

"What's his name?"

"Ahmed Rashaud." Metzler paused. "But the captain died three years ago, and he was just the middleman."

Bailey made a mental note of the name, but her excitement faded. Blaming a dead person was easy and not helpful. But the age of perpetrators was a concern. What if the researcher who developed the drug and/or the experiment had died too? Still, someone was protecting the secrecy of the project by killing certain subjects. That person had also likely kidnapped or killed Lopez. Bailey took out her phone, tapped the microphone icon, and started recording. "Just taking notes," she said with a half smile.

"Who else is dead?" The doctor's voice quivered.

"Three of the children you delivered. All male, or at least they identified as male. Do you know why they were targeted?" Wilson could have been wrong about the pyromania reason.

"No. I've tried not to think about those babies. I still don't even know what the drug was really for." The doctor shuddered. "They told me it was an immune system booster, but I knew that was a lie when the second hermaphrodite was born."

Hermaphrodite was an outdated term, but the doctor was old-school.

"If the intersex issue was a side effect," Bailey countered, "what was the drug's real focus? Something hormonal?"

"I don't know. Pharmaceuticals can do bizarre and unexpected things to the body, especially in utero."

The primary reason the FDA regulated clinical trials. But ImmuNatal had clearly never been sanctioned. Had they even tested the drug in animals first? And who were *they*? "Was Captain Rashaud at Fort Carson?"

"Yes. And I think the ImmuNatal development took place there."

"At the base hospital?"

Metzler pressed his lips together for a long moment.

Bailey wanted to slap him. Instead, she waited him out.

"No, but once when we were having drinks, another doctor on staff mentioned an underground research facility. When I probed for details, he buttoned up."

"Any names associated with the facility?"

Dr. Metzler shook his head. "I wasn't privy to classified information."

"So you gave pregnant women a drug you knew nothing about? Just following orders?" She was feeling something unexpected. Disgust? Because the doctor was immoral? Or just weak? "How much was your bonus pay for the experiment?"

He stood. "It doesn't matter now."

Bailey jumped up. "You're not going anywhere. I need a written statement from you. And I want details. How was ImmuNatal administered? How many patients took it? Did you report their names to your boss? Their babies' names?" She stepped forward and locked eyes with him. She could outstare anyone and often got what she wanted simply by making the other person squirm. "If you cooperate, I may be able to keep you from being prosecuted."

Metzler glanced away. "Let me get some paper to write on."

She followed him down a hallway with dim recessed lighting. He turned at the second door. "Do you mind? I need to use the restroom." The doctor went in and turned the lock.

He was stalling and probably regretted his confession. She'd seen a shift in his eyes when she asked for written details. Did the bathroom exit into a master suite . . . one that opened to an attached outdoor patio? Bailey rushed through the kitchen and out a sliding glass door. She didn't see the doctor, but the yard had staggered sections that followed the shape of the house. She crossed the flagstone, then a stretch of grass, and rounded a corner to the left. Another small patio with a hammock nestled against a master bedroom. Metzler wasn't in that yard either. She'd probably overreacted. Her heart settled down, and she strode calmly into the house, stopping in the kitchen for a glass of filtered water. She could feel her skin drying out from the plane ride, lack of sleep, and too much coffee.

Bailey took a seat at the kitchen table, expecting the doctor to join her there to write his statement. A glance out the picture window revealed the first few snowflakes coming down. *Oh hell.* Searching for the entrance to an underground facility would be challenging enough. Snow would make it impossible.

The house was eerily quiet. Did anyone else live here? The neighborhood was hushed too, with only the sound of the wind rattling the dead leaves in the tall aspen trees.

A gunshot blasted through the silence. *Fuck!* Bailey

bolted to her feet and down the main hall. The bathroom door was still locked. "Dr. Metzler!" She knew in her gut he'd killed himself. A career military man, he probably wore a gun on his body somewhere, or kept several in the house. Why hadn't she seen this coming? Loyalty and honor were everything in the armed forces. Just because the doctor had cleared his conscience to make himself feel better, didn't mean he would testify against superior military officers.

Metzler might not be dead. And it was only a bathroom door. Good thing she'd worn sturdy ankle boots in preparation for Denver weather. Bailey brought up her right leg in a tight bend, then extended it with all her body weight. Her foot slammed near the doorknob, and the force splintered the wood around the locking mechanism. She slammed the door again in the same spot, and it popped open.

Metzler was on the floor, slumped against the glass shower. Blood ran down the back of his head and dripped on the white-tile floor. The coward had put a handgun in this mouth and blown out his brain. At least she'd recorded his confession in her phone. She worried about the audibility of the volume, but bureau tech people could do amazing things to enhance recordings. The bigger concern was how to handle this.

Her boss would want to be the first to know. Bailey opened her phone's short contact list and pressed the first number. No name attached. The director of the Critical Response Team didn't answer. Maybe that was for the best. Lennard's idea of how to proceed might slow Bailey down. She left a message: "It's Bailey, and we have a situation. A retired military doctor just confessed to his part in a secret medical experiment twenty years ago. Then he went into his bathroom and killed himself. I'm looking at his body right now. Please send a Denver agent to handle this. I don't want to get trapped here talking to the local police. I'll file a report as soon as I can."

She signed off, knowing Lennard would call back soon, demanding more information. Bailey started for the front door then stopped cold. What if the doctor was more involved than he'd admitted, and Taylor Lopez was being held here? Bailey turned back. She had to at least check closets for secret doors and scan for breaks in the floor that might indicate a trap door. It wasn't logical that Lopez would be here, unless this house was a temporary holding place before she was transferred to another facility. Maybe that explained the doctor's suicide. Plea deals were never offered for kidnapping.

After a fast but thorough search, Bailey called her boss again and left a second message, asking that the field agent take the doctor's home apart to search for the missing woman. It needed to be done—just in case—but not by Bailey. Instead she would take Metzler's computer and scan it for contact names.

Someone knew where the underground research facility was, and she was determined to find it. If Taylor Lopez was alive, that had to be where they were holding her. If they were also conducting medical experiments, the girl was likely being treated like a guinea pig. Bailey didn't feel Lopez's pain, but she understood it was imperative to stop whatever the hell was still going on.

Chapter 32

Saturday afternoon, Stratton Research Center

Taylor paced the room, hating its white walls and fake plants. It was the same size as her studio apartment, but without windows it seemed much smaller. Just knowing she was underground made her feel edgy. How did people work down here, day after day? It wasn't natural. And what the hell did they want with her anyway? More medical experiments was what she feared. They might give her untested drugs to see what effect they had. Would she develop painful lesions or grow testicles? How long would this last? The thought of waking up every day in this room for years—or decades—horrified her. Why hadn't she just ignored those bodies and minded her own business? That was how she'd lived her whole life up to that point—head down, no eye contact, no attention drawn. It had worked for her. Mostly. But then she'd decided to look at Adrian Warsaw and see beyond his drowned corpse.

A rap on the door made her jump. Whatever they had in mind was starting. Taylor rushed to the reading chair and sat down. Her only chance of getting out, or at least not getting hurt, was to pretend to go along. She would project as much calm and confidence as possible. She needed them to trust her, so they would drop their guard around her.

Ha! Like she could ever pull that off. Her hands were shaking already.

A young woman stepped into the room and smiled. "Hi Taylor. I'm Marissa." She had flawless, creamy skin over high cheekbones, a small heart-shaped mouth, and wavy strawberry-blond hair.

Taylor stared. Marissa was beautiful and around her age. Was she one of them too? Taylor finally found her voice. "Hello. You're not who I expected."

"I never am. That's why I'm so good at what I do." A sly, seductive smile.

"What do you do?"

"Whatever my country needs." Marissa sat on the bed across from her chair. "You should consider it an honor to be here. The major obviously thinks you have potential."

"For what?" Taylor's pulse began to race. She didn't want to serve her country. Not if it meant spying or seducing strangers for information, or whatever the hell this pretty girl did. Testing drugs would be easier.

"To gather information. Particularly from terrorist young men."

Dear god. It was even worse than she'd imagined. Taylor's throat closed up and she couldn't respond.

Marissa leaned forward and patted her arm. "Don't be scared. They won't send you out until you're ready. By then, you'll be eager." A delicate laugh. Marissa gestured at the solid walls. "And not because of this place. Once you fully understand the threat we face, you'll want to take action."

"You're a spy?"

"That's an old-school term. And limiting. I'm an operative."

"Where? Here in America?"

"Mostly. But I went to Bahrain once, a specialized mission."

197

"I didn't know the military had spies."

The young woman laughed. "You're not supposed to. That's kind of the point." Marissa leaned forward. "Let's get to know each other a bit. Tell me what you do."

Like on a date? Taylor went along. "Uh, I'm a college student and a death investigative intern."

Marissa's mouth opened in mock surprise. "You work in a morgue?"

They obviously hadn't prepped the operative about her. Did that mean the girl didn't know about the experiment? She needed to hear it. "I'm the one who discovered the shared intersex features of the men who'd been murdered. Did you know about the assassinations?"

"I can't talk about our projects yet." Marissa brushed off the subject with a wave of her delicate white hand. "Tell me about you. What do you like to do for fun?"

This was so weird! "Uh, I'm pretty busy with my internship and classes, but I shoot pool at the student center on campus sometimes, and I like quirky comedies,." *Where was she going with this?*

"We have a theater here, but we'll mostly be watching training films." Marissa's eyes sparked. "I think we should watch one now."

Training films didn't sound bad compared with the other things she'd worried about.

Marissa grabbed her hand. "Come with me." She led Taylor into the hall. The girl stopped and turned to her with a bright smile. "Don't try to run, please. I'm fast. And deadly."

Taylor believed her.

After a few turns in a maze of corridors, they entered a small theater with a couple dozen seats. Marissa told her to get comfortable, then set up a movie from the computer station at the back.

At first the images were peaceful. Families in a Middle Eastern country going about their lives. Shopping, laughing, hugging. Suddenly, a bomb exploded, and their bodies were torn to shreds. Taylor recoiled in horror. Why were they making her watch this?

"Keep your eyes open!" Marissa's tone was sharp for the first time. "Pretending this isn't happening doesn't make it stop."

Taylor did as she was told, afraid the girl would tape them open if she didn't. The video showed two more scenes and explosions like the first one. The next image was a group of Americans—or Europeans, she couldn't tell—sitting in a restaurant. A bomb blast killed them as well. *Dear god.* How often did this happen around the world? But the film got worse. Men in black hoods torturing people. Beheadings and stonings. How could anyone do this? Taylor kept closing her eyes, and Marissa kept shouting at her to watch. But the violence was too horrifying. Taylor broke down into sobs. The terrorists had to be stopped.

Chapter 33

Saturday, 4:25 p.m.

His desk phone rang, and Blackburn snatched it up. After the shitstorm yesterday with Seth Wozac's stunt, he needed some good news. "Major Blackburn speaking."

"Bruce Montoya." The deputy director of the CIA. Montoya had been deputy director ten years ago when he had assisted the Peace Project with placing and monitoring personnel in the Middle East.

"What's the update?" Blackburn knew it wouldn't be good.

"One of our Saudi Arabia operatives has been arrested."

"Oh fuck. Who and why?"

"Fatima Syed. I don't yet know the circumstances."

The name was like a punch in the gut. "She's the one who called in yesterday to report her readiness, isn't she?" The last operative to do so—giving them the green light to launch Phase 2.

"Yes. So it's likely someone heard or detected the call."

No! "They'll torture her, won't they?"

"Of course, and all of our operatives could be detained within days."

Fuck! This couldn't be happening. Blackburn realized they had an even bigger problem. "The security around the region's water systems will tighten immediately."

"So we act now," the director said. "Is the drug ready?"

"It should be. The lab started scaling up batches weeks ago."

"Better get it shipped out to our people before the door slams shut."

He realized that. "Update me if you hear anything further." Blackburn ended the call. For a moment, a cacophony of emotions overwhelmed him. Twenty fucking years he'd been working on this project, nurturing it along step-by-baby-step. Now the whole thing was about to implode. Their best opportunity to end terrorism was on the edge of disaster because one woman got careless.

Fuck! He grabbed a stapler and threw it against the wall. It wasn't enough. He lifted his in-basket and threw it too. The metal container hit the wall, and papers scattered everywhere. The side door opened slightly, and his assistant peeked through. "Everything all right, sir?"

Blackburn got control of himself. "Yes. Close the door."

The officer obeyed, and Blackburn snatched up his work cell phone, grateful he'd broken himself of the habit of throwing it. He scanned through his contact list for the manager of the lab. He could walk or take a cart down to the facility, but he didn't want to spend the time.

A pleasant voice answered. "Bill Blessert speaking."

"It's Major Blackburn. We need to transport ImmuNatal ASAP. So get it ready to ship.

"But sir, nothing has changed since you called yesterday. We're still working on the moisture issue with the packaging—we need more time."

"We don't have it, and I don't give a shit about moisture. Our window of opportunity is closing fast."

"But if the drug degrades en route, it might not be fully effective."

"Find a workaround and get it done!" Blackburn slammed the phone down before he started swearing.

After decades of watching the offspring to ensure they would be passive adults, plus years of patiently waiting for the operatives to work themselves into positions of accessibility, it was time to carry out the goddamn mission. The production facility should have been ready with the drug a year ago, but he and Rashaud had delayed the scale-up of ImmuNatal to develop another pharmaceutical aimed at suppressing the fear receptors in the brain. The decision had seemed sound at the time because several Peace operatives had seemed a few years from being ready. He couldn't have predicted they would be in this time crunch now. If the mission failed, he could only blame himself.

Blackburn pulled a bottle of vodka from the small refrigerator in the office corner and downed a few swallows. He needed to stay calm until the ImmuNatal had been delivered to the operatives and the Peace drug slipped into water supplies around the Middle East. Even beyond that, it would be years until they knew whether they'd been successful in creating a generation of nonviolent children who wouldn't join ISIS. The beauty of ImmuNatal was that it would stay intact and potent for years, and through irrigation channels would also end up in the food supply. Their research had shown it to bind with hormones and stay in people's bodies for half a decade. The birth of passive babies would continue for at least five years beyond the original insertion in the water supply, possibly more. A decade beyond that, the jihadists would suffer a recruitment problem that would last five to ten years. During that window of opportunity, they could be defeated.

Blackburn finally sat back down, guilt eating at him.

A loud rap on the door. "It's Rashaud."

"Come in." His co-researcher had a right to be informed.

Rashaud had a new worry line on his forehead as he took a seat. "Bill Blessert just called. He needs more time. Why the rush?"

The weasel! Blackburn suppressed his anger at the lab manager and spoke calmly. "An operative in Saudi Arabia has been arrested. She was the final one to signal her readiness yesterday. We have to assume her communication was discovered and that's why she's been detained."

Rashaud slammed a fist into his other palm. "Goddammit! This could jeopardize the whole project."

"That's why we're going forward immediately."

Rashaud's eyes narrowed. "We are going to warn the other operatives, correct?"

"No. Fatima Syed doesn't know any names."

"But she knows the others are out there, and she knows the plan. They'll torture her until she tells them everything."

Blackburn refused to focus on the individuals. "The Saudis will assume it's region-wide and inform other governments. We have to move past this."

"They'll also use her phone to find her handler, and he knows names. The operatives will be discovered! Rashaud's distress was palpable.

"It'll take time." Blackburn knew their people would likely be captured and killed after they carried out their missions. He'd been through the possibilities in his head and made peace with the outcome. "Once the ImmuNatal is in place everywhere, we'll warn everyone."

Rashaud shook his head. "It'll be too late. They'll never

get out."

"They can go underground. We all knew the risks when we placed them." Blackburn was trying to placate himself too. They'd sent some of the first operatives to the Middle East when they were teenagers, so they could assimilate. The CIA had trained and sent others. The Peace Project was the most important mission the U.S. had ever undertaken. "We're not going to compromise the mission. The lab will ship out the drug today. This will go as planned, and we'll have peace in our lifetime."

His co-researcher stood. "It sure as hell better. I hear Fatima's screams in my head already."

"Hundreds of thousands of lives will be saved. Most of them Shia Muslim. We're doing this for *your* people even more than mine."

Rashaud nodded and strode out.

Chapter 34

Saturday, 4:45 p.m., Colorado Springs

Bailey drove away from the doctor's house, wondering if he had a wife who would come home and find the body before the Denver agent showed up to process the scene. Not her problem. Her priority was to locate an underground complex that the military didn't want anyone to find. *If* she found it, then what? Even with a dozen agents, breeching the structure could prove impossible. The perps could also kill the girl and dispose of her before the FBI team made it in. Unfortunately, Taylor Lopez was probably a lost cause. Bailey's best hope was to track down the names of the researchers and have the bureau director use his clout to obtain arrest and search warrants.

Her only lead was a dead man named Ahmed Rashaud. But he had lived and worked at Fort Carson, so she would start there. Maybe the captain had left notes in his personal papers or confided in someone. It was even possible Metzler had lied about his commander being deceased. The doctor had paused between giving the man's name and saying he was dead. Perhaps Metzler had regretted exposing his superior, maybe even enough to take it a step further by killing himself and avoiding a court martial.

The trip to Fort Carson took only twenty minutes, but by the time she pulled up to the checkpoint station, snow was blanketing the ground. She rolled down her window and smiled at the pimply-faced kid in a crisp blue uniform. "Special Agent Andra Bailey, FBI." She pulled out her badge and federal ID.

"We don't allow visitors without clearance. Do you have a pass from the information office?"

"No, I'm a federal agent. I shouldn't need one."

"Sorry, ma'am, but everyone does." He pointed at a building on the right. "Just go into the visitor's center and show your ID. They'll run a background check and issue a visitor's pass."

Seriously? The impulse to ram her car through the bar-gate overwhelmed her. Bailey fought for control, visualizing herself being fired. She had nothing to gain by the action, and everything to lose. "I'll be back." She retreated, parked in the visitors' lot, and hurried inside.

Empty folding chairs filled the small room, all facing a long counter. Four monitors, plus the thirty-something chairs, indicated that the visitors' center was often a busy place. But not at the moment. Another uniformed young man with a shaved head sat alone at the counter, yawning. When he heard her come in, he snapped his mouth closed and pulled his shoulders back . "How can I help you ma'am?"

"I need to talk to Captain Ahmed Rashaud." If the man were really dead, she would know in a moment. She handed the clerk her federal ID. "Agent Andra Bailey."

He didn't react to Rashaud's name or her credentials. "I need your registration and car insurance too."

Bailey bit her tongue. "I'm in a rental, and I'll see what I have. Get this going. I'll be right back." On the way out, she noticed the sign listing the required documents. Car insurance? What the hell was that about? Did visitors routinely crash into military vehicles?

As she retrieved the paperwork, the snow started really coming down, and her smoldering rage picked up heat. Snow was one of the reasons she'd listed three other places besides Colorado as her choice for bureau assignments. Her success on the job had landed her in the D.C. headquarters in a few short years.

Back inside, Bailey took slow measured breaths and kept her face impassive as she handed over the documents.

"This will take a few minutes while I run a criminal check."

Bailey sat stiffly in the chair. No one had run a background on her since she'd applied to the bureau. She checked her cell for the time. She wanted to see exactly how long the damn process took.

Four minutes later, the young clerk made a call from a desk phone, asking for Captain Rashaud.

So the doctor had lied. His commander wasn't dead.

After a short moment of listening, the clerk hung up and said, "I'm sorry, but you've been denied clearance."

Stunned, Bailey resisted the impulse to slap him, then searched her brain for the correct social response. "It must be a mistake. I'm a federal agent with the FBI. I can get the director on the phone if I need to."

"I'm sorry, ma'am, but I'm just doing my job, and I can't issue you a visitor's pass."

The guilty asshole Rashaud was shutting her out. Now what? She had to get out before she lost her cool. Bailey strode across the parking lot, climbed into her car, and called her boss. Lennard finally picked up. "Bailey, it's about time.

What the hell is going on?"

"I was just denied entry to Fort Carson. The man suspected of running the illegal drug test, Captain Ahmed Rashaud, is on the base, and I need to talk to him. Or get a warrant for his arrest."

"Oh fuck me. This will get complicated."

"People are being killed to silence them about this experiment."

"How do you know it's Rashaud. Anything solid?"

"The doctor giving the pregnancy drug named him."

"Then killed himself," Lennard reminded her. "So our witness can't corroborate your claim."

"I recorded his confession on my phone."

"Can you send me the file?"

"Of course."

"Good. I need something solid to even get you into the military base. A captain has a lot of clout, and the military prefers to investigate their own."

"We still have a missing woman. I think she might be inside Fort Carson at a secret underground facility." That kind of urgency could get a judge to sign a warrant.

"Send me the confession recording, and I'll take it to the director."

"Any update on the doctor's suicide scene?"

"It's handled. The Denver bureau sent an agent, and she's coordinating with the local police. They'll keep the news suppressed until we give them the green light."

"Good." That reminded Bailey that she needed to check in with the Denver agent investigating the deaths of the intersex people. Maybe there was a witness who could identify the killer. But the fact that Agent Zane hadn't contacted her probably meant he hadn't found anything significant. "I've got to get going."

"Good luck and keep me posted." Her boss ended the call.

Bailey noticed a new text on her phone, opened it, and read: *What's up? Any news on Taylor?* It had to be from the reporter. She hadn't bothered creating a contact entry for Wilson, but texted back: *No news. Following a lead.* She hoped it would keep him at bay.

Before leaving the visitors' lot, Bailey scanned the area, scoping out the perimeter. The base wasn't fenced. A person could walk in, if they dared. She just couldn't drive in without a clearance pass. Good to know. She cranked up the heat in the car and headed back into town.

Bailey bought a sandwich at a fast food place near the motel and took it back to her room. After wolfing it down, she realized it wasn't enough food. She hadn't eaten since the airport early that morning and didn't know when she would have the opportunity again. A little sleep would be nice too. Could she take a break and nap for a few hours? Not yet. The doctor's laptop might contain useful intel. She grabbed the computer, sat down at the small desk, and turned it on. No passcode required. *Nice.*

She checked email first and found that the messages were all personal, family and friends offering their condolences after 'his loss.' Apparently Metzler's wife had died recently, which might help explain his decision to commit suicide rather than face consequences. None of the current messages were helpful, so she searched the archives for the oldest email he had on file and found one from ten years earlier, a thank-you note from a patient.

Bailey switched to searching folders on his hard drive. Bank statements, tax PDFs, and personal correspondence.

Except for pay stubs, nothing seemed connected to the military. She was about to move on, when she spotted a folder inside a folder labeled Will and Testament. His family would need this document, but she intended to peruse it first. The only point of interest was a reference to a wall safe behind a painting in the dining room, including the code. She'd missed the safe when she searched his house, because she hadn't been looking for valuables, only information. Now she had to go back and open it. Who knew what could be in there?

She stopped at St. Vincent's thrift shop on the way and bought a long overcoat, a wool cap, and gloves—items she would recycle before flying home. It had been seventy degrees in D.C. when she left, and she hadn't expected the snow or to spend much time outside. But if she had to access Fort Carson on foot, the extra layers would be welcome. Cold, heat, and pain didn't bother her as much as they did empaths—because she could focus her mind on other things—but she still liked to be comfortable.

A sedan in front of Metzler's house indicated an agent was still there. Good. She wouldn't have to break in. As Bailey walked up the driveway, a woman came out the door carrying a stack of paperwork. Of course they'd sent a woman. Handling an agent-witnessed suicide was a no-brainer. Sexism at the bureau was deep-rooted and often subtle.

Bailey introduced herself and added, "I was here when Metzler killed himself."

"Clare Renfro." The agent shook her hand. "The medical examiner picked up the doctor's body about twenty minutes ago."

"What are those?" Bailey nodded at the papers Renfro held.

"Documents from a file cabinet. I was told this was part of an active investigation and that I should gather anything that might be useful." Renfro shrugged. "But I couldn't find a computer."

"I have it." Bailey gestured at the front door. "Let's go inside."

Once they'd stepped in, Renfro asked, "What's this case about?"

"An illegal medical experiment from two decades ago and the current murders of people who knew about it."

Renfro's eyes widened. "Do you need help? I was headed back to Denver soon, but I could stay." She set the papers on a foyer table.

Bailey hesitated, then handed the agent her phone. "Enter your number in case I need backup."

Renfro keyed it in, then pressed the call button. "I'll stay here at the doctor's house tonight and wait to hear from you."

"Then you might as well search those documents. I'm looking for anything that mentions a drug called ImmuNatal or someone named Ahmed Rashaud."

Renfro pulled out a notepad and jotted the names down. "Anything else?"

"Not yet. But let's see what I find in the safe." Bailey walked into the dining area, her legs suddenly heavy with fatigue. She would rest for a while back at the motel.

The painting, a hideous abstract, was heavier than she'd expected and she set it down with a thud. At the sound, Renfro hurried over. Bailey ignored her and opened the safe with the code she'd found in the doctor's will.

Inside, sat a stack of cash, an expensive watch, some

bonds, and a plain leather-bound book. Bailey picked up the book and flipped it open. A journal with handwritten notes. *Please let it go back twenty years.* She tucked the journal into her shoulder bag, resisted the urge to touch the money, and closed the safe. If the other agent hadn't been standing behind her, the cash would have been tempting. It was unlikely anyone knew it was there or would miss its absence.

Bailey turned to face Renfro. "I'm headed back to my motel. Let me know if you find anything."

"Will do."

Bailey hurried toward the door. Halfway across the room, she stopped and turned. "Thanks for staying." Renfro could be useful if the investigation got sticky.

Back in her motel room, she ate the protein bar she'd picked up and washed it down with black coffee. She pulled off her jacket, unholstered her weapon, and sat on the bed. No point in taking off her clothes. She needed to be ready to rush out of the room if anything broke open with the case. Eager as she was to read the journal, she had to send Metzler's confession to her boss first. It proved to be easy—simply tap the recording and hit the Share icon.

She pushed the laptop aside, leaned back against the headboard, and opened the journal. The first page was dated May 3, 1995, and the last page with writing said September, 2016. Last month. Bailey started skimming the handwritten text, the sloppy penmanship making her strain. Every entry had two sections, the first revealed personal thoughts, goals, and accomplishments, while the second contained cryptic references to the ImmuNatal experiment. The notes indicated the drug was intended to improve his pregnant patients' immune systems as well as their babies'. The mentions were brief, referring to new shipments, occasional side effects, and the money he received.

After a few minutes, Bailey's eyes hurt and her brain wanted to shut down, so she skim read, looking for names. On a page dated February 13, 1996, she found a detailed personal entry that overlapped with the drug-trial information.

I delivered the Lopez baby this afternoon and was surprised, maybe a little horrified, to discover that the baby had mixed genitals, a tiny penis and a vagina. I consulted with the parents, and they were distressed. The father wanted me to perform a surgery to close up the vagina, but mother disagreed and refused consent. They named the baby Taylor, which is not gender specific. Mariah Lopez was the first patient I gave ImmuNatal to, and I wonder if there's a connection. I certainly hope not.

The doctor's musings continued with speculation about how an immune booster might have an effect on genitalia and concluded that it couldn't. Bailey flipped ahead several pages, and read an entry dated six months later.

A seventh intersex baby had been born to an ImmuNatal mother, and the doctor had been distressed enough to question Captain Rashaud about the drug. His commander had admitted they were testing it for other effects, and the intersex babies were unexpected, but welcome.

What the hell? Bailey closed her eyes to rest for a moment. Why were military medical researchers pleased with intersex offspring? Messing with human reproduction was serious business, and she suspected it had implications related to the army's main focus—war. But how? And what other effect had they wanted?

The numbers were a puzzle as well. The list sent by the clinic receptionist held thirty-three names. Were they all intersex? Or just the names of those born to mothers who took ImmuNatal? Perhaps some looked gender-specific at birth, then developed gender identity issues later. She might never know, unless the researchers had documented everything and she managed to access that data. Bailey knew that all embryos started out as female, so gender seemed to be a biological afterthought. ImmuNatal clearly exploited that weakness.

Bailey forced herself to open her eyes and scan a few more pages further into the journal. One entry caught her attention.

I went to Captain Rashaud, demanding more information about the drug. He offered to reveal details if I was willing to monitor two of the intersex children over the next twenty years and report anything significant. When I objected, he reminded me of my part in the trial and his ability to deny me an Army pension. So I agreed to go along. I admit, I'm curious about how their lives will turn out. Rashaud told me he and Major Blackburn were developing psychotropic pharmaceuticals in a secret lab on Fort Carson and that Blackburn was fascinated with intersex offspring. I find this very curious.

Yes, indeed. Bailey found it intriguing as well. Exhausted, but fascinated, she kept reading. Below the personal entry was Major Sam Blackburn's bio: a medical doctor and helicopter pilot. He'd flown Medevac missions during the Gulf war, and developed a clotting drug to save injured soldiers. He had a son named Devin, who was also in the military.

What was the major's interest in non-gender-specific people? Did he think they made good soldiers? She grabbed her phone and texted Havi, her bureau analyst: *Get everything you can on Major Sam Blackburn and Devin Blackburn, including photos.* Havi would be at home, but he would get right on it anyway. That was the job.

Bailey couldn't think straight anymore. She needed to rest until the morning. Then she would access Fort Carson on foot, visit the base hospital, and find Major Blackburn, one way or another.

Chapter 35

Hours earlier, SRC

Blackburn finished his meal and poured a drink, the good stuff this time. He briefly considered leaving his quarters to watch a movie or play pool in the rec room but decided against it. The Peace Project was at too critical a juncture now to take his focus away even for an hour. Tomorrow he had to show up at the hospital for a budget meeting, and it would be good to get out of the complex and get some fresh air. By then, ImmuNatal would be on its way to complete the mission, and the loose ends would be wrapped up as well.

But where the hell was Devin and why hadn't he heard from him? Blackburn called his son again, leaving another harsh message. He called the lab next, and Blessert answered, sounding less pleasant this time.

"Is the drug ready? It needs to go out on a helicopter now if it's going to make it onto the next transport plane for Kuwait."

"I'll inform you as soon as it's packaged, sir." The call went dead.

The insubordinate little shit. Blackburn clenched his fist, relaxed it, and clenched again. He took a big pull of scotch and stared at the desk photo of Devin's mother. Their affair had been brief but beautiful. She'd broken it off without telling him she was pregnant. He'd only learned of his child after she died giving birth to Devin. After one look at his son, Blackburn had known Noreen had been given ImmuNatal at the obstetrics clinic. The discovery had outraged him, and he'd fired the doctor who'd included her in the trial. Unfairly, of course. The poor man hadn't known Noreen was his girlfriend. No one had. Blackburn had done the right thing, filed for custody, and raised the boy as best he could.

A knock on the door interrupted his thoughts. Blackburn jumped to his feet, his aging body slower than it used to be.

"It's Rashaud."

Blackburn unlocked the door and let him in, the first person to enter his private quarters in years. The psychologist's eyes were distressed.

"What's going on?"

"A clerk at the visitor's center just notified me that an FBI agent was seeking entry to the base and wants to talk to me specifically." Rashaud walked over to the desk and poured himself a glass from the bottle Blackburn had left out.

"Well, fuck. That can't be good. Any idea what it's about?"

"No, but I denied her a pass. I also called my contact at the FBI, but I haven't heard back yet." Rashaud gulped his drink. "We have to assume they sent someone to investigate."

"It's probably about the Lopez disappearance." Blackburn shook his head. "I regret bringing the girl here. Maybe it's time to dump her body somewhere and make it look like a serial killer abducted her." An unseemly idea, but Lopez shouldn't have been so nosey. A disturbing thought hit him. "How did the FBI agent come up with your name? Especially in connection to Lopez?"

"I don't know." Rashaud looked grim. "Maybe it's not about the missing woman. Maybe it's about the dead subjects."

"Goddammit. Only the doctors you gave the drug to know about your involvement."

"I called Metzler and he doesn't answer."

"His wife died recently. Maybe he's becoming unhinged." *Damn.* Would they have to terminate Metzler too?

"Have you heard from Devin about the others?"

Rashaud meant Seth Wozac, the fourth fire-starter, and Wilson, the reporter. More loose ends. "No, but I will. I'm sure my son is handling it."

Rashaud wasn't appeased. "I think we need to cover our tracks on the original subjects. Notify the monitors that it's over and tell them to destroy all documentation."

"Agreed. We need to destroy files at the clinic too. If I don't hear from Devin, you'll have to handle that yourself."

Rashaud was silent.

"I'll contact Devin again now." Blackburn nodded at him. "I'll keep you updated."

After the captain left, Blackburn finished his drink, did twenty pushups to work off some anger, then called his son.

After six rings, Devin finally picked up. "Hello, sir. I see that you've called a few times. Sorry, I've been ill." Devin spoke slowly and didn't sound like himself.

"What do you mean by ill? What's going on?"

"I'm behind on my assignments." A pained tone now. "Things didn't go well. I'm sorry. I'll get it done."

"Just fucking tell me!"

He heard his son take a deep breath. "I intended to give Jake Wilson an overdose, like we discussed. But he was with Wozac. Wilson picked him up from the hospital."

Oh christ. Could it get any worse?

Devin continued, his voice gaining some strength. "I saw it as an opportunity to take care of both at the same time. So I followed them to Wozac's home." A pause. "As I was preparing to enter, a dog attacked me, and a witness started screaming. I had to abandon my plan and get away."

"What a clusterfuck!" Blackburn had a moment of concern. "Were you injured? Is that what you mean by sick?"

"No, sir. I had the heroin needle in my hand, prepared to inject it upon contact with the target." A longer pause this time. "But the dog bite interrupted me, and I accidentally shot myself in the wrist with a dose. I had to go to a motel and sleep it off. But I'll get back on task immediately."

Blackburn held back another reprimand. Some missions just got FUBAR—Fucked Up Beyond All Recognition. No one could predict or control everything. "I have another assignment that's equally important. The computers at the clinic need to be destroyed and removed. Yes, it'll create havoc for the staff for a while, but it's time to shut down the Peace Project and eliminate all trace of the patients who participated." *Maybe the remaining doctor too.* He would call the monitors in Washington and Alaska too. Blackburn wanted everything done right fucking now, but getting someone else involved at this point seemed counterproductive. The fewer people who knew, the better. Rashaud could take care of the doctor. Blackburn tuned into what his son was saying.

"I think it's best to enter the clinic in the middle of the night, then make it look like dopers broke in and stole the computers."

"That's acceptable. Locate Wilson and Wozac in the mean time."

"Yes, sir."

Blackburn gave him the clinic's alarm code. "Keep me updated."

"I will, sir."

They both clicked off. Blackburn poured himself another drink. The most important objective was to get ImmuNatal on a transport plane and into the hands of the operatives—even if he had to fly it out himself—before they were compromised and twenty years of research and resources were wasted. If he accomplished his Peace goal, whatever happened next would be worth it, even if the FBI showed up to arrest him. But Blackburn would never let himself be court-martialed or imprisoned. Death would be better.

Chapter 36

Sunday, Oct. 16, 3:15 a.m., Colorado Springs

Jake woke and couldn't get back to sleep. He finally got up, made coffee, and got online. He'd been up all night the evening before worried about Taylor, then finally crashed late that afternoon after switching motels and hearing no news from Agent Bailey. So his sleep schedule was off, and he was wide-awake in the middle of the night.

He shut the laptop off and paced the room, feeling hyper, cooped up, and frustrated. He had to get the hell out of this room and do something! If he couldn't be productive, he needed to smoke some weed and calm down. Did he have any more stashed in his backpack? He searched every pocket and came up empty. Relieved and disappointed at the same time, he started pacing again.

What could he do to help Agent Bailey? Find the researcher who'd devised the experiment! That name had to be in the clinic somewhere. He'd searched for it in the files he'd downloaded, but they were all medical records and didn't include any administrative details. Maybe he should go back to the clinic and try again. The FBI agent probably wasn't willing to break any rules or laws to get information, but he was. Taylor's life was on the line, and he was willing to risk a few months in jail to save her. Jake grabbed his backpack and headed for the door.

Jake stepped out of the motel room and sucked in the cold, fresh air. God, it was good to be outside. The dark stillness should have made him feel less visible, but instead, it enveloped him with a sense of dread. The assassin could be looking at him right now through the scope of a rifle, waiting for him to take one step forward. The man had come after him twice, so he'd earned the right to be paranoid. Keeping his back to the wall, Jake stepped sideways until he reached his car. *Taylor's car,* he reminded himself. What would happen if she never turned up? He would have to contact her family somehow—if he could find them. She hadn't mentioned anyone she was close to. If he found a relative and told the truth, would they believe him?

Don't think about it!

Jake ran the ten steps to the vehicle, bracing for the sound of gunfire. No shots rang out. He jumped in, cranked the engine, and backed up. Was that more snow hitting the windshield? *Shit.* The last thing he needed.

The five-minute drive to Carson Obstetrics made him feel alone in the world. A dark eerie silence surrounded him. No lights flickered in any buildings, and no cars were on the road. He shut off his headlights, pulled into the clinic, and drove to the back, not wanting to take any chances—especially the possibility of a police officer cruising by. He also planned to leave out the back by driving over the strip of landscaping that separated this lot from the one behind it. Even with his escape mapped out, this was probably the riskiest, stupidest thing he'd ever done. But being arrested and jailed was better than sitting alone in the motel room feeling helpless—

or running back to Denver like a coward. He couldn't live with himself if he abandoned Taylor.

His plan was to break in with a credit card. If that didn't work, he would use a crow bar on one of the doors or windows. He fully expected an alarm to go off, but he figured he'd have enough time to grab the computer from the director's office, run to the car, and drive out the back. Drug addicts and burglars pulled off these kinds of stunts all the time.

The sight of another car parked behind the building startled him. A dark SUV. *Oh shit.* Was that the assassin? A flashlight flickered inside the clinic. Whoever it was had access but didn't want anyone to know about their visit. Jake sat for a moment, paralyzed with indecision. Self-preservation told him to stay in the car and wait to see who came out. But what if the clinic director was deleting files and hiding evidence? Or it might even be the military researcher who'd conducted the experiment. They might be destroying the only link to their involvement and the only path to Taylor's location.

Jake forced himself to get out of the car, then reached back inside for the crowbar. The clinic's rear door was likely still unlocked, but he wanted the tool for protection. If the armed assassin was in there, the crowbar might be pointless, but it made him feel better anyway.

At the door, he pulled on wool gloves and reached tentatively for the handle. It turned easily, and no alarm sounded. Jake let out the breath he'd been holding and pushed open the door. He hesitated a moment, decided no one was lying in wait, then stepped inside. Two night-lights along the wall at the floor level illuminated the back hallway. He hurried to the administrative area, stepping lightly. But his footsteps seemed to echo in the empty building. Tucked behind a tall filing cabinet he tried to mentally pinpoint where he'd seen the flicker of the flashlight.

The sound of metal crashing into metal made him flinch. Was that a computer being destroyed? While the noise muffled his presence, Jake rushed to the center of the building where the nursing staff desks were located and ducked down behind a counter. During the short run, he'd spotted a man crossing a hallway. Dark clothes and a hoodie. *Shit!* His instinct was to run from the building.

Jake inched up and peeked over the counter at the hallway. He saw the man smash a computer with a hammer and throw it onto a wheeled cart. It wasn't the first machine in the pile. He was destroying—and likely intended to remove—every digital file in the building.

No! Jake's legs trembled. The guy had to be stopped, but he didn't know how. He wasn't a cop or superhero, and he would probably die trying but he had to try. Jake slipped his phone from his pocket and texted Agent Bailey again: *Need help at clinic. Man smashing computers.* He pressed Send, hoping she was a light sleeper.

He thought about calling the police but changed his mind. How would he explain his presence at the clinic on a Sunday morning before dawn? He needed Agent Bailey to get here now. If she didn't arrive in time to arrest the perp, Jake would keep out of sight and follow him. Hopefully, the guy would lead him to Taylor.

Footsteps thundered in his direction.

Jake's heart missed a beat as he scrambled around on his knees, looking for a place to hide.

Legs appeared in the opening between two desks, and a soft voice whispered, "I've got you this time."

Oh shit. He had to do something now or he would die, cowering on the floor. Jake tightened his grip on the crowbar and lunged. A sharp blast rang out, followed by intense pain. He dropped the crowbar and grabbed his chest, knowing it was over for him.

Chapter 37

On the ride to Carson Obstetrics, Seth blasted his favorite indie rock band. The heavy beat filled his mind with kinetic energy—to go with the pain-numbing rush of the meth. Just what he needed to carry out the burn. This would be his greatest blaze yet—if the snow didn't interfere. It might even be his last. Once he'd torched the clinic that had spawned him, maybe he would lose the impulse to watch fires. Or not. As long as no one got hurt, he didn't see a problem. That was why he was doing it now, in the middle of the night when no one would be in the building. The place would be locked of course, but he didn't need to get inside. He had a bag of bricks and Molotov cocktails. He would throw his sweet little firebombs in through the broken windows, then run like hell to a place where he could watch in safety.

He drove past the clinic, turned onto a side street, and looked for a secluded place to park. *There.* Behind the health food store. Its roof looked accessible. The store would be open later, with other cars in the parking lot, so Ray's crappy car wouldn't be noticeable if he had to ditch it and leave on foot to avoid the police. He parked the Toyota, adjusted his satchel, and jogged across the strip of grass to the clinic on the other side.

226

Surprised to see two cars in the back lot, he stopped, mouth open. *Well fuck.* What the hell were people doing here? Were they inside the building? He didn't see any lights on. His mind raced with possibilities and his pulse kept pace. They could be lovers who met here and walked to a nearby motel so no one would see their cars together. Or party people who took their action somewhere nearby. *Whatever.* He was too jacked up to abandon his mission. This fucking freak show had to go. Every nerve in his body hummed with the need to watch it burn. If anyone was in there, they would run out as soon as the first firebomb went off. The Molotovs were noisy motherfuckers.

Seth charged toward the windows in the front. He wanted to start with a big target, a sure thing. As he rounded the corner of the building, he grabbed the first brick from his satchel and hurled it with all his might at the lobby window. *Goddamn, that felt good!* The crash of breaking glass gave him another jolt of pleasure. He reached for a firebomb, lit the gas-soaked rag, and hurled it through the hole in the glass. It exploded in a sharp blast. Flames burst upward, and Seth watched through the window, mesmerized.

Keep moving! He could enjoy the whole blaze in a few minutes—from a safe distance. Sprinting again, he charged around to the side of the building and hurled another brick, followed by a second firebomb. The flames fed his soul, and he stayed to watch for a moment. The light, the orange glow, the danger. So beautiful.

Keep moving! Seth sprinted toward the back of the clinic. One more. The sound of a car approaching made him slow down. He glanced over his shoulder. Not a cop. *Good news.* But what the fuck was everyone doing here? A damn staff meeting? He hurled the last brick-and-firebomb combo but didn't stop to enjoy it. He had to disappear for a minute in case the person in the car had seen him.

He darted behind a dumpster and bent over to catch his breath. He could smell the blaze now, the intoxicating aroma of hot carbon. As much as he wanted to stay close, he would wait for the car to leave, run across the median, and climb to the roof of the health food store. If he lay flat to keep out of sight, he could watch the blaze until the fire trucks arrived. He'd earned it. In the darkness, another vehicle started. Someone leaving? From his hiding spot, he couldn't see the back parking lot. The engine roared and seemed to race away. A few minutes later, another car sounded like it followed the first one. Was it safe to make his break? Seth stepped to the edge of the dumpster and peered out. Two of the cars were gone, but the piece-of-shit Jetta was still there. *Oh fuck!* That was Jake's car.

A weak cry for help drifted out the broken back window. *No!* Jake was in there, hurt. Not by the fire, he hoped. But what if he was trapped? His new friend cried out again, a little more desperate. *Oh fuck.* Seth had never hurt anyone with his burns, and he couldn't let this one get ruined with fucked-up guilt.

Seth sprinted for the back door. He would get Jake out of the building, then run like hell. If the cops were on the way, he might have to watch this fire on the news.

Chapter 38

Twenty minutes earlier

A beep from her phone made Bailey sit up in bed. A text? She grabbed her cell and pressed the icon. A message from Jake Wilson: *Need help at clinic. Man smashing computers.*

What the hell? She blinked and focused on the time: 3:43 a.m.

Bailey bolted out of bed and pulled on her shoes. What was Jake doing at the obstetrics office, let alone this early on a Sunday morning? And who was destroying evidence? She secured her Glock, pulled on her jacket, and bolted out of the room. Snow was coming down in a steady white sheet. She wasn't dressed for this shit, but the extra layers she'd bought were still in the car. Bailey rushed to her rental and climbed in. Did she need backup? She reached for her phone, then changed her mind. She would check out the situation first. Getting other agents out to Colorado Springs would take hours. What if the man destroying files at the clinic was just a meth-crazed burglar? Or a janitor acting on orders from someone else? She didn't need help with either of those scenarios. In fact, she preferred to operate on her own as much as possible. Especially since she was willing to ignore the rules to get the job done.

A few inches of snow had piled up, and the short drive down Nevada Avenue was surreal. Deadly quiet with moonlight glinting off the white powder. No vehicles traveled the streets, but fresh tire marks in the lane indicated someone had been through recently. Wilson? She'd just passed his new motel.

As she approached the clinic, bursts of orange light radiated in the dark. Was that a fire? *Holy shit!* Bailey pressed the accelerator and skidded into the empty parking lot. Where were the cars? She drove around the building and spotted the Jetta she'd seen in front of the motel when she'd met with Jake. Nearby was a large SUV. Glock in hand, Bailey climbed from the car. The fire unnerved her. Was the intruder burning the clinic to destroy evidence of the experiment? Was Wilson still inside?

A fast-moving figure caught her attention. Dressed in dark, the skinny man sprinted around the corner and hurled something through a window. Glass shattered as the man stopped and reached in his pocket. He drew his arm back and threw another object through the broken window. A second later, a small boom shook the night, and flames shot up inside the glass.

Molotov cocktails! The intruder was burning down the clinic. Bailey processed her options. Go inside and check on Jake or apprehend the unsub. The fire-starter might know where Taylor was or had been hired by someone who did. The pyro might even be the researcher who'd conducted the illegal drug test, or the killer who'd killed the other subjects—and might kill more. She sprinted after him. He was fast, but so was she. If he stopped to hurl another firebomb, she'd catch him and take him down.

Three seconds into the chase, an engine started behind her. Bailey slowed and glanced over her shoulder. The SUV, running without headlights, barreled straight at her. She hugged up against the building and stared at the driver. Another young man in dark clothes. This one with a short buzz cut. Was he the one who'd been inside destroying files? She tried to read the license plate but it was too dark, even with small fires burning inside the clinic. She processed her options again. The military-style haircut of the driver made him more likely to lead her to Lopez—or the secret complex. The fire-starter was already out of her line of sight now anyway. She'd lost him when she leaped out of the vehicle's path.

Bailey turned and sprinted for her car. She would follow the second perp and call for backup.

Chapter 39

On the road, Bailey pressed the newest entry in her phone and willed Renfro to answer. Finally, the other agent said a sleepy, "Hello?"

"It's Bailey. I need assistance. Alert the police to a fire at Carson Obstetrics, then get in your car and drive toward Fort Carson. I'll update you on my location." The military base was just a guess, but the SUV ahead of her was traveling south in that direction.

"What's happening?"

"Unsubs are destroying evidence, and I'm following one now. He might lead me to the missing woman. Call the Denver field office as well. We may need a whole team."

"Will do."

Bailey hung up.

The darkness was frustrating, but she kept her headlights off, so the SUV driver wouldn't see her behind him. No other vehicles were on the road, yet, so it wasn't much of a risk. But daybreak would be coming soon. As they drove south, the snow tapered off, then finally stopped. *Thank god.* She called her boss, unconcerned about the time. Lennard was quick to pick up. "Damn, Bailey. Do you ever sleep?"

"Things are breaking here. The clinic is on fire, I'm following an unsub, and the missing woman could be in a secret complex on Fort Carson. I might need a SWAT unit to rescue her."

"It's the military. You'll need a damn presidential phone call."

That worried Bailey too. "So start working on it. They're destroying evidence right now." Bailey wasn't even sure why this case had become so important to her. With all the shortcuts she was taking, it could ruin her career instead of helping it. But she wasn't capable of giving up.

"Are you sure the woman is there?"

"Yes." *A small lie.* "Even if she's not, the mastermind of the experiment, the person who likely ordered the murders, is there. His name is Major Sam Blackburn, and who knows what else he's got going on?"

"The audio file you sent doesn't mention the missing woman or a secret complex," Lennard argued. "Do you have anything else I can use to get a warrant or executive order?"

She didn't have time for paperwork! "The doctor's diary mentions Major Blackburn and a secret lab, but I'm in pursuit and can't fax anything right now." She held back a string of swear words.

A long silence from her boss. Finally, Lennard said, "I'll get a SWAT unit on standby and talk to the director about protocol for raiding a military base."

Not good enough. Bailey glanced at the road ahead and realized the SUV had disappeared. "I have to go. I'll try to keep you updated." She pressed her earpiece, turned on her headlights, and punched the accelerator. Where had the damn vehicle gone? The highway was relatively straight, but other vehicles were traveling now, so maybe the SUV was still ahead. She spotted a sign for Fort Carson. Maybe the driver had turned off already.

When the checkpoint station came into view on the left, Bailey slowed and scanned for the SUV, but didn't see it. She made the turn and parked at the outer edge of the visitors' lot. After pulling on the overcoat, she took off running across the grassy slope that separated the highway from the first row of military housing. She needed an easy-to-steal vehicle. Jeeps were quick to hot wire, and the base probably had them sitting around.

She ran past two streets lined with perfectly maintained new homes and apartments, a quaint image with the snow-covered ground and sun peeking over the horizon. No slobs or slackers allowed in a military neighborhood. But no Jeeps either, so far. Almost no vehicles on display at all. They had to be tucked into garages. Bailey kept moving, her feet already cold from the wet snow.

When she hit the main road leading into the community, she started scanning for vehicle storage lots. Every base had them. She spotted one on the next block. A vehicle was coming down the road in her direction, so she jogged behind a building and cut across the side street. In the distance, engines started, lights flickered on, and heat pumps generated white noise. She had to do this quickly before someone spotted the anomaly that she presented—a forty-year-old, non-uniformed woman running on base in sensible work shoes.

The lot was only partially fenced, so Bailey sprinted around the barrier and ducked in between two oversized vehicles that that looked like bigger, stranger versions of tanks. Beyond those, she spotted three Jeeps and a Humvee. Excellent.

She jumped into the smallest Jeep, pried off the dashboard cover, and pulled out the jumble of ignition wires.

Yellow to red. It was that simple. The engine roared, giving her an old familiar thrill. She'd stolen plenty of cars in high school to take joy riding. She'd returned all but the one she'd wrecked. Joy riding had been her favorite of the many self-indulgent activities she'd pursued until she'd gotten control of her impulses. But taking what she wanted was natural to her—and often fun.

The feeling passed quickly. This was a military base, and she was an intruder. She would be lucky not to end up in a windowless room with expressionless armed guards. Bailey eased out of the lot and instinctively headed away from the base's entrance. The hospital was at the back. Her earlier map study had provided a visual layout to work with, but it wouldn't help her locate the secret complex. Still, she expected a medical research lab to be near the hospital, perhaps below it.

The base intrigued her. Numbered buildings with open spaces and rolling hills in between. No clutter or trash, no pedestrians, and nothing that looked aged or run-down. She noticed a pub, a behavioral health clinic, and a fire station. Looking down a side street for the SUV, she noticed a cluster of fast food restaurants. A self-contained community.

Five blocks ahead at the T-intersection, she noticed the big dark SUV make a right turn. *Yes!* She gassed the Jeep, no longer worried about being seen. The driver wouldn't be concerned about a military vehicle behind him. Beyond the intersection, the three-story hospital sat on a small hill, with a gently-rising wilderness area behind it. Was the unsub headed into the hospital parking lot?

She exceeded the 15-mph speed limit, raced to the last stop sign, and turned right. The SUV had skipped the hospital entrance and was driving past a golf course into open terrain.

Now that she had the big vehicle in sight, Bailey reduced her speed and hung back. While she followed, she worked through possible scenarios. If they were headed to the secret lab, it was probably gated, guarded, or difficult to enter. Following the unsub inside might be impossible. Apprehending him before he reached that point might be more logical. Once she had him in custody, he became leverage, a bartering tool. She was on her own for now, so the rulebook was moot.

Still, it would be nice to have backup. Using voice command, she called Agent Renfro again. "Bailey here. I'm inside Fort Carson, but leaving the main base on a back road headed southeast. I'm still following a dark SUV, driver unknown, but he's the one I caught destroying files at the clinic." *Close enough.* She needed a solid reason for pursuing him and making an arrest.

"I'm headed your way," Renfro said. "About five miles out. Does the base have a checkpoint?"

"Yes, but I went around on foot after being denied yesterday. Tell them you're picking up a friend or something." *Damn.* Renfro's stop at the visitor center would slow her down. Maybe even block her backup cold. Hopefully, the Denver team or SWAT unit—if either arrived—would bring a warrant or official paperwork that would bypass the clearance bullshit. But in case Renfro made it through, Bailey gave her basic directions. "Once you're inside, come straight to the back of the base, turn right, and stay on that road." She clicked off.

Her phone beeped with a text from Havi. With one hand, she opened it. No message, only a photo of a handsome man in his late fifties with military-cropped graying blond hair and the caption *Major Blackburn*. It helped to know who she was looking for. Another text followed with an attachment, but now was not an ideal time to read the major's background profile.

The snow clouds began to part, and the morning sky brightened. Bailey hung back, not wanting to spook the driver or move in before they were within striking distance of the complex. How would she know? She typically relied on logic as her operating mode, but this one might call for a gut instinct. Fortunately, even her hunches were better than most people's. More important, she needed a plan. At the moment, all she could think of was to run the other car off the road.

Chapter 40

Devin took another gulp of coffee and rolled down her window. The cold fresh air helped, but she was still woozy and sick to her stomach. How long would the effect of the heroin last? Once she dropped off the computers at the complex for incineration, she had to find and terminate Wozac. How could she do it feeling like this? Grabbing and smashing data storage at the clinic had been mindless and easy in comparison. At least until all hell broke loose. Finding the reporter in the building had surprised her, yet it made sense that he would be there, searching for the evidence she was sent to destroy. It had been a lucky break—after chasing and failing to terminate him twice. Putting two bullets into Wilson had felt victorious.

But the breaking glass and firebombs that followed had been a complete shock, so she'd fled the scene in a still-high-on-dope state of panic. Devin didn't know what the hell had happened, but once she was safely on the road, she'd burst into rare laughter. Another lucky break. The clinic would burn to the ground, not only destroying all trace of the Peace Project, but giving her some peace of mind too. As proud as she was of her service to her country, she hated the damn drug that had made her this way.

And as much as she respected her father, she hated him

too. At the age of six, she'd tried to tell him she was female, but he'd shut her down and threatened to beat the girlishness out of her if she brought it up again. She hadn't. The major wasn't abusive very often, and she liked to keep it that way.

The violence issue troubled her. The Peace Project's mission was to end the horrible violence of Islamic terrorists. But she'd killed five people in their quest to keep the project going forward. *Five lives were nothing,* she told herself again. Nothing compared to the thousands and thousands who would die over the next twenty years—either from direct warfare, Sharia law, or the disease and starvation that plagued the refugees fleeing the terrorists. Yet the five deaths bothered her now, and she didn't want to be a fixer anymore. Did she feel this way because of the heroin? She hoped the guilt and revulsion would go away when the drug finally wore off.

One more, Devin told herself. After she terminated Wozac, she would get her last tattoo and tell the major she wanted a transfer. Living under the radar—and under her father's direct supervision—wasn't how she wanted to spend her life. She would always serve her country, but there had to be something better for her. The major had started his military career as a doctor, a healer. Maybe she would become a paramedic or Medevac pilot like he had been.

Another wave of nausea rolled over her, and Devin stuck her head out the window. Frigid air slammed into her face and pushed the sickness down. When the heroin had first hit her system, she'd been euphoric, experiencing a pleasure and sense of wellbeing she'd never known. She'd stopped at a park and sat for an hour, marveling at the beauty of nature and the diversity of people who came and went. But she'd soon become drowsy and had checked into a motel and slept until the major called. During the wait to carry out her clinic assignment, she'd walked around, eaten what she could stomach, and drank a shit-ton of coffee. Maybe the caffeine was making her sick now.

Twenty minutes later, as she neared the entrance to the research complex, another wave of nausea hit her. Devin pulled off the road, climbed from her car, and vomited.

Chapter 41

The SUV suddenly swerved to the side of the road and stopped. *Oh shit.* The driver had probably spotted her. Bailey braked and pulled her weapon. She eased to the edge of the gravel but kept moving forward. She rolled down her window, transferred her Glock to her left hand, and stuck the gun outside the car where she could fire it.

Fifty feet ahead, the driver stepped out, bent over, and started puking. *What the hell?* A ruse to lure her in close? Not likely. Bailey slammed to a stop, shut off the engine, and sprinted toward the incapacitated unsub. Rather than risk a chase or physical confrontation—or be forced to shoot an unidentified, possibly unarmed man—she would simply slam into him, knock him to the ground, and cuff him. *Did she have handcuffs in her jacket pocket?* Yes.

The man looked up seconds before impact, but he didn't have time to brace. Bailey put up her free hand at the last moment to minimize the impact to herself and hit him broadside. They both went down, her landing on top. She registered pain but ignored it. With her forearm pressed against the side of his neck, Bailey got up on her knees and rolled the man face down. As she grabbed for the handcuffs, he suddenly bucked. To shortstop the altercation, she slammed the butt of her Glock into the back of his head, then cuffed him before he could recover.

She pushed to her feet. "Roll over so I can see you." She stepped out of reach and kept the Glock aimed at his head. He didn't comply, so she rammed a foot under his shoulder, lifted, and shoved.

The face staring back at her was young, sharply defined, and strangely pretty. In fact, the kid looked a lot like the photo of Major Blackburn, only more feminine. "Who are you? Devin Blackburn?"

The man, or boy, was silent. He had to be a soldier, otherwise he wouldn't have made it through the checkpoint. Did he have a weapon? "Roll back over."

This time, he did as told. Bailey dropped onto his back and searched under his jacket for a weapon, but found a phone and a magnetized key-card. A security pass? That might come in handy. She slipped both into her pocket, then patted down his legs and confiscated a small handgun from an ankle holster. Was this the weapon used to shoot Zion Tumara?

She stood. "Don't move or I'll put a bullet in you." Bailey stepped over to his SUV and looked inside. A military-issue rifle sat on the passenger's seat. On the floor of the vehicle, she spotted a roll of duct tape and a pair of plastic handcuffs. Materials used in restraining someone—like a kidnap victim. *Interesting.* Maybe Lopez really was in the complex. Bailey glanced at her detainee. He hadn't moved. She remembered his vomiting. What kind of sick was he? Poisoned? Such as with a suicide pill? That seemed extreme, and she had no knowledge that soldiers carried such things.

Bailey reached in and grabbed the duct tape. She needed to get him into his car, which she would appropriate. They wouldn't go anywhere just yet—she had other objectives to accomplish—but keeping him out of sight seemed wise.

She squatted next to his feet, grabbed his ankles, and began to apply the tape. He kicked at her, and she rocked back. Bailey caught herself with one hand, and felt a burst of rage. *The little shit!* She squeezed his Achilles tendon between two fingers until he lay still. But he didn't cry out. A tough guy. Good for him.

She wrapped the tape in a loose figure-eight pattern, leaving enough slack in the middle so he could walk with tiny steps but not escape. She jabbed her Glock into the back of his calf. "Get on your feet."

He didn't respond.

"Hey, I can cut you a deal if you cooperate. Otherwise, you're going to prison for life. I caught you with the weapon you used to murder Zion Tumara, and I'm sure the bureau's forensics team will find Taylor Lopez's DNA in your SUV."

If she could manage to get the vehicle off base to have it processed.

The man was silent.

"Get on your feet and shuffle back to your car. It's damn cold out here." Actually, the morning sun was warming the air and melting the snow, but after lying in it for a few minutes, he had to be wet and cold. Still, he was a soldier, so hitting him or threatening him with pain was probably pointless. Bailey tried again with persuasion. "Work with me. Tell me who gave you the kill orders. Save yourself."

The man finally brought his knees up and struggled to his feet.

Bailey locked eyes with him. "Who are you?"

"First Lieutenant Devin Blackburn."

The major's son, as she thought. She repressed a smile.

Perhaps his father would be interested in a trade.

"Agent Bailey, FBI." She nodded and gestured at his SUV. "I'm detaining you for questioning in the disappearance of Taylor Lopez."

"You have no jurisdiction here."

"I will. The bureau director has made a call to the commander-in-chief. A team will be here with an executive order soon."

Devin shuffled toward his SUV. While he inched his way over, Bailey took his rifle and stashed it out of reach in the back, where she found a pile of smashed computer hard drives. From the clinic? A technician should still be able to recover the files. Only a powerful magnet would completely wipe out digital data. She searched the rest of Blackburn's vehicle and found a grey-canvas duffle bag, and a black, hard-plastic box. A look inside the duffle bag revealed more duct tape, lock picks, tools, and a variety of hats, sunglasses, and shirts. For disguises? What the hell was in the black box? It was locked, so she suspected weapons. An assassin's treasure trove.

She checked on her detainee. He'd made it to the car and stood there, looking pale and ill.

She opened the back door. "Get in."

Devin climbed in and rested his head against the upholstery. He was clearly not well. She might as well take advantage of that.

Bailey got behind the wheel, found the key in the ignition, and started the car. "Let's get closer to the complex where you were headed and call your father. I want to trade you for the kidnapped woman."

Behind her, Devin grunted. "You're outnumbered and wasting your time. You'll be shot on sight."

She weighed the threat. If it were real, she should take her detainee and evidence and get the hell off the base as quickly as she could. What if it was a bluff? Retreating without Lopez was tantamount to surrender. She was too close to winning the whole thing—rescuing the girl and apprehending the mastermind. Her ego and tenacious nature were fully in control. She recognized it, but couldn't self-correct.

Renfro would be here soon, she told herself. Maybe a whole team of agents. Bailey eased the SUV back onto the road and drove forward up the slope. "Tell me when we get close. And if someone starts shooting at me, I'll use you for a shield."

A long pause, then the young soldier finally said, "Pull over after you round the next bend."

They were already in proximity, and he seemed to be cooperating. She knew better than to trust him, so she drove slowly, her weapon out the window, ready to return fire.

No shots came, so she pulled off behind a massive boulder. She turned to face Devin. "Tell me about the Peace Project. I've already figured out most of it, and you're going to prison either way, so what's the harm?" Bailey had a vague idea what they intended for ImmuNatal, but she wanted confirmation.

Devin looked startled. "Where did you hear that name?"

"Dr. Metzler gave a full confession, and he put all the blame on your father, Major Blackburn." She gave the kid a quirky smile. "Tell me what I want to know, and you could walk away from this without a court martial."

Devin shuddered. "You have no idea how important the Peace Project is. Stopping the major now would be disastrous for the United States. For all of the civilized world."

She'd suspected this was about terrorism somehow, but she suddenly realized how the military mission would play out. "The drug is intended for the Middle East, correct?"

Devin didn't respond, but his eyes signaled that she was on the right track.

"It makes people passive and non-reproductive, doesn't it?"

The soldier shrugged.

Incredible idea, but challenging to execute and not one she would have had the patience for. "So they tested it here first to see if they got results they wanted." But how would they target women all over Iraq and Syria where the terrorists had their stronghold? "Talk to me, Devin. You have nothing to lose."

He was silent.

It all came together for her. "The Peace Project has operatives in the Middle East who are prepping and waiting to get the drug, correct? The plan is to put it into the water supply or a food source?"

A small smile from her detainee. "That would be smart."

"Why not just produce a sterility drug?"

"We're not them. We're not trying to annihilate a population."

But they intended to radically change a whole culture. Ambitious and brilliant. She admired Blackburn's audacity.

She needed one more piece of information. "Who killed the pyromaniacs? And the receptionist who leaked information?"

"I don't know what you're talking about." The soldier slumped back.

He'd shut down. Obviously, the murders were Devin's role in the project, but he was smart enough to keep that to himself. With luck, DNA evidence would convict him.

It was time to rescue Taylor Lopez. Bailey grabbed the duct tape and tore off a short strip, then turned to her detainee "Does your father have a sense of humor?" She was feeling wicked, almost giddy. Either she was about to die or her blood sugar was dropping.

"No, he doesn't."

"Too bad." She secured the tape over his mouth, then used Devin's phone to call Major Blackburn.

On the second ring, a harsh voice cut in. "Devin! What's your report?"

"This is Agent Bailey with the FBI. I have your son, but I'm willing to trade him for Taylor Lopez. Don't bother denying that you have the girl. Devin already admitted that you did."

A full five-second pause while the major weighed his options. "Where are you?"

"Just send Lopez out of the complex, and I'll leave Devin and drive away. A backup team of agents will be here in a moment, so if you hesitate or fuck with me, the negotiation is over, and Devin will spend the rest of his life in prison. This is your only chance to save your son."

Another long hesitation. "How do I know you really have him?"

"I'll send you a photo."

"How do I know you won't go back on your end of the deal?" The major was smart enough to not admit anything.

"I want Lopez alive. If I cared more about prosecuting Devin, I wouldn't be talking to you."

"Give me a minute to consider." The major disconnected the call.

Bailey calculated his possible responses. Blackburn might

simply flee out another exit and disappear into the wilderness. Or he could wait it out and see if she really had a backup team. But if he was like most parents—based on what she'd observed—he would put his child first and send out Lopez. Bailey still couldn't determine why they'd taken the girl, and that made the major unpredictable. Also, he might not be like other parents. If he'd trained his son to be an assassin, Blackburn might even be on the sociopathic spectrum.

Bailey took a picture of Devin, mouth still duct-taped and sent it to Blackburn. She pulled the tape off, in case her detainee wanted to share more information.

The kid made a throaty sound. "My father will never compromise himself to save me. I'm not that important to him." Devin shrugged. "No soldier is."

His tone was stoic but his eyes registered pain. Even she could perceive that. Not good. If Blackburn didn't send Lopez out, Bailey would have to go in. Where the hell was her backup?

Chapter 42

Blackburn called Rashaud, then shouted "Meet me in my office" and hung up. He scanned the bedroom. Where were his damn pants? He'd just stepped out of the shower when he'd taken the call he thought was from his son. How the fuck had Devin let himself be caught by an FBI agent? More important, had his son destroyed the computer files at the clinic first? Or eliminated the reporter? Not that Wilson mattered now anyway, with the damn FBI on their trail. The bureau didn't have jurisdiction on the base, and Blackburn wondered how the agent had gotten in past the checkpoint.

He walked to his clean clothes hanging on the back of a chair. As he pulled on his shorts, he stared down at his body. *Disgusting.* A penis so small women sometimes laughed when they saw it. Except Noreen. She'd wanted him, or at least his child. But why? His face? His authority? Certainly not for his body. He had man boobs, for god's sake. He'd developed them at thirteen and had been mocked and pinched and tormented in school locker rooms. But he'd learned to fight and had joined the military to prove to himself he was as masculine as everyone else. Yet, he'd never made peace with his body, and eventually, he'd gone to medical school to learn everything he could about gender biology and how pharmaceuticals, hormones in particular, affected genitalia.

Blackburn shook off the old feelings. He was facing the worst crisis of his life and needed to focus. Head pounding with pain, he pulled on his clothes. *Damn.* He shouldn't have drunk so much the night before. But now, the only way to get rid of the headache was to pour a little vodka into his orange juice. Only he didn't have time for juice. Blackburn took a short swig from the cold bottle, strapped on his favorite handgun, and headed next door to his office.

He opened the entry to the hallway, and Rashaud was waiting, as he'd expected. Blackburn motioned him in and held out the photo he'd received. "An FBI agent has detained Devin, and I think they're right outside the complex."

Rashaud stared, open-mouthed. "He looks like a prisoner."

"The agent, probably the woman who was here yesterday, offered to trade him for Taylor Lopez."

"How did they know she was here? Devin must have been sloppy."

Blackburn bristled. He could criticize his son, but Rashaud never should. "They may have been following Devin." Blackburn would never tell anyone that his son had accidentally drugged himself with heroin. Was that what had made his son so careless? *Fuck!*

"We can't let the feds ever know the girl was here." Rashaud bounced on his feet. "We'll spend our lives in prison for kidnapping."

Blackburn stiffened and glared at him. "But they already do. If we make the exchange, Devin has a chance to escape and start a new life somewhere. Then we can hire the best military lawyers we know for ourselves."

Rashaud shook his head. "Devin is already compromised. They probably have evidence against him. Let him take the blame for everything." The captain raised his voice. "Don't let misguided emotion cloud your thinking. Cut your losses."

Rage boiled in Blackburn's veins. "Fuck that! We're not sacrificing my son. I'll take the blame. You can run out the back exit like the coward you are."

Rashaud grabbed Blackburn's shirt with tight fists. "Don't ever call me that."

Before Blackburn could react, Rashaud pushed him away and backed toward the door. "I'm taking Lopez to the incinerator. She's the only real problem for us." He pointed a finger. "You're the one who brought her here, and now you're the one who doesn't have the courage to deal with her." Rashaud turned and bolted through the door.

The insubordinate, ungrateful prick. Blackburn charged after him. Once he put the captain in his place, he would grab the ImmuNatal from the lab, get up to the helicopter landing pad, and pilot the drug out of here. He didn't care what happened to the girl, and Devin would understand that the Peace Project had to be his priority. The safety of the world depended on it. Blackburn couldn't believe he'd forgotten that for a moment.

Chapter 43

Taylor woke again after a restless night of horrific dreams. What would her captors make her do today? Except for the films, they'd been civil to her, even offering food she had no appetite for. She brushed her teeth, then tried to read the magazine she'd found on the desk, but it held no interest for her. The torture images she'd had to watch haunted her. She could see why Marissa had become an operative who dedicated her life to stopping terror. Someone had to. The terrorists were horrific, and she'd learned that they planned to take over Europe, then America, through violent warfare. But she didn't feel capable of being a spy. In some ways, she realized she was a perfect candidate, no family, except an aunt in Virginia she never saw, and little chance at a normal life. She would never marry or have children, and her goal was to become a forensic technician or coroner—someone who focused on death. Even if she escaped this horrible place, her future held little promise.

Depression overwhelmed her, and Taylor lay on the bed. Maybe she should go along with the training and give her life some meaning. A soft rap on the door made her sit up.

Marissa slipped in. "Hello again."

Taylor jumped to her feet. "Hey." The young woman was prettier than she remembered. Did Marissa use her sex appeal to extract information from terrorists? Did she infiltrate radical cells? Taylor didn't think she could do that.

Marissa came over and touched her face. "You've been crying."

"Those films were horrible."

"They're real. You can't forget that." Marissa stroked her hair. "But I'm sorry I made you unhappy."

Taylor stepped back. "No, you're not sorry. That was the point. You're manipulating me."

The pretty spy smiled. "Yes, but I would rather make you happy."

"Then tell me what the gender experiment was all about. Why did they give that drug to all those women? Why make intersex babies?"

"I can only tell you that it's an integral part of the war on terrorism. The results won't be seen for many years, but there will be peace."

How? Taylor's mind struggled to match up the two ideas. "Is the drug intended for the Middle East? To make people passive?"

"You're on the right track, but let's not talk about that. I want to cheer you up." Marissa grabbed Taylor's hands and pulled her close. "I know you're attracted to me. I see it in your eyes."

She'd tried hard to suppress those feelings, but sexual attraction wasn't something she could control. *Walk away.* "No." Taylor shook her head and stepped back. "I'm not into women."

"Like hell you're not. You're one of us." Marissa moved in again and whispered. "I sense your hyper-sexuality."

So Marissa *was* part of the experiment too. Taylor wanted to see her body... just out of curiosity.

The girl leaned in and pressed her lips against Taylor's mouth. Gentle, yet urgent.

Oh god. No one had ever kissed her like that. The one prostitute she'd been with had been perfunctory, and the only boy who'd ever kissed her had been stiff and awful.

Marissa wrapped her arms around Taylor and stroked her back. "You're going to like training."

This was the last thing she'd expected. Maybe she should just go along, as part of her escape plan. Marissa ran her fingers lightly over Taylor's breasts. The shock and pleasure overwhelmed her. In the next few moments, Taylor saw flashes of the rest of her life. Seducing strangers, stealing data, using drugs to make herself forget the ugliness and fear.

She didn't want it!

With everything she could muster, she shoved Marissa against the wall, slamming her head on the concrete. The girl made a soft cry, then slipped down to the floor.

Taylor froze. *Oh god.* What had she done?

Run! Her brain screamed, even though her feet didn't want to move.

Get her ID pass and run! This is your chance.

Taylor knelt down next to Marissa's slumped body, snatched the ID she wore around her neck, and bolted from the room. *Go left!* She'd made a point to remember how she'd come in. She wanted to sprint, but worried she would encounter other soldiers or spies in the hall and look suspicious. She walked rapidly instead, keeping her head up and her face deadpan. *You can do this.* Just act like you belong and keep moving to the front of the complex. She would take a golf cart from the foyer, open the door with her pass, and drive right out. Unless Marissa regained consciousness and alerted the guards.

Taylor came to an intersection and glanced sideways. Down the hall, she saw a tall man in a blue uniform punch a smaller brown-skinned man in the face. Was that the major? What the hell was going on? Picking up her pace, she entered the long hallway separating the maze of interior rooms from the entrance foyer. They'd driven in on a cart, so it would take longer to get out on foot. How far was it?

Heart pounding with fear and hope, Taylor sprinted up the empty passage toward freedom.

Chapter 44

Devin couldn't believe she was trussed up liked a pig for roasting in the back of her own vehicle. But at least she'd managed to slip the handcuffs down and over, so they weren't behind her back anymore.

None of this was her fault. The major had given her too many assignments too quickly, not allowing time for careful planning. And all those back-to-back deaths had connected back to the obstetrics clinic. No wonder someone besides the morgue attendant had caught on. Or maybe Lopez had called the FBI before she'd been arrested and abducted. Either way, it was the major's decision to bring Taylor into the program instead of shutting her down and dumping her body where it might never be found. Devin rubbed the tape between her ankles more vigorously as the stressed thoughts invaded her brain.

When the second phase of the Peace Project had finally come close to fruition, the major had started to make irrational decisions, especially about terminating the wildcard subjects. Devin could see that now. And she would be the one to pay the price. Her father would never give up his own freedom and reputation to save her. Not a chance in hell. She was on her own, and if she ended up in court, she would put all the blame on him. She was just a soldier, taking orders from her commander. A military jury would struggle to convict her. The FBI had no jurisdiction over her at all. The agent was here, but she wouldn't make it off the base alive.

Devin was determined to get loose. If she did, she might even make a break for it. She'd been working the tape between her ankles since the moment she entered the back seat. Now, at least twenty minutes had passed since the agent called the major and offered the deal. Rubbing the tape against itself was forcing it into a frayed, rolled-up mess in the middle. Time to test it again. Devin yanked her legs outward, trying to bust the tape. She heard a small rip. *Booyah!* She almost had it. She looked up at the agent. Bailey was sitting against the passenger door—where she could see Devin—but currently looking down and texting someone on her phone. The agent hadn't heard the ripping sound or noticed the activity.

Devin rubbed the ankle tape harder for a moment, then jerked outward again. Another tiny ripping sound. *Yes!* She would break her legs free eventually. If she could run, she could escape.

The agent stepped out of the car and yanked open the back door. "Let's go."

"What's your plan?" Devin hadn't spoken since Agent Bailey had called her father. She regretted some of what she'd said but didn't think it would matter. Hearsay wouldn't sway a military jury.

"I'm going in and you're my shield."

Devin shook her head. Bailey was stunningly brave. Or stupid. No, they were both going to die. Unless the duct tape on her ankles gave before they entered the complex.

The agent grabbed her arm and started across the clearing.

Chapter 45

Bailey knew her plan was reckless, but she was tired of waiting for backup that might not be coming. Leaving without Lopez was failure, and letting Blackburn get away was unacceptable. He'd ordered the murders, and Bailey worried there would be more. What if he'd tested new versions of ImmuNatal on other generations at other military hospitals? She was also incredibly curious about the complex and what other kind of research was going on in there.

Keeping Devin in front, she approached the flat-roofed, metal building that looked like a big mechanic shop in the middle of nowhere. But she knew it was just camouflage for the real entrance. Would there be any guards? The only way to reach this location was through a gated military base. Or maybe hunters on horseback might wander through. Bailey spotted the security post and waved Devin's card in front of the camera. An overhead door opened, and Devin shuffled inside, his feet still bound. Bailey stayed behind him, Glock drawn. She had Devin's stun gun in her pocket in case she encountered a guard. She didn't want to shoot a U.S. soldier who was just doing his job.

The mostly empty room smelled like a mechanic's shop too.

"Stop right there!"

A uniformed guard stepped out from his post at the back of the building.

Oh hell. Bailey called out, "FBI. Drop your weapon." She peered around her human shield.

The guard, another young male, blinked in surprise. "What are your orders, Lieutenant Blackburn?"

"Stand down. She's armed."

Devin's cooperation surprised her. Then she noticed his handcuffs were now in front. *Oh hell!* There was nothing she could do about it at the moment. The guard lowered his gun but didn't drop it. Bailey pushed Devin, and he moved toward the shiny panel next to the soldier's post.

Suddenly the door opened, and Taylor Lopez ran through.

Holy crap! Blackburn had decided to trade.

At the sight of them, the girl stopped, her expression crushed.

The guard started to lift his rifle. Bailey pulled the stun gun and let the double prongs fly. They landed in the guard's chest and thigh. He dropped to his knees, then sprawled out flat, moaning. His weapon clanged against the cement floor. "Stay down!" She turned to Lopez. "Special Agent Bailey, FBI. Come with me." Now that she had the kidnapped woman, Bailey would retreat.

She spun Devin around. "We're going out," and she shoved her captive toward the exit.

"You said you would release me if the major let Lopez go."

Bailey laughed. "I'm not always a woman of my word." She pushed him again, and he shuffled forward, cursing. Bailey glanced back at the guard. He was still down.

Lopez rushed ahead and activated the overhead door, then stood under it to hold it open for the two of them. When they'd cleared the building and the door slammed shut behind her, Bailey breathed a sigh of relief. Now she just had to get them all safely off the base.

Halfway across the clearing, she heard the distinct sound of chopper blades. Bailey turned back. From behind the building, a helicopter rose into the air, and it looked like Blackburn was piloting it. *Shit!* The major was getting away, and probably taking the ImmuNatal with him. For a moment, she wasn't sure how she felt about that. What if the drug and the mission worked as planned? Wouldn't that be a good thing?

Devin suddenly spun around and head-butted her in the nose. Pain overwhelmed her and she made an involuntary grunting sound. With stars flickering around her watery eyes, Bailey brought up her Glock. Devin body-slammed her, and she went down.

The roar of the helicopter thundered as it came closer, low to the ground. Bailey clambered to her feet.

Devin sprinted for the center of the clearing, duct tape flapping around his ankles. The chopper hovered above, a rescue line dangling. The soldier leapt and caught the line with cuffed hands, and the craft started to lift again.

Hell! The major and his son were both getting away. Bailey gripped her weapon with both hands and aimed at Devin, clinging to the rescue line. Could she justify shooting him? The young lieutenant was probably a killer, but she had no proof.

Gunfire ripped through the air. The major was shooting at her.

Bailey raised her Glock to aim at the helicopter and pulled the trigger three times. The chopper started to spin out of control. As it dropped from the sky, the swinging rescue line slammed into a massive boulder and Devin

Blackburn fell to the ground.

Moments later, the helicopter crashed and burst into flames. Major Blackburn would likely not have survived, and neither would the ImmuNatal. Next to her, Taylor Lopez gasped and burst into silent tears.

Behind them, engines raced, and tires crunched on the gravel road. They both turned to see a fleet of dark sedans rushing toward them.

Chapter 46

Monday, Oct. 17, 8:45 a.m., Denver

Bailey set her laptop on the tiny desk at the motel and opened Skype. She had a conference call scheduled with her boss and the new deputy director. Because of her swollen nose, she would have preferred a phone conversation, but they wanted an update on yesterday's events at Fort Carson, among other things. She wasn't looking forward to it. She'd already been debriefed by the head of the Denver bureau and two separate military investigators. The second session, which had taken place in a windowless room in a numbered building on the Fort Carson base, had lasted until midnight. At that point, tired of Colorado Springs, she'd driven to Denver to find a nicer motel and be near the airport.

Bailey poured another cup of crappy motel coffee, sick of it too. But her body was bone-tired and she had a red-eye to catch at the end of the day. And yet she hummed with a slow-brewing anger. Her investigation had been blocked. In response to her call for backup, the deputy director had arranged for a military investigator to accompany the Denver team into the base, which she was thankful for. But they'd been given limited access and told their only focus was to locate the missing woman—which she'd already done. Not one agent had set foot inside the hidden complex. Whatever the researchers were doing in there would remain a secret. The military investigator had confiscated all her files too, including Dr. Metzler's journal. Bailey still had the thumb drive with patient records from 1995 and '96 but no authority to continue the case.

Her computer vibrated with the Skype ringing sound, so she stepped over and sat down. She knew she looked tired—and beat up—but at the moment she didn't care. She would do her best to be pleasant and courteous. Bailey tried to smile. "Good morning."

Alan Rogers, the new DD, spoke first. "Excellent work, Special Agent Bailey. Locating the kidnapped woman the way you did demonstrates superior investigative skill."

"Thank you." Lopez had practically rescued herself, but there was no reason for Bailey to downplay her own role. Rogers was the one person who could promote her to the job she wanted. "Finding the doctor's journal was particularly helpful."

The DD nodded. "I understand that the military is spinning certain events to protect their research, and I appreciate your cooperation in letting them do that."

As if she had a choice. "I would like to know if Captain Rashaud will be prosecuted for his part in giving unapproved drugs to pregnant women." She wanted someone to be held accountable for what they did, detail by detail, in front of a jury. Lopez and the others deserved that.

Agent Lennard cut in. "Ahmed Rashaud was gone from the complex, and the military investigators found no trace of any drug called ImmuNatal."

No surprise. Rashaud was probably on his way to the Middle East to carry out their mission with a second batch of the drug. In another twenty years—if she lived that long—

she would know if he'd been successful. She had no proof of their intention to contaminate water or food supplies in the Middle East with this gender/passivity drug, and she wasn't foolish enough to share that theory. Not without someone to corroborate it. "Is anyone pursuing the captain?"

"That's up to military investigators, and they're not communicating with us anymore."

"What about the damaged clinic computers? Have our tech guys had any luck recovering data?"

Lennard's brow creased. "The military confiscated those. This case is closed for us."

Bailey had expected it, but the cover-up still infuriated her. *Let it go.* She'd found and apprehended the murderer and rescued the abducted woman. This investigation was another success for her. There was nothing to gain by pissing off military commanders. "I'll file a full report when I get back."

"Take a few days," Lennard said. "Do some skiing for me while you're there."

Not a chance. "I'll be back Thursday." Bailey shut down the connection.

Skiing was dead last on her list of ways to spend free time. Walking into a jail voluntarily was right there at the bottom too. But she might do it anyway. She called the Denver facility and learned that her father's visiting hours were Mondays and Wednesdays from 3:15 to 3:45 p.m. That would work out with her flight. She would stop on the way to the airport and spend thirty minutes with her dad. Considering how reckless she'd been—and might be in the future—she might need the old man to do the same for her someday.

Chapter 47

Tuesday, Oct. 18, 2:05 p.m., Colorado Springs

Taylor walked into the hospital cafeteria and looked around for the man she was meeting. Despite everything she'd been through, this conversation made her nervous, like only it could. Was that him near the back wall? He was the right age and the right complexion. She started toward the man in the crisp blue shirt. He saw her and stood. "Taylor?"

"Yes."

Her father was handsome in a rugged sort of way, and she recognized herself in his high cheekbones and narrow chin. But fortunately, she had her mother's small nose.

"Thank you for coming. I know this is awkward." He reached out his hand.

Taylor shook it, grateful he hadn't tried to hug her.

"Please sit down. Can I get you anything?"

He was nervous too. She could tell by how fast he spoke. "No thanks. Let's just get this over with."

His cheeks sagged, and he slumped back into this seat.

She'd hurt his feelings. But what did he expect? Taylor sat in the plastic chair across from him. "So what happened? Why did you leave us?"

He nodded. "Fair question. First, let me say I'm sorry. I

know it was wrong to abandon you. But I had to leave your mother. She changed, and I couldn't handle it."

"Don't say anything bad about her or I'll walk out right now. Just tell me why I never saw you again." Or heard a single word from him until yesterday when he'd called.

"The military offered me a job I couldn't refuse. The opportunity was tremendous, but required a deep commitment and total secrecy."

"I know about the research complex and ImmuNatal. That's why my body is this way." Bitterness oozed out of her voice, and she didn't try to hold back.

He leaned forward and spoke softly. "I wasn't involved in the Peace Project, and we can never talk about it. I was simply tech support for the research facility. But you have to trust me that some wonderful medical discoveries came out of that place."

She'd been debriefed by military investigators who'd pressured her to sign papers saying she would never publicly talk about her experience. She'd refused. They'd said they would contest her account and that her version would make her sound crazy. She hadn't yet decided if she would tell anyone. But it was comforting that her father knew the truth.

Still she had to confront him. "That doesn't explain why you never called me or came to see me. I can't believe they wouldn't let you see your family."

Miguel Lopez sighed and hung his head. "I know. I was rattled by your gender issues. Your mother and I disagreed about how to handle the situation, and she won the first big decision. We fought all the time about whether to treat you like a boy or a girl. I finally gave up and walked away."

Hurt and confusion overwhelmed her. "You mean you wanted to raise me as a son? So, if I wasn't male you didn't want to be around me?"

"No." He shook his head. "I wasn't rejecting you. I was just afraid of the confrontation and confusion and decisions that needed to be made. I didn't know how to support you emotionally."

His eyes were watery, and Taylor had a moment of sympathy for him. But she was also glad he hadn't been part of her childhood. It might have actually been worse. "I have to go. I'm really here to see my friend Jake." She'd only agreed to meet her father because she was going to be in Colorado Springs anyway.

He reached over and grabbed her wrist. "Please give me a few more minutes. I want us to have a relationship."

"Why? Nothing has changed. I'm still who I am."

He fought back tears. "But *I've* changed. Give me another chance."

"I'll think about it." Taylor stood and walked away. She would probably come around someday and spend time with him, if only out of curiosity. But not today. She hadn't had the explosion dream the night before and felt at peace for the first time since her mother died. She would hold on to that for as long as she could.

A few minutes later, she walked into Jake's room in the ICU, feeling nervous about this meeting too. She didn't really know Jake either. They'd spent an intense day and half together—all of it focused on the investigation. What would she say to him? Besides "I'm sorry." She hadn't wanted to ever return to Colorado Springs, but she owed Jake a personal thank you.

Another young man was in the room. Longish blond hair, bone-thin, and with a terrible complexion. Both men turned to her.

"Hey, Taylor." Jake sat up, beaming. "I'm so glad to see you." He pushed back the white sheet, swung his legs to the floor, and stood.

"Don't get up on my account." Taylor hurried over, worried about his injuries.

"I'm fine. They want me to move around. And I need to give you a hug."

Taylor stepped in and gently put her arms around him. He squeezed her back and whispered, "I was so worried about you."

She let out a small laugh. "I was too." She glanced at the other man.

Jake grinned. "Taylor, this is the illusive Seth Wozac. Seth, this is Taylor Lopez, the reason you're still alive."

Seth shook her hand with cold fingers. "Thank you. That was some crazy shit. But it was also just what I needed."

She didn't know what to say. "I'm so glad Jake was able to warn you in time."

"It's all good. I finally know why I am the way I am." Seth turned to Jake. "I'll get out of here and leave you guys alone."

"Don't leave on my account." Taylor wanted to be polite.

"I have to go. My mother's picking me up." He blushed. "And taking me to rehab. I want a real life, if I can."

Thank goodness. He looked kind of gray. "Best wishes."

"From me too," Jake said. "And thanks for saving my bacon. I owe you. If you ever need a favor, call me."

"Nope. We're good." Seth gave a funny salute and walked out.

"How did he save you?" Taylor asked, sitting down.

"I can't talk about it. Because Seth wasn't actually at the clinic that night." Jake winked and eased back onto the hospital bed.

What did he mean? The FBI agent had told her that Devin Blackburn, the assassin, had damaged computers and burned the clinic. But Seth had an obsession with fire, and if he'd really been there . . .

"Don't think about it," Jake pleaded. "Just know that I owe him my life."

"Now I really am glad he's getting treatment."

"Me too." Jake scowled. "So why the heck did they kidnap you? The military investigator who debriefed me said you were found wandering around the back of Fort Carson. And they have no idea who took you or how you ended up there."

What a load of bull. Taylor tried to keep her anger under control. "It's a cover-up." She scooted her chair closer to the bed. "They don't want me to go public with this, but I have to tell you. Devin Blackburn kidnapped me and took me to an underground research complex. They wanted to train me to be a spy in the fight against terrorism."

"No shit?" Jake laughed, then grabbed his chest in pain. "Why you? Because you figured out what they were up to?"

Taylor shrugged. "The guy in charge said he liked my spunk." The image of the crashing helicopter flashed in her mind. The major and his son had both died, and she'd felt nothing but relief.

"What's wrong?"

"Nothing. It's just been a rough week."

"Sure as hell has." Jake gave her a brave smile. "Just be glad you're alive." He reached over and touched her hand. "I hope you'll tell me the whole detailed story of what happened to you. The Denver Post wants me to write a three-piece article for them." He looked tired, despite his good cheer.

"I will when you're feeling better. The military will deny

it and say I'm crazy, but I don't care."

"Good." Jake grinned. "The Post offered me my job back."

She squeezed his hand. "That's wonderful."

"I'm pretty damn happy about it." His eyes clouded. "I almost died though."

She knew the feeling. "So what happened?" She hadn't heard his story yet either, only that he'd been injured.

"I went to the clinic in the middle of the night, hoping to find information that would help me locate you. Instead, the assassin was there, trashing computers. And he shot me. Twice."

"Oh no." She brought her hands to cover her face. "I'm so sorry. It's my fault you got involved."

"No." Jake locked eyes with her. "I found Zion's body, remember? And called you. Besides, I'm okay. Seth pulled me out of the building and called 911. But you can never tell anyone that."

Because Seth had set the fire, and Jake was protecting him. "I hope Seth gets his problems figured out."

Jake nodded. "He will. He's been troubled by his gender issues, but that could be over now. Or at least a lot better."

She might as well tell him her news. "I just saw my father for the first time in sixteen years. He was an IT person at the research complex all this time."

"Get out! That is too fucked up."

"I know. I'm still coming to terms with it. But he says he had nothing to do with the experiment, and I believe him."

"Are you going to see him again?"

"Probably. But not yet. I have something more important to take care of first."

"What's that?"

"I'm contacting everyone on the list and inviting them to

a group meeting. Maybe even ongoing meetings. I think we all need each other."

"Great idea. Maybe you can find a counselor to join you."

She laughed. "You think I'm messed up?"

"No!" Jake flushed with embarrassment. "I just thought it might be helpful."

"It's actually a good idea, but my real purpose is for us to meet others like ourselves. Maybe even find someone to date. I'd like have a partner who would accept me for who I am."

Jake smiled. "That should be easy. You're pretty terrific."

L.J. Sellers writes the bestselling Detective Jackson mysteries—a four-time Readers Favorite Award winner. She also pens the high-octane Agent Dallas series and provocative standalone thrillers. Her 19 novels have been highly praised by reviewers, and she's one of the highest-rated crime fiction authors on Amazon.

Detective Jackson Mysteries:
The Sex Club
Secrets to Die For
Thrilled to Death
Passions of the Dead
Dying for Justice
Liars, Cheaters & Thieves
Rules of Crime
Crimes of Memory
Deadly Bonds
Wrongful Death
Death Deserved

Agent Dallas Thrillers:
The Trigger
The Target
The Trap

Standalone Thrillers:
The Gender Experiment
Point of Control
The Baby Thief
The Gauntlet Assassin
The Lethal Effect

L.J. resides in Eugene, Oregon where many of her novels are set and is an award-winning journalist who earned the Grand Neal. When not plotting murders, she enjoys standup comedy, cycling, and zip-lining. She's also been known to jump out of airplanes..

Thanks for reading my novel. If you enjoyed it, please leave a review or rating online. Find out more about my work at ljsellers.com, where you can sign up to hear about new releases. —L.J.